The

LOOM

The

LOOM

A NOVEL

SHELLA GILLUS

Guideposts

The Loom

ISBN 978-0-8249-4816-0

Published by Guideposts
16 East 34th Street
New York, New York 10016
Guideposts.org

Distributed by Ideals Publications, a Guideposts company
2630 Elm Hill Pike, Suite 100
Nashville, TN 37214

Library of Congress Cataloging-in-Publication Data has been applied for.

Cover design by Laura Klynstra
Cover photo by Getty Images
Interior design by Müllerhaus Publishing Group | www.mullerhaus.net

Printed and bound in the United States of America
10 9 8 7 6 5 4 3 2 1

DEDICATION

*T*o the One who knows and loves me anyhow.

ACKNOWLEDGMENTS

I would like to say thank you to my agent, Joel Kneedler. I am honored to be among the best. Thank you for your diligence in finding a home for this novel so quickly; Editor Beth Adams, Marketing Director Carl Raymond, and the entire team at Guideposts for believing in this story and working so hard to see it in print at its finest; Editor Adrienne Ingrum for posing just the right question that sparked a whole new vision; Rusty Shelton for an incredible social media campaign; Author Sharon Ewell Foster and Author/Actor Blair Underwood, my mentors from afar; the following spiritual leaders who have laid a strong foundation on which I stand: Rev. Amos L. Lewis, Bishop Alexis A. Thomas, Bishop Kenneth C. Ulmer, and Pastor Terrence Autry; my friend, Rev. Allen Parr, thank you for sharing your biblical insight and answering endless questions with patience and grace. Thanks to a team of women who encouraged and supported my effort to complete this task: Alisa Swinger, Viveca Bonner, Lisa Autry, Cheryl Savage, LaShon Anderson, Taiwan Brown, Kafi Nsenkyire, Melanie Quick, Shanise Pugh, Teresa Isaias Park, and my wonderful mother-in-law, Joyce Gillus.

I would also like to thank Gwendolyn Potter, my fairy godmother. I have recently discovered just how much of who I am comes from the wisdom and love you have showered on me since my infancy. I could never repay nor could ever be convinced that we do not have the same blood running through our veins. I love you.

Lee S. Chamberlain, you have supported every idea I have ever contemplated and believed in every one of my dreams since I can remember.

From questioning unjust music teachers to cheering every one of my performances, you have been at my side. There is no greater father.

Minnie L. Chamberlain, you are an amazing woman of God, one of the world's greatest givers, and the best mother a girl could have. I thank you for your fervent prayers and your unwavering love. There is only one Minnie. Never will the world have another like you. How did I ever receive such favor?

Alisa Chamberlain Walker, what can I say? You are more than my sister. You are my very best friend and I cannot, will not imagine my days without you. I don't know another soul who has labored through every challenge, every line, each story idea of this book like you have. But I know why. We are knit together. You are my treasure. I love you with everything.

Thank you to my precious little ones, my dear children, Spencer and Staci, who pretend to be me, hushing the house "'cause I'm writing." I'm sorry for the many weekends I spent locked up in a room behind my computer away from you, but I am here now and I cherish every moment.

And last but never least, I want to thank the man the Lord has placed over my life. Stacey L. Gillus, none of this could have been possible had you not believed, supported, and allowed me to write the story of my heart. If it had not been for your love and patience (not once in two years of this process did you complain. Not one bitter word between us), there would be no *Loom*. Your sacrifice epitomizes what it means to love me as Christ loves the church. You're doing it. Every day you're doing it and I am grateful for you, a man of incredible honor and strength, the earthly vessel through whom God has chosen to love me in ways I never imagined. There are no words....

My days are swifter than a weaver's shuttle,
and are spent without hope.

JOB 7:6 KJV

PROLOGUE

*E*very push for life pulled her closer to death.

With tears, Lydia pressed her way forward through the black night, through the maze of oak and hickory, through the path of pines, over stubble, patches of worn blue grass, fallen twigs, moss. The beauty of the things that bred around her, these natural wonders she had first come to recognize as a child, now as familiar as her own scent, she could not see. Through the wiry thicket she ran, her breath catching in her chest until it rose to her lips in a desperate pant.

With every step toward freedom, Lydia was bound. She knew it, even now, in the midst of her flight, she knew there would be no unleashing from all she left behind. Every mumbled rainbow wish; every broken branch she raised, stretched out over the creek she demanded to part; every black-eyed Susan she plucked and bunched into a bouquet for a brown boy she longed to marry; for every dried, white crusted tear she'd rubbed clean from her eyes in the cold water of the river, shivering when she discovered not one dream of them would come true. Every crinkled brown sack hand she'd clung to, squeezed, soothed, Daddy's right-cocked smile, Grandma Lou's feathery touch, all would remain, reside in her until they smothered her to death.

Lydia swatted past oak limbs and evergreen branches, scratching her arms against them and the coarse wool of her cloak. *Push!* She pushed against the cool April air whistling in her ears until it chilled her, caused her to dip lower into the hood that slipped from her head when she whipped around every few feet. Sweat slipped down the nape of her neck, slithered down the bumpy road of her spine. Hot in this cold. She pushed for life.

Bondage could not hold her.

Only a couple of hours had passed since her first step toward freedom. Her heart thumped at the thought of that first move, the choice that brought her here alone scrambling through the forest searching for the light, the safe house she'd heard about. Already she had rested, collapsed against an oak, bark crumbling over her shoulder as she glanced up at the Maryland sky. No moon. No stars. No light. Nothing in the heavens guiding, leading her. Not one sparkle, one glimmer on her side.

She knew she was running too fast, muscles tensing so soon, moving much too quickly in the dark, her hissing breath now clipped, but she was stirred, compelled, drawn to something that had once lived outside of her but somewhere along the way had entered in and now pulsed boldly through her veins, pumped her very heart. The alluring call of life swelled within her, and its echo. Death.

Tonight Lydia was ready to die for it. Death would surely come. Not a death of nothingness, for death was never that, but a cruel, unbearable unrest one couldn't do a thing about. And yet still, she pushed because there was not one without the other. Death rode the wings of life, swarming in just as sure as night followed day. It was the way of the world. She had seen one too many mothers panting, their bloodstained thighs pushing out babies only to slip away themselves. Every prize had a price. For everything she wanted, there attached to it like the thorn of a rose was the thing she didn't. But life was worth the risk no matter what was lost.

Lydia smoothed the woolen hood from her head and looked around. She would miss the words, the music. Here was just the sound of her own feet and the crunching of leaves. And crickets, night creatures. Was this the right path? She was near the river, she knew, several miles north of the Kelly Plantation.

She picked up the pace and began to sprint again. Bent arms and knees swinging hard, pressing, pushing. For every thrust forward, she left behind every friend she ever loved, ever bloody back she helped heal. She had to make it to the light. She gasped. Determined, she moved through the woods, panting, panting. She couldn't breathe.

Truth was, she hadn't breathed in months. She hadn't breathed in years. Lydia had never breathed a single breath her whole life. Not one gasp of air in two decades. Not one moment of filling her lungs with life. Not one. That's just how it was. Just a life without breath. No life at all.

The night's wind and the salt of her tears burned hot streams down her cheeks. The cotton slip of her dress caught in the thicket, tearing her hem loose so it hung lifeless, dragging against a soil that housed the bones of her people. *Run, Lydia, run!* Dragging like little Jacob's body behind Master's wagon.

Life. Death. Life. She needed it. *Push!* She gasped for the breath of life. Lydia ran for her life.

Somewhere it was there. This life, this breath she needed. She knew because she had seen it with her own eyes. She had witnessed in some, not the up-and-down movement of their chests, but their souls rising and falling, lifting. And color didn't have a thing to do with it.

Not all White folk were free. Some were just as bound as she. White didn't no more make one free as black made one bound. Lydia knew because her skin was as white as theirs, her eyes as green as many, and all of them were as bound as her enslaved grandmother was free.

Born to two light-complexioned mulattos, Lydia's skin was cream to their beige. With her father's eyes and her mother's hair, no trace of her African blood flushed through her pigment. That was only in her spirit.

As the night passed, she grew weary. Arms that had hours before swung with vigor rose to swat tree limbs with exhaustion. She scraped her cheek against a lower limb and winced when the air stung her pierced skin. Wiping the blood away with the back of her hand, she dragged through the woods. *Push!* The night seemed suddenly noisy, the distant sound of barking dogs, the scurrying on dry leaves all around. She looked behind her. Furry feet shot across the torn leather of her shoe. She screamed, swung around, and slammed into a thick hanging branch. A thundering pain shot through her skull, watered her eyes. Lydia gripped her head and tried to steady her balance. She was frightened, lost.

And then she saw it.

One small round, dim light. High and far away. She staggered toward it, dazed and weak. She dragged toward it. But when she was close enough to see the circle did not grow in size, it was too late. She was blinded by the beam in the hands of a man.

"Well now, boys, what do we have here?" The words poured out of his mouth slow as molasses as he lowered his torch. Through bleary eyes, Lydia saw three White men standing in front of her, one with rope, the other two with guns. The butt of a rifle cracked high against her forehead and sprang blood down her brows, showered her lashes until the men were blurry ghosts of red. Lydia collapsed at their feet.

O death, where is thy sting?

CHAPTER ONE

*F*ree folk relished the day. Bond folk cherished the night.

A lit sky was one to endure. Bent backs and broken spirits. *Make it through. Make it through.* But when darkness fell, lovers laughed, they danced, swirled, and swayed, fingers to backs, hands to waists, flesh to flesh; daddies jostled sons on bruised shoulders and willed them to higher places; mamas cuddled babies, tickled fat feet, and dreamt dreams for their young they no longer dreamt for themselves; misty-eyed granddaddies whispered hope into tender ears; and grandmas soothed the wounded with salve and hot water cornbread. One dark, sweet sliver of life filled them by night, but like chocolate, melted by morning.

Lydia tugged the straw bonnet forward over her scarf and shielded her eyes as she glanced up at the position of the sun. *Halfway to evening.*

For the second time since dawn, she lugged a large wooden bucket up the hill several yards behind the Kelly manor, working twice as hard as most days. With Cora stricken with fever in the night, Lydia rose early to empty chamber pots and fetch wash water. After starting the fire in the kitchen, she swept floors of oak and maple wood and scrubbed bed linens until her fingers were red and wrinkled. She wiped the drops of sweat collecting above her lip with the sleeve of her dress and sighed. Still she needed to bring water to the workers in the field and tend the main garden and by evening, sit at the loom.

When she reached the top of the hill, she slouched over the empty bucket, resting her hands on her lower back, her elbows pointing to the sky like wings. Even the simple duty of fetching water several times a day was no small feat for a girl as young as Cora, nor one as petite as she.

How Lydia managed any of it after the beating amazed her.

Left for dead in the woods, she awoke a few days later safe in slave quarters on her plantation. She recalled nothing of those early days of healing, except one word spoken three times. *Live.* Whispered. *Live.* Hovered. *Live.* Breathed over her.

Lydia swept her arm over her damp forehead, over the silvery scar she kept hidden under her scarf, and pumped. Gripping the handle with both hands, she raised the splintered bucket to her knees and waddled toward the Big House.

Water swished against her dress and soaked her feet muddy. She jiggled the bucket down and rubbed the early white patch of a blister on her palm. Squatting, she wiped her face against the folds of cotton across her lap, and squinted. Less than a hundred feet to go. She sighed and closed her eyes.

Let it be night. Music played in her mind before faces appeared. Daddy. Grandma Lou. Lizzy. Funny her White friend should come to mind.

Suddenly, she felt a tickle on the back of her neck. Her fingertips slipped under the nape of her braid, dropped as paper-thin legs danced across her knuckles. She screamed, leapt forward, and tumbled the bucket to its side.

Kicking against the river of water streaming around her, she fussed herself weary. *Get your own water!* Her head hurt. The ladybug lifted its tiny wings and flew up, high above her head. She wallowed in the dust for several minutes, watching it flutter and fly, fly away. *Free.*

When she could no longer see it, she gathered herself, yanked her lopsided, soiled hem straight, and trudged several yards back up the hill.

Pausing between pumps, Lydia scanned the land. The colonial sat center front next to a tobacco field in which several slaves labored. What field slaves did every day put her to shame. Lydia watched them hover over the leaves they would soon dry in heavy bunches in the tobacco barn near the slave quarters. The supply house and an empty barn were adjacent, but across from it, a breathtaking garden in the valley. Rows and rows of Indian corn, turnip greens, and tomatoes led to vibrant magnolias, marigolds, and roses of every hue.

Lydia looked up at the pale sky. *More than halfway there.* She picked up the bucket, leaned back under its weight, and trotted down the side of the mount. The swooshing of water mirrored her thoughts: back and forth, back and forth from the day's duties to night's rest.

Behind the Kelly manor, Lydia filled a washbasin with water and poured suds of lye over her hands, scrubbing under the white tips of her nails, her fingers, and her wrists until they were streaked pink. With her elbow, she pushed her way inside the house, jamming her foot against the door before the screen slammed shut and the smell of crackling pork roused her hunger.

Cora's knife rested on a slab of ham as wide as it was round. She smiled when she looked up, her deep-set, large brown eyes sparkling in a face as dark and sweet as molasses sugar. With more flesh on her cheeks than her chest, she was merely a girl no more than twelve or thirteen.

Her mother, Beatrice, had been Mrs. Kelly's favorite, had nursed the Missus's child as her own. A sleek, coffee-colored woman with long limbs and a solemn soul, Beatrice was as connected to the earth as any plant that sprouted from its soil. Her palms were as dark as the back of her hands no scrubbing would wash clean. Every autumn evening, she would sit in the Kelly garden with seeds pinched between long fingertips, digging, sowing, weeding, her knees bent on each side of her like petals, her back curved, swaying in the wind like a rose. During the harvest of 1847, her spirit dried out and she was found wilted on her side, her cheek pressed against the damp red clay. Word had it she was buried in the slave graveyard several miles behind the Kelly barn, but Lydia believed otherwise, because the following spring and each year following, in the garden, a single black rose emerged among the lilies.

After Beatrice died, Mrs. Kelly kept the slave's newborn under her roof and was particularly solemn in the fall. All obliged to be in her presence knew well enough to speak softly during the season, and most certainly to not make mention of the woman whose presence still sparked in her daughter's spirit.

"I didn't expect to see you up, Cora."

"Fever's gone. I'm as good as new." She nodded toward the hearth. "Got the grits on already."

Lydia tied an apron, frayed on the edges, around her waist and leaned over the pot of bubbling white hominy. She stirred, scraping a clump from the bottom of the pot. "They up yet?"

Cora nodded. "The Missus and Lizzy."

Of course. Mother and daughter dined alone morning after morning though Mrs. Kelly insisted the girls prepare as if her husband were likely to join them. But rarely did his evening outings in the slave quarters stir a hunger for food. Lydia tugged the front of her cotton dress higher at the thought of his eyes on her, grateful he harnessed his desires in the arms of the field women. Her cheeks burned the moment she thought it. They no more wanted his touch than she wanted his stare.

"Lydia!" Lizzy sprang into the kitchen swooning. Several blond tendrils fell from the chignon at the top of her head as she spun around the sunlit room in a yellow gown of satin. She bumped into Lydia and wrapped her arms around her neck, giggling. "I love it."

"Oh, Lizzy, you know I'm not finished." Lydia swiped her hands across her apron and shook her head, but smiled. "I still need to add several buttons to the back."

"I know. I just couldn't wait." She twirled, draping the fabric out around her like a fan. "What do you think, Cora? You like it?"

Cora smiled and nodded.

The three girls turned when Mrs. Kelly entered the room. Her thin face and frame were nothing more than a withered Lizzy. Her sunken cheeks, lined neck, and hands, spotted brown, aged her more than her husband, though he was several years her senior.

"Lydia and Cora, I'm waiting. Is breakfast ready?"

"Yes, ma'am."

"Well, get a move on, please. I'm starved." Her eyes shot over the length of her daughter. "Elizabeth, what are you doing in your dress?"

"Just excited, Mother."

"Out of it at once before it's soiled."

"May I take it to Richmond?"

"That's nearly three months away. We'll see if you're even as fond of it by summer's end."

"I will be." Lizzy smoothed her cotton-white hands over the fabric. "I'm going to love it just as much."

"Is my gown finished, Lydia?"

"Yes, ma'am, it is. I just have a little more work on your shawls and Lizzy's—Elizabeth's buttons left."

Mrs. Kelly stared at her. A most indifferent woman. Although she often spoke words of concern, the weight of them carried no emotion, as if they lay dead deep inside, buried like Beatrice. She nodded and returned to the dining room.

Lydia and Cora whipped around Lizzy, setting each dish of grits, eggs, ham, and biscuits on a silver platter.

"Fix your scarf." Cora tapped her own yellow handkerchief and pointed at her head just before she stepped out of the room.

Lydia smiled her thanks, ran her hand over the single braid down her back, and adjusted the faded brown gingham over her scar. She hated that thing. That awful, ugly keepsake of a lost dream. It teased her endlessly, peeking out from its cover unashamed, reminding her of her state in the world. Grabbing the tray off the counter, she walked into the dining room, set the food on the cherrywood table, and drew the drapes.

Sun rays spilled onto a stew of pink and yellow as Mrs. Kelly mashed her ham and eggs together and drummed her fork between small breaths that caved her chest, rounded her shoulders.

When the missus dismissed Lizzy, Lydia cleared the half moon of bread her friend left and waited. Minutes later, Mrs. Kelly frowned and tossed a rumpled napkin over her full plate and screeched it away, across the table, until it clanked against her husband's breakfast. The congealed grits jiggled, untouched.

"You may go and see to the field."

"Yes, ma'am."

Out on the front porch, Lydia squinted against the sunlight and waddled out to the field workers under the weight of a bucket she held against the slightest curve of her hip.

She searched the rows of tobacco for the one she wanted to serve first. She smiled when she saw him, his back to her, his overalls torn on the back left pocket. She would mend them when she had the chance. Her father turned when she grabbed his arm. He squeezed her with his gloved hand into his shoulder, reeking of nicotine and tar, and kissed the top of her head.

"Good to see you out here. On your feet again."

She looked up at the tall shadow of a man. His right-sided grin usually made her smile, but today it pierced. Sadness crinkled his eyes. He was thinking of how she had been.

"I'm all right, Daddy. Doing fine now. Here." She offered him the gourd. "You thirsty?"

He stooped over the bucket and drank for several seconds. "You almost done out here? I want you to hurry up and get on back inside. Don't want the sun making you weak."

Lydia laughed. She hadn't seen the sun for nearly a month. Couldn't make her weak if it tried.

She watched him work, breaking the flowers off the top of the plant, gleaning tiny shoots from the leaves. His drenched skin, high yellow like the white corn she shucked for dinner most nights, blazed against the other men and women on his row. All the shades of her people. The beauty of butter cream to the darkest shade of midnight.

Lydia froze.

Midnight. That space when all the world was still and she felt alone with the thoughts she wouldn't dare think in the day. Those same thoughts came the first time she saw him.

John was as beautiful as midnight.

"Water?" she asked, bending a tobacco leaf from her view. When he saw her staring, his dark face lit with the kindest smile and the deepest dimples. She lowered her gaze.

"Sure."

Gently, he clutched the gourd, his fingertips grazing hers. She watched him. His eyes close. His lips part. He was not a boy. Three or four years her elder, she reckoned. This was a man. When he opened his eyes, she blushed. His gaze met hers then traveled higher to her brows, her forehead. Lydia's stomach flipped when her fingers found her scar uncovered. She tugged her scarf over it and looked away.

"I'm glad you're better. Your father speaks of you often."

How much did he know? "But you're new here, right?"

"Somewhat. Yes." He wiped the water from his mouth with the back of his sleeve.

Lydia watched the sweat gather across his forehead and sweep down his temple, his cheek, the square of his jaw. A hard worker. She glanced at the other men and women in the field. She supposed they were all hard at work. She was just close enough to see him dripping, hear him breathing, sipping.

"More?"

He nodded.

Lydia dipped the gourd into the wooden bucket and handed it to him.

"Lydia right?"

"Yes…" He knew her name.

"I'm sorry. I'm John."

John. *John.* How many times would that name play in her head tonight? More than she could count.

CHAPTER TWO

*L*ydia slipped through death's door.

Inside, orange rays shone through the cracks of the tiny log house and bronzed the smooth chocolate cheek of the old woman at the loom.

"Baby, is that you?" Ruth turned her head toward the door when it shut but her eyes stared ahead.

"It's me." Lydia smiled at the couple sitting in the center of the room waist-deep in a colorful sea of fabric.

Spun cuts of cotton draped over the low three-legged table in the corner like clouds over a rainbow of material in lavender, gold, crimson, slate. Colors Lydia had only seen on the petals of roses and in the deepest of dreams, and yet sadness prevailed in the mosquito-ridden cabin. The three knew as well as she, this was it for them. They would not leave this place. Life as they knew it would soon be over. Their cooling board prepared. Their cloth, their winding sheets.

She moved toward the table and allowed her fingers to touch the yarn of the spinning wheel and wealth of cloth surrounding her, showering them. She ran her hands down the length of rough wool and let them slide over a small patch of slippery silver. Bolts of cloth lay in each corner of the room, like barricades, like borders.

Abram leaned against the hunched shoulder of his wife and held a cloudy silver spoon of stew to his lips. Lydia stared at the scar in the middle of his palm, the back of his hand, his arm ashen brown and dull, as shriveled as dry wood. He paused when he saw her and nodded his smooth head. The corners of his white moustache and half-moon beard curved around the slightest of smiles.

Lydia acknowledged the wise one with a bowed head and a reverent utterance of his name. *Old Abram.* A chief, a sage, a spiritual warrior among her people, her father had shared. Respected and sought after for his wisdom and his knowledge of the Great One and His ways, he was father of the young and the old. For years, ailing children were sent to his side, draped in his arms, laid in his lap. Word had it, Abram would mumble, sometimes for minutes, at others near an hour, until his lids fluttered, his palms trembled, and power soared through him to little limp bodies that would rise, their eyes opening and blinking wide and round at the gathered worshippers on their knees. When the praise turned to him, he was quick to correct, "It is God who heals." And heal He did through him countless times, but only for the young. For the older folk, there was no hope. The moment a boy's voice deepened or a girl's body curved, Abram was helpless to aid, as impotent as the rest. Too much time away from the source of life, too many tainted, tired years, he reasoned. For them, all he could offer were words that healed on the inside, and these verbal morsels men and women savored eagerly, sitting silently at his feet to listen to words deep in tone and nature, hoping to glean guidance that could carry them one step farther down the road of life.

Lydia had never witnessed any of it. Abram was old when she was born and set aside by the time she was of age. She wanted to, needed to believe in the power that raised spirits, that lifted heads, but all she knew was the shriveled man who nodded and offered few of the many words he had once spoken.

Even the greatest withered away.

It hurt. This ending to his life. Nothing could be easy about losing awe, the admiration of ones who believed in a life set apart only to discover that it would dry out as deeply as it had flourished. When the healing faded, it burned, but when the seekers ceased to come and he was thrown away in The Room to die, it seared. A leader reduced to a weaver of cloth like all who could no longer serve in the fields. It was the fate of the old, the disabled, and it had fallen just as surely in Abram's lap as it had the rest.

It hurt. Lydia knew. She saw it in his misty eyes quick to turn away when they met hers. She heard it in the quiver of her father's voice when the elder's name was spoken. She felt it in her heart when she tried to catch her breath within the walls of her people's purgatory.

"Lydia…" His wife Odessa nodded her crown of gray hair. Her fingers intertwined with Abram's free hand like knotted tree limbs. Of the three, she was the one who looked the oldest, who spoke the slowest, who broke the easiest. Often tears slid down the sandy-brown grooves etched around her eyes, down her cheeks, beside her mouth like every treacherous road she had traveled, like tracks through a hard ground that couldn't bring forth life if it wanted to.

A nervousness moved through her, darted her eyes like flies in a web of wrinkles, quivered her lip, nodded her head even when she said no. But "no" was rare, hardly ever spoken by the oppressed, even less by the time he or she entered The Room.

Lydia walked to Ruth and squeezed her shoulder.

"How's our girl today?"

"Fine. Just fine." Grazing the back of her mentor, Lydia watched the miracle of weaving hands, the gathering and threading of slivers that would create a world as soft and warm as the arms of love. She stood for several minutes before sitting next to the leader of the loom, the blind woman with blue eyes.

The first time she saw Ruth, she ran.

Lydia had been a girl, not quite as old as Cora, charged by Beatrice to carry food to the loomers. It was a big task for a young one to deliver anything, so she did it proudly, happy to have been asked.

With her fingers gripping the handle of the woven straw basket, she held the rations with taut arms as she tiptoed across the cornfield, sweat slipping down the front of her stifling burlap dress.

It was scary even then. The Room. It was fuller in those days. A room of eight or nine old folk she had never seen before. Foreign faces of life long past, gaping at her, staring through her. Bony wrists grabbing for the cobs of corn she had no idea how they would chew with empty, wide mouths beneath sunken cheeks. And it smelled, not of chamber pots, for the children of the aged prided themselves in keeping them emptied and clean. No, this stench was a humming still, dry musk like the clawed dead that hung from the ceilings in the smokehouse.

There was only one in the corner Lydia hadn't served, a woman sitting on a bench at the loom. Even from behind, she was different from the others. Her back straight, her body agile with only thin slivers of shiny silver through dark locks bound by the bandanna tied at the back of her head, stretched against the top of her ears.

"Ma'am, would you like something?"

When she turned, Lydia gasped. *Still blue skies captured in the face of the darkest night.* She dropped the basket of food and stumbled over bare feet, bent knees, and wounded legs struggling to move out of her path, the sound of cracking joints and her apologies ringing in her ear as she ran out.

It took several weeks before the patience of the eldest house slave ran dry and Lydia gained the courage to return. In time, she sat under Ruth, a profound teacher without sight who taught her to see designs as intricate as they were beautiful before they were ever formed at her fingertips.

"You ready, baby?" Ruth asked, removing her foot from the pedal and sliding off the bench to a wooden chair she felt her way into.

"I am."

Lydia sat inside the loom with her stomach pressed against the front beam. She stretched out her legs until her foot reached the heavy pedal of gourd and pressed down, flexing and pointing her toe. Two pairs of shafts, she decided. When she threaded the white weave pattern 1-1-1-1-2-2-2-2 with four threads in each heddle, she smiled. The black she threaded in a plain weave with single threads, passing each one through both pairs of heddles, creating an equal amount of warp and weft—a balanced weave.

She was always ready for the loom. A time to sit at the massive wooden machine of posts and beams that filled most of the space of the small shack was her pleasure. It was peaceful, a journeying away, a chance to dream. Often she sat for hours, unaware of the time passing or the light sounds of sleep from the three nearby. All she heard, all she saw, all she felt was the newness. A new creation, a new design that would thread a new experience that could fashion a new life. She weaved a world of possibility each week until her lashes tapped against her lower lids and her head bobbed, her foot stopping and starting against the pedal.

By nightfall, she completed the shawls. When she released her foot, her pulse raced. One more task. Just one more and she could escape to another world.

As secret as it was kept, Lydia was a lady.

In her quarters, she glanced at the gown Lizzy had worn at breakfast, ruffled on top of her bed. *Her gown.*

From the light of the kerosene lamp, she was surrounded by the shadows of her bed covered in old linens, a cedar stool, a rough-hewn chair, a wobbly, three-legged wooden table much like the one in The Room, and a large mirror, a treasured gift from Lizzy.

She moved to the stool with the satin dress in hand, her lips jiggling a stick pin in the corner of her mouth. Fastening the yellow knob buttons in place, she threaded the needle and whipped it in and out of the fabric with skill until twenty buttons, one on top of the other, adorned the gown she spread across her lap. It was ready.

She was ready. Lydia looked around, felt her heart thump as it did each time. Now, all these years later, she couldn't remember the first time she had done it. All she knew was she couldn't stop. She wouldn't.

She let her fingers dance over the slippery fabric of yellow and caressed it against her cheek. She thought of Lizzy dancing in the gown, spinning and twirling carefree in the kitchen. And tomorrow night with a gentleman. The sweet dance of love. What it would be like to spin and twirl in a gown like this for John.

Tonight she would dance for him.

Each article of clothing she made for Lizzy and the missus she wore first. Every dress, every chemise, every shawl, every cloak first slipped over her shoulders, slid against her thighs. She saw herself in each piece first. So though it seemed she obtained their old attire, they in fact acquired hers. She was the first lady of the house, even if only in her mind or in the few minutes she stood before the antique mirror.

Lydia rose and dragged the stool behind her. Quickly, she looked out the door and, when she saw no one, creaked it shut, pushing the seat against the wooden frame.

She and Lizzy were the same size, both thin, petite girls, though her friend was slightly taller.

She shrugged out of her worn slip of a dress and stepped into the gown. As she brought the satin up over her knees, her thighs, she lifted the bodice over her breasts and slipped her arms through. Holding the back of the neckline together, she inched to the mirror.

Though she had tried it on before, she was now certain this one was better on Lizzy. If it were hers, she'd need to raise the hemline and tighten the waist some. She tugged the dress down over her shoulder and glanced up at her reflection. She closed her eyes. *Darkness and dimples.*

She was a lady.

CHAPTER THREE

*O*h, Lizzy. It's perfect." Outside on the steps of the Kelly manor, Lydia
studied her friend from head to toe.

She was sunshine in darkness. Her blond hair, the pearls against her
throat, and the yellow dress shined, but they were no match for the joy that
made her face glow in the moonlight.

"Thank you, Lydia," she gushed, grazing the strand of pearls. "I sure
wish you could come."

Why'd she say such things? *Why?* Lydia looked down. Her faded blue
dress trimmed in thick white lace was still pretty though she wore it often.
Not pretty enough for a ball. But it was more than a dress that would keep
her away. "It's all right, Lizzy. I'm going to see my daddy tonight."

"Elizabeth!" Mrs. Kelly called from the carriage. "Come now."

"Bye, Lydia." Lizzy paused before she smiled, squeezed her hand, and
walked down the steps to her mother, wrapping her shawl around her.

Lydia rubbed her arms against the breeze. A shawl would do her good
tonight. She would grab it quickly and head to the slave quarters. Though
the days of late summer were warm, the nights were still cool enough for
covering.

She turned, stumbling into Dr. Kelly, a tall, burly man with deep-set
brown eyes, tonight dressed in formal black attire.

"Lydia…" He twisted an unruly strand of his moustache, rubbed his
beard. His wild curly hair desperately needed a trim, but she had to admit,
the look fit him just fine. Loose and untamed. Where women curved, he
bulked rough and rigid to their softness, straight and simple to their com-
plexity, downright masculinity in body and breath.

"Dr. Kelly." She dropped her head in respect.

"How are you this evening?"

When she looked up at his smile, her heart fluttered.

"Fine, sir." She glanced at the carriage and wondered if Mrs. Kelly and Lizzy could see him. She swallowed. And if they could?

"Where's Cora?"

"Already down at the cabins, sir."

"I see." His voice was lower, gritty. "Looking nice tonight."

She rubbed the back of her neck, could feel his eyes on her. Folding her arms, she looked at the ground, the narrow toe of his black leather shoe tap, tap, tapping.

"Thank you, sir."

He nodded and skipped down the steps to the carriage. A chill came over her she couldn't shake, not even after she had retrieved her shawl.

Passing a dozen slave quarters behind a wooden fence, Lydia walked until music and laughter floated through the air. *Field slaves.* The style, the rhythm, the texture and tones made it clear these were her people. Her grandmother, her father. Ten years in the Big House hadn't kept her from being one of them, the only people bold enough, bright enough to loose themselves from iron shackles at least some of the time. She walked toward the sound, felt her feet moving as quickly as the strumming beat.

Right in the middle of an open field, more than fifty bondservants gathered in a half circle around a fire, some standing, some sitting, others clapping and singing a song Lydia had never heard. In the corner sat a reverent, white-haired fiddle player in suspenders, tapping his foot to the music he plucked with care. A bearded bald man swung and dipped a woman whose hair stood full and wide around her like a halo. A small peanut of a child clucked around, his elbows flapping faster at the growing attention. Brown skin in bland clothing created the most colorful scene of the night.

On the perimeter, cotton-white men stood near, planted by the master to guard their safety against the uprising of a Moses and a people eager to plot the exodus of a lifetime.

Suddenly, Lydia felt breath on the nape of her neck. She spun around and stumbled. Strong arms steadied her.

"Sorry. With the music, I didn't think you'd hear me."

"John."

A glowing smile of white teeth greeted her in the most handsome face she'd ever seen. Had he grown more beautiful in a day?

"Lydia."

"I was looking for my father."

"He's here. I saw him earlier."

Lydia followed his gaze over the crowd. She spotted Cora near the banjo player giggling into cupped hands with two other girls her age. Her father stood several feet away, drinking from a tin cup. He waved when he saw her, made his way over.

Lydia wrapped her arm around her father's waist. He nodded at John. "I see you met my daughter."

"Yes, sir." John smiled at Lydia, glanced back at her father.

"Daddy, where's Grandma?"

"Asleep. She didn't feel up to it tonight. I think it's just too much noise for her sometimes." He looked around and chuckled. "Too much noise for *me* sometimes. I'm heading in myself. You coming by tomorrow, ain't you, Lydia?"

"I am."

"Good night, Baby Girl." He squeezed her to him and kissed her cheek. "John. See she gets back safely, hear?"

"Yes, sir. I most certainly will."

When her father slipped through the crowd, she turned to the man at her side.

"He's a good man. Your father."

"Yes. Yes, he is." She looked at this stranger her daddy had entrusted her to. She could see why. There was gentleness in his eyes. She wanted to know him. Everything about him. Wanted him to be a stranger no longer. "What about you? Your father?"

"Never knew him." He said it matter-of-factly. "My mother died a few months back, just before I was sold here. I've been moved around a few times."

"Why?"

He shrugged. "A male like me is worth a lot."

Lydia thought back to the day before, seeing him out on the field, working. Even tonight, in his thin cotton shirt, she could see the outline of his tall frame, the muscles in his arms, the evidence of strength.

The near sounds of a harmonica rose above the final tune of the fiddle. A young man with closed eyes and thick lashes leaned into the solemn song he blew through the wooden rectangle. Each note hunched him lower.

"My mama died early too." The slow music, the words carried weight, a sadness. Joy was quickly setting like the evening sun. She willed it to rise. "But I have my grandmother. My daddy's mama. She's good to me. I get to be with her by week's end."

"Let's sit. You hungry?"

John returned with a wooden bowl of chickpeas and cracklin' bread. He straddled a chair in front of her.

"So you work inside. What's that like?"

"It's fine." Lydia ate a few bites of bread before she continued. "My sleeping quarters are nice, but I still miss staying with my daddy and grandma."

"You can't miss sleeping on a dirt floor."

"Well, no, I don't miss that."

"How are they? They good to you in that house?"

"The Kellys? They treat me all right." If she ignored her master's gawking. "Their daughter, Lizzy, Elizabeth, is a good friend."

He raised his brows. "You sure about that?"

"Yes." This she knew for sure.

He nodded slowly. "Well, good."

Lydia balanced the half-empty bowl on her lap and looked back into his eyes. "What about you? What's life like for you here?"

"Haven't been here long. I don't know. Like any other place, I suppose. Except one." He looked down. When he looked back up something had changed. No smile, just eyes focused in the distance.

She moved in closer to him, waiting. "Which one is that?"

"The one place I'm going." The words hovered between them until they floated away like sparkling dust. "Let me take that." He reached for her bowl like they were never spoken. Like she had imagined them and this other man with the serious eyes. She watched him, his back to her, and a pang shot through her chest. He wouldn't be here for long.

"You ready?" he said much too cheerfully. "It's getting late." A tall couple entangled like the branches of the tree they stood under remained and a handful of youth.

"Sure."

They walked in silence until they reached the back steps of the Big House. She looked up at him and smiled.

"I enjoyed the evening," he said.

"Yes. So did I."

"I'll tell you the truth. I've never seen nobody like you. No girls I know carry themselves like you."

"Is that right?"

"That's right. You're different."

"In what manner?" She hated to ask, knew what he was going to say. The same thing everyone said. "You mean because I'm a White Colored."

"No."

"No?"

"That's not what I mean at all." He stuck his hands in his pockets and shrugged. "It don't much matter to me what shade a woman's skin is."

"Really?"

"You don't believe me?"

"Well, you'd be the first. You're the only one in the whole world who don't care what color skin is."

"I don't think so."

"What do you mean, you don't think so?"

"I mean, I can't be the only one. There's nobody else out there who can see a little deeper?"

"A little deeper?"

"Yeah, a little deeper." He tilted his head and flashed a smile. He leaned forward on the balls of his feet. "I'm trying to see what's behind them green eyes."

"Is that right?" she asked too softly. She bit her lip and looked down, could feel warmth flush her body.

"Good night, Lydia."

"Good night." She walked up the steps. One, two, three, four, five, six, and opened the door. Was he watching? Just before she stepped inside, she turned around. He was. She waved. He nodded with his hands still in his pockets and turned away.

Twice in one night, his back to her. It was a sight that already stung.

CHAPTER FOUR

$\mathcal{L}$ydia sat on the dirt floor in the unlit cabin across from her father, tugging on the itchy burlap against her neck and the new patch of denim now securely fastened to the pocket of his overalls. She placed them beside her and stretched. The smell of cornmeal mush still clung to her dress hours after the supper Grandma Lou prepared.

The old woman kicked up gray puffs of dust around her thick ankles, pattering her way back to the only other room in their home. Stringy raven locks swung behind a thick frame. Though Lou had seen too many harvests to count, her hair remained black as the night.

"Grandma, don't forget I need you to do my hair." Lydia always felt like a child here, like nothing had changed.

"Wake me up when you ready." Grandma's voice faded when she was no longer in sight. "I'm just gonna lay down a minute."

She turned back to her father.

"She all right?"

"She's fine." He tapped her nose. "Stop that worrying."

Daddy propped himself against the log wall, beside the hearth. In the dark, Lydia could make out the withered wooden table, the stool, and a crate, but something was missing.

"Where's the bench?"

"Cracked. Needs to be replaced altogether, but I don't think it's right here. Makes this space too tight."

"You could put it out front."

"Could."

She looked around the room and felt the familiar rise of guilt that always climbed up the back of her throat when she was here. They had so little. Little food. Little space. Not even room enough for a bench, a place for a seat. Not even room for rest.

She swallowed the shame of living away from them, eating, working, sleeping in the Big House. She had so much more than they ever would. And even what she had was not enough.

Lydia heard stirring in the other room and could see her father shift toward the coughing. She watched him in the dark. He crossed his legs and reached for the hands she hid in her lap, blew air into them. The hard calluses on his palms scraped against her skin.

"How are your hands, Daddy? Still numb?"

Even with gloves, the poison of tobacco seeped into his pores, stiffened his joints.

"I'm fine."

"Why you quiet, Daddy?"

He shook his head, twining his fingers with hers. "Just tired."

Their house grew silent again, except for the chirping of crickets. Lydia spotted one, hopping, hopping toward the window. *Why did hopping look so happy? So fun and free?* Even the crickets were free.

"Why you think God made us to belong to somebody?"

"I don't think He did." Daddy paused. She could barely hear him breathing. "I know we ain't meant to. One day…"

"God's gonna do it." Lydia nodded and squeezed his fingers, thought of the raising of rods she had lifted, she had hoped, believed would part the creek as a child. One day, He would let her people go. "I think so." When he didn't respond, she released her hand from his and patted his knee. "What do you think freedom's like?"

"Listen, Lydia." He sighed. "You're not thinking about running again, are you? I'm not willing to lose you over nothing."

"Don't worry, Daddy." If she could, she would. Given the chance, she'd be gone before night turned to day. With everything in her, she'd run free. "Don't worry, all right?" She scooted closer until her knees were against his and whispered. "Come on, tell me. What do you think it's like? I know you think about it."

"Good." His head dropped. "Real good."

"Like heaven?"

He chuckled. "Not *that* good."

"Well, that's funny."

"What's that?"

"Dead is better than us alive."

"I didn't say that."

He didn't have to. She already knew some things were worth dying for.

Daddy didn't say another word. She could see his face turn away. He pressed his palms against his eyelids.

"Daddy." Lydia inched next to him and stroked his back. "I'm sorry, Daddy. Let's not talk about it."

"We almost lost you." His words, each syllable, broken.

"Let's not talk about it."

After a few moments, he wrapped his arm around her and squeezed her shoulder. "I better get some shut-eye, Lydia. I got tilling to see to first thing in the morning. Kelly's orders." He stood up, stretched, and pulled her to her feet.

Lydia hated to leave him. No one, nothing in her world was warmer, sweeter than Daddy. She stood shivering for several seconds, looking up at him.

"Cold?" Her father rubbed her back. When she nodded, he reached down and grabbed a dark, worn blanket. Wrapping it around her, he kissed the top of her head.

She dragged several feet toward the back room. Her father yawned, already stretched out on his back beneath a quilt, his feet flexed against the hearth.

"Good night, Daddy."

"Good night, Baby Girl. Love you. It's always good to have you here with us even if it is just for a day or two."

She swallowed hard and nodded. "Love you too."

Lydia inched forward, sweeping the dirt with the tattered blanket as she walked away.

In the next room, draped in the dark covering, she wiggled under a thin patchwork quilt with her grandmother. She lay still, perfectly still, a game she liked to play as a little girl to see how long she could remain. She recalled not having a clue whether she improved each time, but she praised herself if it felt longer and it always did. She smiled at the memory. She turned and watched the woman next to her snoring on her back with the cover shimmying a nervous dance above her nose. It moved in short rainbow waves, up and down around her, and just when it looked like it was going to fall and cover her completely, the breath in her lifted it and kept it from coming any closer. Lydia watched until she dipped in and out of drowsiness before plunging into a world, light and fuzzy around the edges.

Daddy's laughing face. He was walking toward her, reaching for her. Then he startled. His smile slid into anger, slipped into sadness. He froze. *What is it? What is it, Daddy?*

A ladybug crawling, fluttering, flying away. Then just as suddenly, the crushing sound of a rifle against skull.

Lydia shot straight up and shook the picture out of her head, but tiny wings fluttered and flickered in the pit of her belly for the rest of the night.

⸻⸻•◦•⸻⸻

It was the cold breeze, the cover she was stripped of that woke Lou. She wrestled up next to her wide-eyed granddaughter.

"Lydia. You all right?"

Lou shook her head. Dreaming again. About them men and their guns, she knew it. What she'd give to wipe out the whole bloody nightmare. She shivered. "I thought you was gonna wake me?"

"I was but you were sleeping so good, I couldn't bring my heart to do it." Even though it was dark, Lou could see her smile. "I must've fallen asleep myself."

Lydia lit a large candle in the corner next to the low wooden stool that Lou found near impossible to lower herself onto. She managed somehow.

The girl wiggled between her knees like a child. "Plait it straight down the back," she said.

Seeing Lydia sitting on the dirt floor in the dark, her head resting against the burlap between yawns and stretches, made her smile. No matter where the missus made her sleep, this old cabin was still her grandbaby's home.

"You know and I know you can do this yourself, girl."

"Not like you can."

She wasn't lying. Years ago, Lou made sure every strand was woven. *Every* strand. *Whatever her hand found to do...*But now she raked her crinkled hands over the girl's frizzy braid not knowing how she would muster the strength to complete the task. She could barely see a thing in the dim candlelight. "Take it down for me then."

Lydia swung her hair loose. Deep dark waves fell down her back. She laid her head against Lou's knee, wrapped her arm around her calf.

"All this hair on the sweetest face. Always said your daddy should've been a girl." Lou laughed and squeezed Lydia's shoulders. "I got my girl after all."

Slowly, Lou gathered and wrapped lock over lock until she winced. "You finish up, hear?" She wrung her hands and sighed.

"I miss you here with us." She slid to the edge of her chair and smiled at the girl at her feet. "I ain't never got used to you not being here. Sometimes at night, it's like I can still feel you right here with me." It hurt. She wasn't sure what hurt more. The girl being gone or the feeling she was near when she wasn't. Would never be again. *This life!* She shook her head. *Soon.* Her only comfort rose inside her, lifting her spirit. Soon it would all be over. "Don't imagine it will matter too much longer."

"What do you mean?"

Oh, Lydia. She would miss her. And her son. *Isaiah and Lydia.* Hoped to meet her other children again on the other side.

"I mean, don't nobody live forever."

"Don't say that." Lydia gripped her knee.

"Don't say it?" She laughed. "It's all I should be saying. Best hope I got going."

"I'll come by more." Lydia grabbed her hand, held it against her cheek. "Much as I can. I've been spending too much time at the loom."

Lou hated the thought of that place. She had sat at the loom on her old plantation like all the women heavy with child, no longer able to work in the fields, but this place here was different. The images she conjured about The Room haunted her, kept her from its grounds, far from ever stepping foot across its threshold. The fact that everyone who dwelled within its walls died there unnerved her. Lou imagined their spirits hovering like breath at first, then swarming in a frenzy, tumbling about the cabin like a gust of wind, trapped in darkness, bound beneath a roof that suppressed sad souls that couldn't even reach heaven. She couldn't allow her mind to think too long of her friend Ruth, good ol' Dessa rotting away in a pit they couldn't escape. The only reason she hadn't joined them was the Lord's favor of a healthy son on the property supplying her needs. Isaiah, her savior from the pit of death.

"Thank You," she whispered.

"Ma'am?"

"I ain't talking to you." She grinned. "You do just fine, baby, coming to see me. And I'm happy for you. Always been happy you living in the Big House. Can't hope for much more." The lie soured in her mouth. She always prayed more, pleaded more for her grandbaby.

"I met somebody." Lydia wound her tresses into a knot at the back of her neck and spun around. "Name's John." Her head tilted when she said it. Oh, yes, Baby Girl was sweet on him. Lou shook her head and chuckled.

"He says I'm different. Says he don't much care what I look like, but still, I wish my skin was like yours. I can't help but wish I looked more like you, Grandma."

"Chil', don't ever wish for nothin' God ain't gave you. Only the fool wanna be what he ain't."

The girl sat up on her knees. "Only fools want to be free?"

Stop it. Just stop it.

"Only fools want to fly away?"

"Lydia…"

"Grandma, I want to be free." The pleading, the yearning in her voice. Lou couldn't take it. *Stop it.*

"I know. Listen to me, Lydia. You don't got to fly away. Life's gonna take you on a path all its own if you just stay put."

She shook her head. "I don't understand."

"I mean *stay put.*" Lou rubbed her crooked fingers and tapped her chest. "On the inside. Stay with your heart and listen real close and let life take you where it whispers. And stop that worrying about what you look like. God made each and every one of us different. And you special. You a perfect pearl. Yes, sirree. Lou's perfect pearl."

CHAPTER FIVE

*L*ydia stepped outside The Room with her latest design, a cream satin weave dress with capped sleeves draped across her arm.

It was perfect. This one, even before it graced her body, even before it ever had a chance to woo her, reflect to her all she imagined a dress could be, this one was special. Made for her and her alone. Never had gathered cloth and stolen hours resulted in a piece just for her. She would wear it, hide it, dream about a day she could present it to the world. For John.

In her quarters, she peeked out her bedroom door. Behind it, her fingers rested against the knob as she steadied her breathing. Holding the dress up against her, she walked to the mirror, wrapping her arm across the waist of the gown.

Slowly, she slid out of the old into the new.

When she pulled the cool graze of satin up over her shoulder, the door creaked open. She shrieked, stumbling over the hemline.

"Lydia?"

She turned to see Lizzy standing on the threshold. Her friend's eyes widened as she glanced over the gown. When her lips parted, Lydia sought to fill them with words, anything, something to say.

"I was just—"

"What? You were..."

"I was just seeing if this would be... I'm sorry. I was— I don't know what I was thinking." She wasn't thinking, had forgotten to block the door with the stool.

Lizzy walked toward her, her mouth still slightly ajar. Would she tell?

Snitch to Mrs. Kelly? Dr. Kelly? Lydia's fingers trembled. She squeezed them steady, gripped them against wet palms.

"Lydia."

"I know. I know I shouldn't have. It won't happen again." She was panicking. "Please don't tell your mother or father about it, Lizzy. Please!"

"Lydia." Lizzy stepped closer. "Lydia." It was all she had said in the few minutes she'd walked in. And as much as her name on her friend's lips had comforted her in the past, it now evoked fear in the same measure, thumped terror through her heart.

"Have you seen yourself in this?"

Lydia stared at her.

"Have you looked at yourself?"

She was standing in front of the mirror.

"No, Lydia. I mean, *really* looked at yourself."

Lizzy gently spun her around toward her reflection.

"Look. Look at yourself."

Lydia looked into the mirror. This one, just as she had predicted, fit her perfectly. Unlike the yellow, it gathered under her bust and creased down the front, billowing around her like a queen upon her throne. Her heartbeat slowed. She unclasped her hands.

"Do you see?"

She could see Lizzy behind her, her large blue eyes blinking rapidly. "Lydia. You look like…me."

She glanced at her blond friend, her own dark hair twisted back in a bun under a scarf. The wide blue eyes, her green ones. Lizzy's round face, her high cheekbones. They looked nothing alike.

Except for one thing.

"Take your hair down."

Lydia hesitated.

"Go on. Take it down."

She yanked the scarf from her head and raked her braid loose with her fingers. Auburn waves tumbled over pale shoulders. Lydia swept strands of hair across her scar.

Lizzy ran to the door and fastened it shut before dragging the stool over to the mirror. "Here. Sit," she instructed. At Lydia's worktable, she grabbed knitting needles and with a few quick strokes of her hand, secured her hair into a tousled chignon.

Lydia rose to her feet at the transformation. Green eyes blinked back in amazement.

"Do you see it?"

She saw it.

"Lydia."

She saw it. Before her very eyes, she was changed. Others had spoken of her beauty, but it was the first time she saw it, staring back at her, boldly in the arch of her brow, in the pout of her mouth, the lift of her breasts. *No longer a slave.* In all the times she had tried on the dresses, she had never thought to arrange her hair. Lady was always in her mind. Never had it manifested before her eyes.

Lizzy slipped the pearl necklace from her neck and draped it across Lydia's. Ivory against ivory. She straightened her back, her neck regal. She grazed her finger over a nose and lips as narrow as any on the side of power. Something flickered in her eyes. And then she knew; she was not *like* them. She *was* them. There was no difference. She was not a slave. She was a lady.

The moment she thought it, that very second, her heart fluttered. Was her African ancestry nothing? Was it nothing to be disconnected from the people she loved? She thought of her father in the tobacco fields, her grandmother in the confined slave quarters. She thought of John. *"It don't much matter to me what shade a woman's skin is."*

Really? What if he saw her now? A sadness overtook the moment. A death of sorts.

"Oh Lydia, you don't look at all like a slave anymore. You're beautiful now."

Was she not the same woman with the same features that she had been only moments before?

"You look White."

But she was not. Not on the inside. She slipped the dress off her shoulder.

"What's wrong, Lydia? Don't you like how you look?"

"I do, but…"

"But what?"

"Never mind, Lizzy."

"No, tell me." Lizzy plopped back on Lydia's bed, her eyes wide with wonder. "I want to know."

"It's hard to make clear." She shook her head. "I love looking like a lady. Just not a White one." She had come full out of the formal dress now and stood shrugging into her old clothes.

"Honestly?"

"Yes."

"I thought everyone wanted to be White."

"Lizzy." Such foolishness.

"Well, I did. I'm not trying to be funny, Lydia. I just thought—"

"You really thought we wanted to be White? We don't want that at all. Just freedom. We want to be free." *I* want to be free. "I've never wanted to be White."

It sounded ridiculous coming from her, a woman as near light as the one on the bed. Even still, it was true. "Never, Lizzy. I just want what you have. I want the same rights as you."

"As me?" Lizzy laughed. "I'm as much a slave as you in this house. Most women don't have their say neither. If you're wanting rights, ask for those my daddy's got. Now those are rights."

They both laughed. The thought had never occurred to Lydia. Dr. Kelly was the only one able to come and go as he pleased. To do whatever godforsaken thing he wanted.

"Lydia." Lizzy slid to the edge of the bed. "I met a man."

She laughed again. They were mirrors. Funny how life was.

"You did? Tell me about him." Lydia joined Lizzy on the bed, sitting on her legs.

"He's handsome. Charming. Just a perfect gentleman."

"And his name?"

"Jackson."

Jackson and John.

"I wasn't even sure if I wanted to go to the gathering and look what happened. I'm smitten."

"*Smitten?* Is that right?"

"Why, I might as well be. I can't get him off my mind."

"Well, when will you see him again?"

"I'm hoping soon. He told me he's arranging a ball at his manor next weekend. I want to go, but he lives in Manassas."

"Virginia?"

"Yes." Lizzy sighed solemnly. "Lydia, I *really* want to go. I need to go. I need to see him again."

Like she needed to see John. Lydia smiled. She followed her friend's eyes as they moved to the rumpled dress on the floor, watched blue eyes beam.

"Come with me."

"What?"

"Come with me. To Virginia."

"Are you out of your mind? No."

"*Please.* Oh, please, Lydia."

"No! Lizzy, what are you thinking? You're *not* thinking."

"I am. It's perfect. It's a perfect idea."

"It's foolish and you know it."

"Oh, it's perfect!" Lizzy climbed off the bed, clapped her hands, and laughed.

"Lizzy, stop it."

"Can you imagine?" She leaned down and grabbed Lydia's shoulders. "Me and you in Manassas? Two White women—"

"No, I can't."

"It's not that far. Less than an hour away."

"I'm not sneaking out of the house, acting like I'm White. And cross the state line? No."

Lizzy pleaded.

But before she could refuse again, Lizzy squeezed her hands. Lydia looked down at their fingers, one on top of the other.

There was no difference.

CHAPTER SIX

$\mathcal{E}$very day Lydia waited for Midnight.

Every day she waited until John found reason to be near. Out, away from the manor, were havens more beautiful than anything that could be housed. John introduced her to endless shades of green on long walks and awakened in her body hungers she had never known she had. She tried to resist but love seeped in.

She smiled at the thought of him. Teeth shone against a skin so smooth and black it looked like the velvet she used to make something rare, something beautiful.

A fine-looking man, women whispered when they thought she wasn't listening. When he came in from the tobacco fields, rags froze midswipe, brooms stood at attention, and even those who'd worked side-by-side with him cocked their heads at his rolled-up sleeves and the peek of muscle when his shirt lifted, wiping his forehead with the back of his hand. *Just doesn't make no sense for a man to look so good,* they purred. What didn't make sense, Lydia thought, was their persistence even in her presence.

Nearly every Sunday after suppertime, some lady, wide-eyed and nervous, would tip into the cabin he shared with Charles, Master's driver, bearing gifts—a crisp apple dumpling, anything hot, sweet, and as oozing as her words—like she was standing on holy ground, setting eyes on Baby Jesus Himself. When John received her offering, she'd rejoice. *No, don't thank me. Thank you! I should've done more.* But Lydia never even received so much as a glance from any of them. Because of it, as soon as the wooden door creaked shut, she was quick to ask for the treat. She devoured every one of those gifts, swallowed every morsel of those traps, until she sat full and pleased that not even a crumb had touched her love's lips, let alone his heart.

On the back porch of the cabin they sat in the dark of night.

"Marry me."

The words warmed her heart. He wanted her. This man wanted her as his own. If only…

"John, I can't. You don't even know me."

"I know enough."

"No, you don't." If he knew the things in her head. The wish, the dream of life in her heart. Never a dream of love.

"All right then, Lydia. Tell me."

"Tell you what?"

"What I don't know."

She laughed.

"I'm for real now. What don't I know?"

"I can't tell you all that."

"Sure you can. Little by little. Go on. Tell me something."

"All right." She wrapped her arms around her legs, laid her head against her thigh. "I love sunrises."

"That's good."

"And the smell of cinnamon on apples."

"Umm. I like that too."

"And sunshine. I love the way it feels when I'm walking in it."

"That's 'cause you're not working in it. I guess I'd love it, too, if it wasn't beating down on my back from the time it got up every morning." He smiled when she giggled. "What else? What about holding hands? You like holding hands?" He laid her palm on his and grazed it with his fingertips. She shivered.

"You cold?"

Nowhere near.

"What else you like?"

"Ladybugs."

"Really?"

"I know it's silly." She straightened her back and stretched her legs in front of her. "But when I was little it's what I wanted to be. So I could fly away."

"It's not silly. Long as you're not trying to fly off nowhere."

If she could, she would. He smiled. *Would she?*

"I bet you don't know many girls who like bugs."

"No. No, I don't, but I doubt it's the bug part you like. It's the lady. You're a little lady yourself."

She stared at him. This man understood her better than she understood herself.

"All right, *Lady.*" He turned her toward him and slid his thumb from her temple to her chin. "Anything you don't like?"

"No." She looked up into moonlit eyes of onyx. "There's nothing I don't like tonight."

———— ·◆· ————

John arrived ten minutes early, watching, pacing, waiting for Lydia at the back of the Kelly manor.

In the month since she'd showed up at the slave gathering, he had spent every Sunday evening with her. But tonight was a weeknight. They wouldn't have much more than an hour together. Studying the night sky, he noted the whereabouts of the moon, the position of the stars, and shook out the crinkled pass from his pocket, reading it for the fourth time, like it had somehow changed since he'd last checked. He needed to do more, rise earlier, get out more crops, anything to get Dr. Kelly to give him more time with her.

He was getting nearer, inching closer to where he was going. Soon this whole state of mind would be a thing of the past.

John watched Lydia skip down the back steps two at a time. One minute she was far from him, the next, near and up close. He wanted her closer.

"Lady."

She smiled. *Beautiful.* His hands wanted to reach for her, but he shoved them deep into his pockets instead. "It's a beautiful night."

"Yes, it is."

He led her through an orchard. The tang of citrus and sweet apple hung in the air, clinging to their clothes. John picked up black walnuts from the ground and tossed one to her. To his surprise, she caught it and giggled.

"Pretty good. You're quick."

She smiled.

"I'm glad we're able to see each other during the week. I wasn't sure the Kellys would be all right with it. Some masters don't allow it, you know."

Lydia walked with her hands clasped behind her back in silence.

"They *are* letting you see me tonight, right?"

"Well…"

"Well?" He laughed. *Hadn't expected that.* "Well, it's best you get on back inside before they discover it."

"They think I'm taking a walk with Cora, but it's all right. They won't come looking."

"You sure?"

"Are you leaving if I'm not?"

"No."

"Well, we're all right then."

She was something. He shook his head and looked at her. Sweet but something else. That something else kept him coming.

Tonight, she was quiet, quieter than she'd been the other times.

They stopped under a maple tree. He sat near the base of the trunk and tugged her wrist. She followed and eased down in front of him. The ground was moist from a late shower the night before.

"You all right, Lydia?"

"I'm all right. Just thinking."

"About?"

"Us."

"Us?" It was all he thought about lately. "Is that right?"

"You think we'll always be slaves?"

"No." *No.* He knew it. Answered her quickly. It was his constant prayer. "I'm hoping one day, not too long from now, we'll see the other side." He looked up at the starry sky. He looked at her. "No." There was too much beauty in the world. "No, we won't always be slaves."

Lydia bent her knees and laid her head against them, stretching the length of her skirt over her ankles.

They sat in silence, the night breeze relaxing him. He pressed back until his spine rubbed against the trunk and bark crumbled onto his shoulder. He closed his eyes but just as soon felt fingers tapping his. Her widened eyes startled him.

"What is it, Lydia?"

Like lightning, he glanced around them, then back at her.

She blinked. Shaking her head, she simply smiled, but when she looked back into his eyes, she whispered, "The night I ran off. I sat just like that." She dusted his shoulder clean. "Just felt like when I looked at you I'd seen it all before."

She hadn't, but he had. Witnessed it all.

"I always wish there was more, John." Lydia swiped her hands through the grass then glanced up at the Kelly manor. "More to our lives. I think about being free all the time."

"I can't imagine there's a slave who don't." John brushed a blade from her wrist, damp from the moisture in the air.

"Oh, there's slaves who don't, John. Plenty of them. Believe me. They just stop thinking about it. They give up. But that's not me. I'm never gonna stop wanting it." She looked into his eyes. "There's nothing I want more."

"Nothing?"

"Nothing."

The statement stung. Not even love, he'd thought to ask, but instead he nodded and added, "I won't rest until we have it."

"I can see that." Her words, her voice waved through him. "I can see that in you."

"Do you?" He leaned closer. "What else you see?"

"I see somebody late for curfew."

"No." He shook his head. "What else do you see?"

Lydia curled her pinkie around his. "I see a man who makes me happy."

"Better. I like that." He touched his lips to the back of her hand, stared into her eyes, and studied her face, promising himself he would hold the picture as beautiful, as perfect when he was alone, until the next time. "Go inside now, Lady. I want to watch you go in. We'll leave together, at the same time."

"All right."

In the moonlight what was soft became softer. How could he let her go? He walked backward until she was several feet away.

"I need you to be safe, John."

"Pray for me."

"I've never stopped."

Right there, right then he knew he loved her.

"I just can't let go," she whispered.

He knew the feeling.

⎯⎯•◦•⎯⎯

One dark night Lydia sat on the back porch of the Kelly manor shucking peas when she heard a deep voice behind her. She turned to see Charles approaching, his long, thin arms swinging at his side.

"Lydia." He greeted her with a wide smile and whispered, "I've come to take you to John."

The sound of his name made everything on the inside flow.

"Come with me."

She hesitated, searching for spying eyes that might witness her departure without permission during the week.

"Hurry now." He glanced behind him. "We've got to hurry." When he looked back at her, she slipped her hand in his, spilling the wooden bowl of peas across the porch, green gems rolling free. She slipped on them as she ran down the steps after him.

The beauty of the night amazed her. She gazed at the star-filled sky as Charles rushed her to a covered wagon several feet away. He flipped a corner of tarp back and lifted her into the wagon. She watched him tie it down from the outside.

It was dark, incredibly dark under the cover. She could hear her own breath and the breathing of one near.

"Lydia."

John. Before she could reach for him, he was there, his arms around her, pulling her to him.

Like a dream.

"I missed you," she breathed the words, wondered if they were even spoken. Only three days apart and she missed him. "Where are we going?"

"Just a ride. I've been looking out, waiting for a good time. When I saw it, I took it. Charles was ready."

"You were watching me."

"I was. You never know when I might be watching."

She laughed.

"Sit back, Lydia. Rest."

Lydia turned around and leaned back between his open legs. His arms wrapped around her, his hands on hers, his mouth, his lips on her ear, the back of her neck.

The wagon was bumpy, much rougher than a carriage ride, and she couldn't see a thing, but it didn't matter. She felt everything. She knew they were passing the slave quarters when the air filled with the smell of sweet potatoes, caramel, and custard. Women preparing for Sunday, the best day of the week. She closed her eyes and thanked God for a sweet sliver of joy. So close she could taste it.

Like a dream.

CHAPTER SEVEN

*T*he perfect pearl.

Lydia gripped Mrs. Kelly's strand around her neck and forced her hand steady despite the bumpy carriage ride that bounced her endlessly into Lizzy.

"Gorgeous night, isn't it?" Her friend beamed.

"I can't believe we're doing this."

"Oh, Lydia, it'll be fun."

"It's foolish." The whole thing was a foolish idea. Lydia's hands shook as she straightened the shawl over the cream dress that had started this mess. Lizzy had arranged her hair again, but this time in a tight chignon at the nape of her neck. "What if we get caught?"

"My mother said yes, Lydia."

"Reluctantly."

"She said yes."

"To my going as your caretaker. Not as…" Lydia looked down at her attire. "If she knew what we've done. How I look…"

"She won't."

Lydia raised her brows.

"She won't."

"What if Dr. Kelly—"

"Don't worry about him." Lizzy dismissed her concern with a shrug of her shoulders.

"If he finds out, what do you think he'll do?" Why had she gone along with this? Lydia balled the cloth of her dress in the palms of her hands. "Lizzy—"

"Oh, stop it, Lydia. Live a little."

It was all she ever wanted to do.

"Enjoy tonight." Lizzy squeezed her hand. "No one will ever know."

Lydia pulled the curtain back inside the carriage and watched as she journeyed rough roads to another world. They were crossing the Maryland state line.

"Tell me more about this Jackson."

"Well, he's as handsome as he is charming. A well-to-do bachelor. The last of his bloodline. His brother was killed years ago. His father was a friend of the family, but he passed recently and left Jackson with everything. Wait until you see this place. I haven't seen it in years, but if it's anything like I remember, you're going to be amazed."

Lydia only nodded because there was nothing to say. Why had she even asked? It wasn't as though knowing more calmed her. In fact, it caused her more anxiety. She had never been in the company of White folk as their equal.

"What do you all say to each other?"

Lizzy's forehead crinkled.

"I mean, you know, when you're talking? The only party I served at was the one your mother had five years ago and I was so nervous, trying not to spill nothing, I don't remember a thing. So what do you talk about?"

"I don't know, Lydia. Same thing you talk about, I suppose. Just people talking. Nothing special."

"Let's practice."

Lizzy laughed.

"Come on, now, Lizzy. You be a lady at the party."

Lizzy straightened her posture and batted her lashes. She flapped the accordion fan in her hand against her chest. "So very nice to meet your acquaintance, dear."

"Oh. Yes, thank you." Lydia shook the tips of her stiff hand.

"Well, I'd be obliged to—"

"Obliged?"

"I'm just kidding, Lydia." Lizzy snickered. "We don't do that. And we don't have a special language. You talk to me all the time! Just be yourself."

But Lizzy wasn't like any other White person she knew.

"We're here."

The forty-five-minute carriage ride was quicker than Lydia was prepared for. The horse clanked to a stop. A lush evergreen meadow sparkled under the starry sky, framing, in the distance, the Whitfield manor.

Lydia could feel her eyes widen, her back straighten at the sight. What would John think of this place?

She had never seen a house more beautiful. The terra-cotta woodwork extended to a rounded front porch with three seamless front windows. A narrow wooden platform extended from the front door to the sides of the manor.

They rode into the center of a circular path of grass worn thin from the frequent travel of wagons and carriages, and waited.

"You ever seen so many steps?" She counted. *Twenty-nine...Thirty.* "Thirty steps, Lizzy."

"Magnificent, isn't it? I remember the first time I saw it." Lizzy stared at Lydia and the moonlit Victorian she admired.

Assisted by the driver, Lizzy stepped from the coach and crossed the dewy meadow to the rear of the manor. Lydia wobbled behind, the smell of blue grass under the ivory kid side-laced boots she struggled to walk in.

"Lydia, you're with me, remember? Don't walk behind me." Lizzy looped her arm through hers. "You're *with* me."

"Oh, look. I see Margaret Dillon." Lizzy released her. "Remember to be yourself." She turned and added, "Oh, and your name is Caroline. *Caroline.*" She winked and walked away.

Be yourself but change your name. Not an easy charge to manage.

Lydia meandered through the crowd, acknowledging fellow guests with a slight tilt of her head, flashing smiles that faded as quickly as they appeared.

Occasionally, she fussed with the knot of tresses at the nape of her neck, until it loosened, but mostly, she focused.

She tried to disregard the faces, the inquisitive eyes, the mouths—it was the mouths, chattering, murmuring, whispering, that crept icy fingertips up her spine. What were they saying? Did they know? Did they sense that she was not like them? An imposter. A Colored amongst them.

She noticed three ladies conversing nearby. She thought back to her reflection in the mirror. There was no difference if she focused, remembered who she was. Rolling the pearls between her fingertips, she joined them and plunged into an act of premeditated nods, grins, and "do tells" for dialogue she hardly heard.

Familiar laughter pulled her to the present.

From the gazebo porch, Lizzy waved her over and rose from the swing she shared with a woman in pink. Blond tendrils bounced against her round face as she made her way to Lydia.

"Ah, well now, aren't you a picture, Caroline? Simply stunning." Lizzy slipped her hand in Lydia's and pecked both cheeks. Her emerald dress shimmered in the moonlight.

"It's a pleasure." Lydia leaned into her friend and whispered, "Where's Jackson? Have you seen him?"

"Did I hear my name?"

Both women turned. Jackson Whitfield, clad in black waistcoat and trousers, laid his hand on the backs of several guests as he edged his way to Lizzy's side. He greeted Lydia with a grin.

Lydia took in this man. His deep sapphire eyes, black, wavy hair, and slender build. He was handsome, a perfect match for Lizzy.

"Hello, Jackson," Lizzy gushed.

He nodded his acknowledgment but kept his eyes on Lydia. "Have I had the pleasure…?"

"Oh, this is Caroline. My friend Caroline."

"Nice to meet you."

"I'm much obliged," Lydia said awkwardly.

Lizzy giggled.

"Are you ladies just arriving?"

"We are. Yes. Just arrived." Lizzy inched closer to the man. "We didn't miss anything, did we?" She lowered her head and looked up with wide eyes.

"You two miss anything? I don't believe it's possible." Jackson looked through the crowd. "Listen, ladies, I would like you to meet someone. Ah, there he is." He stretched out his hand, brushing it against the top of Lizzy's head, and waved over a young man with freckles. "This is Andrew."

Andrew pecked Lizzy's hand, then Lydia's, planting a kiss that seeped through the thin cotton of her glove.

"So Caroline, is it?" Jackson asked.

Lydia nodded, swallowed.

"And from where do you come?"

"She's from Dorchester." Lizzy inserted herself between them. "Her father is a friend of our family, Jackson."

"Good ol' Jack," a balding, heavyset man with a full mustache said, slapping the host on his back, extending his hand with the other. "Henry Sullivan," he said, tipping his top hat to them.

"Whoa, Henry," Jackson laughed. "Hardly recognized you. You clean up rather nicely."

Beside him was a rail of a man who introduced himself as Rex, a close friend of Jackson's. "Henry and I've known Jack since he was eight years old."

"Six. I think he was six," Henry corrected.

"They work for me, my overseers. Actually, Henry's right. I was six. Timothy was eight. Well, excuse me, gentlemen, ladies, I need to tend to my other guests, but please don't slip away." He directed the last phrase at Lydia.

Jackson excused himself, but even from a few feet away she could see him staring at her, stealing glances as he conversed.

She was flattered to receive attention from a man so handsome, but her mind was on John.

"So, nice night, isn't it?" Andrew glanced up at the sky and nodded. He bit his bottom lip then grinned.

He looked tenser than she felt. Lydia smiled. She wasn't alone. By evening's end, her nervousness drifted, sailed away with each conversation, with every encounter. She moved more and more into a world she'd only dreamed of. She didn't even flinch when Lizzy accepted the invitation to a dinner party Jackson extended to them. She was having fun, after all. Living for the first time.

CHAPTER EIGHT

For the first time, she felt it. Something sweeter than Grandma's apple fritters. This was sweet that stayed long after the first taste. Love for a man.

Lou sat on the porch in a grand wooden rocker Daddy had made her. "Girl gone and fell in love." She slapped Lydia's thigh with the rag she used to mop the sweat trickling from her scalp.

Lydia flinched and giggled. She swatted at a fly. It was much too warm out here on the porch. Funny how it didn't bother her as a child. She pulled the sticky front of her dress away from the circle of sweat it clung to and looked up at her grandmother.

"You loved PaPa like that?"

"Oh, honey, yes. I sure did. Looonggg time ago." Her head fell back with laughter as she rocked. "Oh yes, indeed. Had all them babies 'cause of it."

Daddy had been the only one who hadn't been sold off, stripped from her. Lydia couldn't imagine how she was able to bear it. How her people were able to bear any of it.

"Well, I don't want no babies."

"What you say?"

"I don't want not one child."

"Why not, girl?"

She shrugged. "I don't know."

"Now don't you sit up here and tell that lie. You know you know why."

"I don't want to bring another slave in the world."

"Girl…"

"Really, Grandma. Ain't nothing good about being a slave."

"Something good about being alive. I know *that*! How you gonna deny somebody the right to be alive?"

"I'm not denying nobody nothing. I'm just saying *I'm* not having no babies. If they want to come in the world they've got to come from between somebody else's legs."

"Watch yourself, now." Lou threw the rag at her. "Don't be grown."

"You know I know about babies, Grandma. You taught me everything I know."

"Fine you know. You just keep your own particulars to yourself." She smiled and shook her head. "You thought about how you gonna keep yourself from having a child? Lust and limbs got a way of deciding things for themselves."

"I know what to do."

"All right, then." She crossed her arms and swung a good four or five swings in her rocker without a word before she leaned down close like a little girl and grinned. "So tell me. He makes you happy, don't he?"

She hesitated.

"He don't make you happy?"

"Yes, Grandma. He does the best he can." John loved her something good. He would do anything for her, but as wonderful as love was, she wasn't sure it was enough.

———•◆•———

The moment John's foot hit the soil, his heart raced. The warm night breeze of August whipped through his shirt as he crept across the fields, the thin cotton billowing around him though tucked into his faded work trousers. Every few feet, he gripped the handle of the trowel in his back pocket and shoved it further from view.

He searched ahead and looked behind him. If he was caught without a pass, he could face a punishment he didn't want to remember. He would never forget the sting of rope around his wrist, the strike against his back, would always recall how he struggled to break free, but the grip was too tight. Not this time. He was careful, smarter, prepared. He was certain no matter what life brought, no grip would ever hold him again.

Crossing over the tobacco field, he slipped between large green leaves that pressed the musky odor of nicotine into his pores. Working on the row each day, he would reek of the scent for hours. Only after a hard lye soap scrubbing could he cleanse himself from the smell that caused Lydia to crinkle her nose.

At the edge of the field, John slipped through the trees into the forest, safer from the ropes of catchers, the guns of hunters, if he could remain quiet. The rustling of leaves dangling around him, and the ones crunching underfoot, could give him away, could ensure overseers of his exact whereabouts.

He was parched after several miles but the thirst ceased when he saw it. He stopped and caught his breath. It was beautiful, as beautiful as the first time he discovered it and decided it was the perfect place.

John walked toward the tree. The silver maple towered over him, made him feel like a child beneath strong, dark branches raised like arms of Africa to the heavens. He stood under the rounded crown of leaves and exhaled. It was the perfect place.

On his knees, he looked around before removing the flat, metal blade he'd swiped from Kelly's storehouse. He pushed the debris of dry twigs and pebbles away with the palms of his hands until the earth was cleared and smooth, soft, and damp to the touch. He looked around before jabbing the tool into the ground. The soil crumbled with ease as he dug, hollowing out the special spot. For a moment, the thought of his hope being swiped sent a shot of fear through him, but his heart steadied when metal tapped against metal. He scraped the dirt away with the tip of the instrument, paused when the moonlight shone on his treasure.

John forced his fingers into the ground around the box and yanked it free from its grave. Reverently, he lifted it to his heart, to his lips.

——————•◆•——————

She should not have come.

Lydia pulled strands of hair over her scar and stared at Jackson and Andrew across the oblong, formal table she was used to serving. Lizzy sat at her side, oohing and ahhing, grinning and nodding at every statement the two uttered. She would never have agreed to dinner had she known it was to be just the four of them.

A great candelabra sprawled like a spider with crystal legs over them, shone against wine-stained walls, casting a rose tint on White faces. Seemed the men suspected nothing, though Jackson's constant staring was beginning to tickle icicles down her spine again. She pressed against the back of the mahogany chair, shivered when she encountered the house slaves.

James, the butler, a short, sandy-haired man, gazed over her once and then strode swiftly to the back of the room. She didn't even notice when he slipped out, but Annie, a lanky maple-colored girl her age, kept her almond-shaped eyes on Lydia. When she set a plate of roast, steaming potatoes and carrots in front of her, she lingered. Lydia could hear her breathing over her, looking, staring at what? The tight wave of her hair at the crown of her head? The tremor in a hand that served the same meals, wiped the same tears, hid the same scars?

"Wine?" Jackson asked.

Lizzy lifted her glass. "We sure appreciate your hospitality, Jackson. It was perfect timing. We're leaving in a month for Richmond."

"You and Caroline?"

"No," Lydia said, too quickly.

"No. My family and I. Caroline was there earlier this summer, isn't that right?" Lizzy nudged.

Lydia nodded and tugged at the napkin in her lap. She heard few of the words around her, only the pauses and the clearing of throats when she failed to fill holes of conversation directed at her. She ate little, found her hand less on her fork than the pearls she'd once again borrowed, her nails entangled in the strand, grazing each gem. For every thought of John that tugged at her, she pulled, yanked at the white treasure at her fingertips.

"Caroline? Is everything all right? Your supper?" Jackson glanced at her plate. "Is the food to your liking?" His fork lay limp in his hand as he searched her. Steady eyes of blue like the sky she had shunned, just as blue as the one she had wished would turn dark, black—*let it be night*—she stared into, held their gaze.

"Everything's fine." She looked at him, wasn't even sure she had spoken the words, until he nodded and resumed eating.

She watched him, chewing, chatting, lines streaking from the corner of his eyes and a bright smile of a mouth that let out a sound that made her sit upright, take notice.

This sound, heavy in strength yet light enough to fly free, lift to the high ceiling, was sharp enough to enter in, jagged enough to pierce her heart.

"Pardon me." She pushed away from the table abruptly, the legs of her chair scraping against the hardwood. The room fell silent. She could feel their eyes on her as she stood, marched toward the doorway, the neckline of her dress slipping off her shoulder. She pulled it straight and walked through a hall, through a dark sitting room, a study that smelled of pine. She didn't know where she was going, didn't know how she'd gotten where she was until she swung the heavy wooden door open, not waiting for the butler's assistance, and scurried down the thirty front steps of the manor in the heels that made her ankles wobble. She stopped, out of breath, when she heard her name.

"Caroline!"

She stopped for a name that wasn't hers at all.

"Caroline?"

She turned to the one calling. Jackson ran to her, gripped her forearms, his eyes darting from her face, her body. "Are you all right? What is it?" Just as quickly, he lifted his hands and stepped back, his brows crinkled.

"I want to go." She swept her fingers through the hair above her forehead, hoped he hadn't seen, hadn't noticed the thing she was hiding. "I'm ready to go."

"All right." He paused, stared at her, then tilted his head toward the house. "I'm not so sure Elizabeth is ready."

"I need to go."

He nodded. Slowly.

Lydia clenched the necklace, tried to steady trembling hands.

"Do I make you uneasy?"

"No." *Yes.*

"I'm sorry if I do." The truth spoke louder than her lie. "I'm just mesmerized." He smiled. Sharp features softened. "You're a beauty."

Her fingers fell from the strand.

"Truth is, I would love to get to know you. Formally, of course."

She looked down. Why was she here?

"I need to fill this space."

His house? She gazed up at the splendid Victorian behind him. His heart? She glanced at him. He was waiting, waiting for her to look into his eyes. She swallowed.

"I need a wife."

She shook her head. *John.* "I'm not the one."

"Maybe not." He laughed. "Maybe so."

"I'm not." She turned, lifting her dress above her ankles, and walked away, crushing wet blades of grass under her feet.

She could still hear him laughing when she climbed into the carriage. That sound. She recognized it now. Knew precisely what it was.

The sound of life.

In the darkest of night, Lydia sat among the dying.

The Room was still, and though all slept, rest escaped their faces. Sprawled against the back walls, not one of them had the space to recline in the midst of material without touching the foot or the arm of another. Gnats and mosquitoes had come through the gaps of the log walls and swarmed around their heads and the flickering candlestick they had failed to extinguish in the corner.

She sat with an unquenchable thirst, waiting for Ruth or Abram to stir, to utter a word for her to consume, to draw in like the suckling babe's craving for mother's milk, the field slave's need of water after a full day's toil beneath the hot beams of sun under a sky she prayed would darken. She thought of Jackson's eyes. Was it darkness she wanted?

She waited for them to tell her to endure, that everything she needed was right where she was and not in a laughter she could still hear hours later. She needed the old folk to confirm Lou's words to stay put, but they did not wake up and the reassurance never came. Lydia folded into herself and rocked against the churning, the knowing deep down. Wouldn't matter if they had stated every word she craved to hear because she had seen the truth so many times in their eyes, the blinking away of wretchedness, in the tears that filled but rarely fell.

CHAPTER NINE

 ydia, there's something I need to say."

"What is it?"

"Sit down." John helped her settle onto a pile of straw, kneeling beside her. Moonlight streaked her cheek. She lit everything, made even Dr. Kelly's pine-scented storehouse bright.

The space was humid, warm. John tugged on the collar of worn denim, unsure which to blame—the weather or the woman sitting in front of him.

An hour earlier, they had slipped off and wandered around carefree. She begged him to take her somewhere, anywhere to see something different. It was a risk, but he had to admit stealing away with her gave him a rush he hadn't expected.

They walked past the slave cabin to the place he came daily to store supplies for the doctor.

The storehouse was sheathed in weatherboard under an old shingle roof. Inside, the one-room house was divided in half by a stack of pine wood shelves rising seven feet high. Tonight, it acted as a barrier from the real world, offering them something for the first time, a place of their own.

"Lydia, you ever seen a man in love?"

She stared at him.

"Ever seen a man treat a woman like she's everything? Like a rose, making sure she don't get trampled on?" John covered her hands with his. "Ever seen that, Lady? A man in love?"

"Dr. Kelly's not around much, but—"

"I'm not talking about Dr. Kelly." He edged closer. "You're seeing it right now. You're seeing it right now, Lydia."

Slowly, slowly, she smiled.

"You're my rose. But you know what? I can't take care of it. My rose don't got much of a chance, not if I don't protect it. And I can't. Not like this. Dr. Kelly's got the freedom to do it and I've got to have it too."

"What are you saying?" He could see her chest rising and falling.

"I've got money."

"Money?"

"Yes."

"How much?"

"Enough. Enough to get out of here."

"John?" She scrambled to her knees. "John, you think they'll let you go?"

"That I don't know. I'm hoping. I'm going to find out."

"When?" She looked down, bit her lip.

"Soon." He had no idea. "The perfect time."

"There is no perfect time, John. You know that."

"We'll know when."

"We?"

"Yes. I want you to come with me."

"What do you mean?"

"I mean, I have money for both of us. I have enough."

"John…"

"I have enough."

She studied him.

"More than a thousand dollars."

"John, how—where did you get it?"

"It's my lot." He inched closer, her knee against his, and whispered, "Riches gathered, collected from age to age. It was my great-grandmother's plan."

She stared at him, shook her head.

"Yes. MaDora wanted one of her kin to walk free. She hired herself out washing clothes for pennies. *Pennies*, Lydia. Whatever she made, she stored in an old metal box, welded on the top lid, the first three cents she ever earned. She passed that box filled with all her money—didn't spend one penny on herself—to her son, my grandfather, Lee Sanders. He was a carpenter and followed after the path of his mother faithfully. Cutting wood, carving detailed designs into rocking chairs, tables, benches, all things wooden subject to splintered hands and a mind, I believe, powerful enough to create a world. A gifted man who made the most for his children's children. He brought in the most money out of all of us together. I'm telling you, Lydia, he could've used that wealth for himself. Could've bought himself out of bondage, I'm sure, but he remained faithful to his mother's dream. He wanted it more for me, more for those to come."

"That's amazing."

"It is. My mother, just before she died, passed the box on to me."

"Where is it?"

"Here. Buried. She sold vegetables from her garden on Saturdays. I tell you, she never did see a day's rest." He dropped his head, hated to think of the weariness that hung her lids, her shoulders heavy. "Master Ridge let me hire myself out, welding, at the end of the week to small farms near his plantation. And here we are. Finally enough."

The telling of his story, this account of his people whispered to the one he loved, was sacred. It moved him and he found his palm open against his chest, his heart, the thumping, the rhythm of life from kin to kin.

"But with all the trading, the selling, the moving around, how did it stay in your family?"

"That's the miracle, Lydia. It stayed because it was supposed to stay, settled in my hands for such a time as this. For us."

"That money was saved for you. We're not even *married* or nothing." Her words were light and lyrical, but worry creased her brow. Although the world didn't recognize their union, they could, should acknowledge themselves. She rubbed a piece of straw between her fingers. Large green eyes blinked up at him.

Those eyes. Married…Yes. They'd have to do something about that.

"I just need to talk to Dr. Kelly." He pulled at the straw in her hand. "At the right time."

She didn't answer.

"What do we have to lose, Lydia?"

"Nothing."

The word tumbled from her lips too fast, fell deep in the pit of him. She had nothing to lose. Not a thing.

She sat up on her legs and stretched the length of her dress around her, inching forward beside him. Her knee against his thigh.

She smiled and he felt himself breathing again. Had he been holding his breath? He wanted to keep her smiling. What he would do to keep her happy…

John lay back with his hand behind his head and closed his eyes and saw himself answering to no one but God. *A real man.*

Pieces of straw pricked his arm as Lydia slid beside him. When he opened his eyes, hers were closed and he saw the girl in the woods. He would ·carry her again. Take her home. Keep her safe. He slid his arm behind her, around her, and folded her into him.

What he needed was the perfect timing that would lead them on a path out of here, but what he wanted was another miracle, a way to keep the world from ever hurting her again.

He drifted off. Lydia danced in his dreams, light and free. His Lady.

"John…John?"

He awoke to her smile shining down on him. He scrambled up and swiped his face with his palm.

"Lydia, I'm sorry."

"You're fine."

"How long was I asleep?"

"Not long. An hour maybe."

"Why didn't you wake me? I've got to get you back."

"You were smiling."

"Smiling?"

"In your sleep." She grinned. "As close to free as you could be tonight."

CHAPTER TEN

*I*t wasn't easy living without love.

Love was the breath that moved through a body, lit a soul, the spirit that, if quenched, left one empty on the outside of a changing world simply watching.

Emma Kelly watched the girls picking blueberries from the sheer curtains of her bedroom window and shook her head. Their fingers would be stained purple for days, but the ruffled ivory sleeves Elizabeth repetitively shoved above her elbows would be stained for life. She couldn't count how many times she'd warned her daughter of wearing anything she cared about in the fields. No matter how much Lydia scrubbed, dark splotches would fade, but never lift completely. Emma had tried herself once and scrubbed her fingers raw. Giving up, she resorted to lye, pouring the bubbling liquid over the cloth, but it burned her skin until it oozed pus and seared a hole through the fabric. She now knew some things couldn't be saved.

She watched her daughter with Lydia, saw herself in earlier years. The full of their skirts accentuated their cinched waists as they leaned over the bushes, their hands cupped under clumps of fruit they rubbed, loosened until they fell into the bottom of the wooden buckets swinging from their forearms. They were good girls, had grown into nice women. Cora still a baby among them.

Cora.

The pain of looking at that girl had dissipated with all her other emotions. The moment she witnessed what she tried to disregard, she froze like a pillar, her heart now stone.

It was the only way she could rise day after day, nod at passersby, smile at humor that was no longer amusing, sit among the living. If she had continued to feel the truth, every ache, every hurt, process all the anguish and deceit from a man she had loved, the weight of it would have broken her, stripped her mind of understanding, and she would've ended ripped to her core. Like Beatrice.

Emma and Beatrice. Elizabeth and Lydia. Her daughter was likely to suffer the same fate, her husband one day wanting the other, the slave woman in her house.

Emma had been in love, grateful for this gentleman to whom her father bestowed her. She was to be the lady of her own home. She beamed at the thought of it, no more than a girl, three seasons shy of her twentieth year. Her heart warmed at the small smile on Michael's lips as they rode in silence down the dark winding road, to the old colonial her father sold him, Beatrice toggling in the wagon behind them.

Alone in their sleeping quarters, she stared into his big, brown eyes and longed to feel his large arms around her, to lie against the warm fur of his chest, but when she kissed his temple, he flinched. When she wrapped her arms around his neck, he gripped her hands, his thumbs pressing against the small bones of her wrist, and pulled away. Only on occasion did he come to her in the middle of the night, and only for a few moments, only touching as much as needed. She lie like Leah, unwanted, swaddled in cool sheets and hot tears.

Emma wondered what was wrong, why he resisted what was rightfully his. She sat for hours contemplating, painting her lids, her cheeks, her lips, bathing in scents of vanilla, crushed petals of lilac, pouring oils as fragrant as they were sacred, anointing the parts of her body she prayed he'd desire, but nothing drew him to her.

One morning, she sat across from him, Beatrice serving hot steaming flapjacks between them. She spoke to her friend, bid her good morning, and witnessed dark eyes darting from her gaze to her husband's. Beatrice scrunched the buttons between her cleavage into her fist and turned away. Michael cleared his throat and rose, brushed against her thigh as he walked out. It was their last breakfast together.

She hated him. Hated her servant, but only for the hours it took for Beatrice to come to her, late in the night, bowing before her, sobbing into her lap, sorry, so sorry, her tears sticking the thin skirt of her dress to her knees. Emma cupped the back of her head and cried in agony and forgave the worst of sins.

When she gave birth to Elizabeth, Beatrice cared for the girl as if she were her own. Dark hands lifted her, cleaned her, cared for her, held the child, spoke life into her. Elizabeth was her slave's daughter, their hearts knit together from her baby's first breath.

She was too bitter to fill her arms with the babe. That night, Michael took one look at the child that brought her to the brink of death and with a nod, left, out to the slave quarters. That night, she vowed never to allow him in her bed again.

A month later, a bitter root sprang up on the Kelly plantation and it scared Emma speechless.

Each harvest she had watched Beatrice in the gardens. Intrigued by the woman's interest, one dawn she followed her out to the rich ground of soil, setting the soles of her shoes in the footprints of the one who traveled ahead.

Beatrice walked nearly a yard before she paused. Glancing over a bony shoulder, the edges of her lips curved.

"I want to come with you," Emma announced.

"Come." The wide neck of her burlap dress had slipped back against her throat, baring a narrow back and the sharpest of blades. The early-morning rays cast a glow around her as she high-stepped across the field. From behind, her dark brown legs and elbows looked like broken twigs, thin and fragile.

Emma gripped her woolen shawl around her shoulders against the wind and trotted faster until she clipped the back of her friend's heel.

When they reached the rows of vegetation, Beatrice squatted, her skirt hiked up over dark patched knees. Even from the front, she was all angles, except her head, made especially round by the tightly tied gingham scarf covering it. Emma leaned over her and watched. Beatrice teetered forward as she yanked on tiny, feathery branches then steadied herself with her left hand. Plucking the carrot from the dirt, she wiggled it at Emma. "This is a nice one. Nice and smooth, don't you think?" Earth packed into half moons under her nails. "You try it."

Emma looked around. She knew little about gardens, even less about reaping.

"Go on."

She scrunched up her skirt over her calves and knelt beside Beatrice. The damp soil caved around her as she leaned over ruffled green foliage.

"Watch it!" Beatrice warned when Emma's fingertips grazed a purple trimmed leaf. "Look at that. That's no carrot, ma'am." Wide-eyed, Beatrice shook her head. "That there is dangerous. See here." She held her long, curved fingers inches under the limp leaf. "See those four corners and that there purple on the outside, that's not good. That's poison. I ain't seen nothing like this since I been here. Seen it all the time on your father's land."

Emma stared at Beatrice's trembling hands and listened to her fear now bound in whispers.

"Back home, this here plant killed nine folk, Emma. Nine! You remember that?"

She nodded. Scarcely, just barely she recalled the incident.

"Three men, five women, and a child, no bigger than this here." She held her dark palm a couple of feet from the ground. "Barely walking, he was. It was something awful. Nine Coloreds gone just like *that*."

Emma stared at the olive plant. Hard to believe something so small, so fragile, had so much power.

"Look at it real good so you remember."

Later that evening, standing in the back corner of her candlelit dining room, Emma leaned against a cold wall, watching her husband. The brisk night air invaded the room and sent a shiver down the length of her.

When Beatrice served him kale, she thought of what else her friend had placed before him, what more he had eagerly received, taken. When she poured olive oil over crusty slices of bread, she thought of the warm liquid she had drizzled over her own body for him. When she served the cherry pie, she thought of her bleeding heart, the softness of a soul devoured.

Michael's fork pierced the brown crust and a thick red stream oozed onto his white plate. A drip slipped over the edge of the porcelain and splattered into a crimson tear.

Emma's chest pounded.

Her husband spooned pie into his mouth. With each scoop, Emma saw limp olive and purple chopped so finely, diced so obscurely, sprinkled with venom in every bite. She watched the man of the house eating, enjoying each mouthful, and she imagined his pleasure fading, his smile freezing, his heart stopping....

"Emma? Is that you?" Michael leaned back in his chair, his head cocked toward the corner she was standing. "I didn't even see you back there."

But all Emma could do was stare. The vision had strangled her words, smothered her voice.

"Emma?"

She ran out of the room, terrified.

Seasons passed. The poison never erected itself again, except in Emma's heart.

She became bitter, filled with violent images of her husband's destruction. Wagons, tractors, men tearing him apart, limb by limb, piece by piece, as he had done her soul. On the few nights she found him asleep in their sitting room, one leg dangling off the sofa, or passed out on the barn floor, hay stuck to the beads of sweat across his forehead, his mouth ajar, his breathing heavy through thin nostrils, she leaned over him and whispered death, begging the heavens the privilege of witnessing his last breath, the honor of watching him draw in the last bit of air cursed enough to fill his lungs.

Every sign of hatred, every wretched thought of his demise, she kept hidden deep inside, reined under a shawl of grace, the guise of a lady, but inside she raged. She was always able to control her fury, except for one drizzly summer evening.

She was reclining, rocking in the white paint-chipped swing on the front porch of their colonial, watching the sprinkle of rain when the front door swung open and Michael stepped out, a gust of wind blowing the wild curls of his hair back over his forehead.

He glanced at her and started for the steps.

"Where are you going?" she found herself asking.

He didn't answer.

"Where are you going?" she asked again, the question clipped in anger.

Michael stopped.

"Who do you think you're talking to?" He didn't even turn around, just waited for the submissive silence sure to follow, then jogged down the steps, but when his feet hit the gleaming grass below, something in her raced. She saw herself going after him, had thought it was just in her mind, but before she knew it, she was moving to the edge of the porch, walking down planks of wood, marching, running, sprinting toward him, her heavy dress swooshing around her legs, confining her movement only slightly because what was in her burst loose. She sprang forward, leapt on his back, her arms locked around his neck, scrambling, gripping, screeching at him, beating his flesh with tiny fists, pounding him, slapping against his skull. He swung around, grabbed at the legs wrapped around him, but he couldn't shake her. She held on, snatching his damp hair from the roots. Swearing, he stooped, tumbling her forward, farther on top of him now, her stomach curved over the crown of his head, her hands gripping his ears, she grappled, bit down, tasted the hot salt of his cheek. He swung hard, his elbow jamming into her ribs, and threw her off of him, but not before her fingernails dug deep, streaking his neck red.

She scrambled up in the wet grass, heaving, watching, waiting.

He gripped his sun-parched neck, blood dripping down the square nails of his fingers and his cream collar, his back bent as though the weight of her was still upon him. His narrow eyes said everything she felt, but to her surprise no sound came from his lips, just a quiver he bit down against. Not a word exchanged between them.

She swept her hand over her hair, swiped her forehead with her trembling palm, and pulled her dress straight as she staggered to her feet. She took a deep breath and left him in the field alone.

Neither mentioned that day, never spoke of it. In the morning, she had thought it a dream, until she saw the bunched-up shirt in the wicker basket of soiled laundry. She picked it up, the smell of lust still clinging to its fibers, the drops of blood at its collar. She scrubbed it endlessly but never could remove the blemish.

As the months passed, she knew, didn't want to know, there was something growing, flourishing in the womb of the one she loved. She glanced at the small bump under Beatrice's dress, tried to ignore the pouch of life that made her restless, stole the last of what was in her, her slumber, her hunger to live.

Even Beatrice was different. With each month, she grew sadder, spoke less, spending each day in the garden, each night at the loom.

When she went into labor in the fall, Emma sat at her feet, gripping her hand in the midst of slaves, frail chocolate and mocha arms lifting Beatrice, clenching her shoulders, her wrists, as she squatted, teetering on the balls of her feet in the dirt cabin. Among them, an old, gray-haired midwife, Odessa, mumbling, praying something, in tears, but when Beatrice collapsed and the cry of mother and child united, it was Emma who caught the baby's slippery body in the folds of her wool dress, sliding to the ground with the new life, her skirt as bloody as the one who birthed her. She stared into the deep-set brown eyes of her husband and wept.

She didn't know whether Michael knew Cora was his. If he even cared.

Months later when Beatrice was found in the garden, Emma died too. No more reason to fight. Nothing else to give.

She watched the young ladies gleaning the last of the fruit from the bushes, their wooden buckets barely grazed, her husband marching through the fields between them, his boots covered with the juice of everything he had crushed. Emma watched it all.

She saw nothing.

CHAPTER ELEVEN

*L*ydia smiled at John as he crossed his outstretched legs, one scuffed boot on top of the other. When he leaned back on his palms, her gaze followed the bulging vein at his wrist, the bicep of his arm, flexing as he twisted himself comfortable, to the rolled-up cotton sleeve and a smile that made her blush. Three candle flames flickered, danced, cast shadows on his face in the muggy storehouse.

Since their secret discussion, thoughts of liberation overwhelmed her as much as they had that night in the woods. She couldn't shake the idea of being with him loose, boundless, released to stroll through wide rainbow fields of flowers, their locked fingers swinging together against their sides without a curfew or a master to answer to for anything. Sauntering through dark hallways to spacious dining rooms lit with candelabras.

Lydia looked away. It was Jackson's Victorian she imagined, his laughter she could now hear rising and falling around her.

"You're not here," John said.

Was she *ever*? She could feel his gaze on her, studying her face.

"You're thinking."

"I am."

"About?"

"What you said last night. Do you really think it's possible?"

He nodded.

"I need it to be true, John." The feeling was eating at her again. Unrest always started the same way. Bit by bit, bite by bite, it wouldn't be long before she was completely consumed. Soon peace would become as unfamiliar as a stranger. All joy would be wrapped into wanting. She was slipping into that place again, that space in her soul where she knew, was completely aware that nothing would satisfy like the thing that eluded her. She was nothing without it. What was a person anyway without rights, without a choice?

"You need it?"

"I do."

"Why? Why so much?"

Why? She blinked.

"Why do you need it? This is not enough?"

"This?" She glanced around the stuffy storehouse that was not even theirs, their backs jabbed with spiky pieces of straw against paint-peeled walls and a ratty blanket he'd brought. "John."

"I don't know, Lydia. You're with me. I'm with you. I can't seem to think of nothing better."

Carriage rides, elegant wine-walled rooms, the warm savor of beef set before her, her body graced in smooth folds of satin. Better filled her mind.

She looked down, tugged a string loose from her dress, anything to keep from looking into his eyes.

John didn't know, hadn't felt the feeling of running free. The wind whisking around him, the power that pumped his legs through anything, everything against him. Even as scared as she had been, nothing got her heart racing like its call to rise, to fly.

"You don't understand."

"I don't?" He grabbed the white string in her hand and tied it slowly around her ring finger. "I do."

He stretched out on his back beside her and looked up at the shabby tin roof. "I ran twice before."

"What?"

"The first time I was about fourteen, working in Master Seward's corn-field. I started hearing so many men talking about escaping. It became the thing they did every day, all winter. They talked, and I listened. Then finally in late spring, three decided it was time. They left one night, and I never saw them again. I heard one was hung not too far from Seward's land. They said he wouldn't come back without a fight so they killed him, but I like to think the other two made it." He took a breath, his eyes far away. "Every day

I waited to see if they would return. When summer came and went I knew I couldn't wait no longer. One cool night, I said good-bye to my mama and went after the North Star. Got all the way up near the Pennsylvania border before I got caught." John bit his bottom lip and closed his eyes. "The men in the field always said it was better to die than get caught, and I begged the Lord to kill me first before He left me in the hands of a White man."

"Who found you?" Lydia whispered. She wanted to know, didn't want to know. She didn't want to imagine, picture him captured. Too late. She saw him wrestling, straining to break free from the hands of…"Your master?"

"No. Some slave catcher. Told me he'd blow my head off if I didn't tell him who I belonged to. I wasn't going to tell him a thing. Go on, kill me, I was going to say, but one of Master's overseers was up North looking for some of their runaways and he knew me. Knew right off I was Seward's. Umm…" He shook his head. "I got thirty-nine lashes, folk said. Master started off then got tired and turned the whip over to the one who found me. Thirty was the last I recall. Woke up raw and bloody, skin hanging off my back." He sat up and breathed into his palms and for several minutes remained silent, his back curved under the weight of the words. "The pain… My mother cared for me, nursed me back, prayed for me, for my body and my mind. I never did understand why the Lord let me live. Not until now. Not until I met you."

Lydia moved behind him, cradled over him, and laid her hands on his back. Slowly, she slid her fingertips under the fabric of his shirt, grazed raised scars, and wept. "John." She wrapped herself around him, her arms pressing his, her hands against his pounding heart, and whispered, "This is no life for a man. For nobody."

She twisted around in front of him and linked her fingers with his. "What about the second time? You said you ran twice."

"I think that's enough telling for one night."

It was enough for a lifetime. They sat in silence for a moment.

"I just wanted you to know I understand."

"So you know why I have to have it then. Why even this isn't enough."

"Those are your words."

"John."

"Even so, I love you."

She looked up into his eyes. Without thought, she found her hand on his face, her fingers grazing his cheek, his jaw. *Black satin*. Was there anything, anyone, more beautiful?

He tugged the worn blanket across her shoulders.

"Where did you get this thing?"

"What?" He shrugged, laughed. "What's wrong with it?"

"This ol' beat-up rag? You need a new one."

"This suits me just fine."

"You're planning on being a free man with this old blanket? I'm going to make you one. Make *us* one for when we're married."

"Oh yeah?"

She tilted her head. They'd *better* be getting married.

"No, that sounds good." He laughed, pulling her to him. "That sounds good, Lydia."

The thought of her hands at the loom weaving, creating for him, touched her heart.

"It's going to be special, John. A freedom blanket. This time it's going to be different. Isn't it? This time we're going to make it."

Sliding back against the wall, John closed his eyes. Lydia watched a shiny stream trickle down his cheek and bit her lip. She kissed his brow, brushed his lashes with a mouth lost for words. He looked up at her. "Free," she whispered. He smiled, but even in the dim candlelight she could see it, sense it. Sadness in his eyes and a pang shooting through her heart.

CHAPTER TWELVE

*M*iss Ruth?" Lydia whispered in the ear of the old lady in the dark. "You up?" She tapped her fingers against her arm until the woman stirred and turned over on the rumpled blanket.

"Lydia?"

"Yes. It's me."

"What time is it, baby?" Ruth shifted upright and rubbed her eyes. "It's late."

"How do you know that?"

"How do I know? You mean, that it's late?" Ruth laughed. "I can feel it in my bones, girl. Not a minute goes by without it ticking on the inside."

Lydia didn't understand. She never felt life moving through her. For her, it stood still. She glanced at Odessa and Abram sleeping, curled into each other in the corner of The Room. Her life was as still as those who slept, as stagnant as those waiting to die.

"What you doing here, Lydia? You got work to do this late?"

"I just wanted to get started. On my dress." The thought made her smile. "I think I'm getting married soon."

Ruth's back straightened. She turned her face to Lydia. Blue eyes stared past her in the dimness.

"I think I'm getting married."

"Is that right?"

She nodded, then realized Ruth couldn't see the gesture. She was grateful she hadn't. It was a foolish statement. There wasn't a married slave among them, never would be under the law that marked them as property.

"And you're making yourself a dress?"

She didn't answer. *Weaving a dress for a make-believe bride.* She sobered. No. No, she would not. Gowns were a custom reserved for White women.

"Lydia?"

"I'm going to wear something simple. Nothing special."

Ruth nodded and gripped her hand, squeezing Lydia's knuckles together against her palm.

The moment rested between them.

"Is he good, Lydia? Is he a good man?"

"He is. The best."

Ruth turned aside, her shoulder resting against Lydia's, her breathing slow and steady.

"What is it, Miss Ruth?"

"Ain't nothing, baby. I was just thinking what it must be like."

"What's that?"

"Love. What it must be like to be loved. By a man."

"You've never…?" Lydia blushed. Why she thought to ask something so intimate of her elder, a woman she respected, stuttered her words. "I—I haven't neither. I've never—"

Ruth chuckled and gripped Lydia's knee. "I've been with a man. One man plenty." Her laughter stopped abruptly, swallowed in silence. "I ain't talking about that. I'm talking about being *loved* by one. What's that like?"

What was it like? This love?

Lydia was surprised how suddenly her mind filled with images, how quickly her lungs inhaled the feeling. Love was like the heat of summer, she thought to say, a sweltering that left her warm and wet, but she would never allow those words to leave her lips. It was like the chilling touch of winter tingling her spine until she shivered. Certainly Ruth would understand that, as cold as the cabin had been in January. Or was love more like springwater quenching a thirst she hadn't even known she had? Better yet, it was the red and orange leaves of fall, bold and bright against a washed-out world. It was beauty at its best.

Lydia looked at the woman sitting erect, waiting. This one whose time had passed, whose life would end within these walls without the very thing needed to sustain it. The one thing Lydia possessed. "It's something," she said simply.

"I hear you." Ruth nodded. "It's everything."

⸻ ◆ ⸻

She was late.

It was several minutes after the eleven o'clock hour when Lydia dashed up the back steps of the colonial. Easing the door closed behind her, she crept down the dim hall to her room.

She heard heavy steps behind her, but when she swung around, she saw no one. It wasn't until her thumb gripped the doorknob, slipped from the cold metal and her elbow was grabbed, she knew she wasn't alone. She spun around.

"Lydia." Dr. Kelly towered over her, his dark brows raised over eyes steady on hers. The ends of his moustache curved around a grin.

"Dr. Kelly."

"You're just coming in?"

"No." He had seen her, hadn't he? "I mean, yes."

"Me too." He smiled wider as he laid his large hand high against the door frame, leaning against the wood. Knuckles covered in hair clawed above her, his prey.

"Well, good night, sir." Her pulse raced as she groped once again for the knob.

"May I come in?"

"I don't think so. No."

"Oh, just for a moment." He swung the door open, plowed inside, bumping into her three-legged table. It wobbled against his knee. "I won't stay long."

Lydia stood in the doorway, unsure of what to do. *Run?*

"Aren't you coming in?" He chuckled. "These are your quarters, aren't they?"

She didn't move.

"Oh, I see. You want me to come after you." He strutted toward her.

Please, no.

"You were out in the slave quarters, too, weren't you?"

"Yes." No reason to tell she was in his storehouse without permission. "I was."

"For?"

She hesitated.

"With whom?"

"Sir?" She could feel the ball of her foot lift against the soft leather of her shoe, her leg starting to bounce under the pressure.

"Oh, never mind that." He stood close, his tar-scented breath drifting over her, his gaze leaving her eyes, her mouth, traveling down the length of her. "You look nice."

She glanced down at her russet dress. Far from nice. Hot and grimy, the cotton clung to her moist skin. She gripped the front of it, pulled it away from her body until it tented around her, hiding all signs of femininity.

"I've noticed your glances."

"Sir?"

"I've noticed, Lydia." He reached for her. "Just a little timid, are you?"

Like lightning, he slid his arm around her waist, nestled into her shoulder, his wet mouth pressed against her neck, his hand, his solid, heavy hands, grappling, pulling, tugging at her.

She squeezed his fingers, dug her nails into the flesh of them until she felt bone and shoved him away.

He stumbled back and looked at his hands, gawked at the ruby wounds.

Lydia's heart raced. She tried to run, but fear locked her feet in place. She was certain he would slap her, kick her, kill her, but when he finally looked into her eyes, she saw no signs of anger.

"I'm sorry." His hands flew into the air, his palms up toward her. "I'm sorry. I didn't know."

She waited.

He swiped his hands through his curls and took a breath. "I misunderstood—I thought you…" He shook his head. "Never mind. Look, I'm sorry, all right?"

Astonished, she rested against the wall, trying hard to steady her breathing.

"I'm sorry, Lydia."

He looked troubled. Worried. His eyes, round and wet, like a child before the finger wagged and the swinging rod landed. "Please. Please don't tell anyone. Elizabeth…"

She nodded her head. Hurt her friend? Never.

"This is just between us."

She swallowed.

"Please. Please!" He was begging. Not demanding. She stared at the pleading one who had transformed before her eyes, this man she didn't know.

She nodded.

He took a deep breath and swallowed, the knot in his throat at rest. "Thank you."

She heard him walking back down the hall. When his steps faded, she collapsed against the wall alone.

The next morning when she went to the field, Lydia walked slowly toward the workers, swinging the bucket low against her knees. She cared little how much water was lost on the way, just kept moving forward down the path toward the men and women like her. Folks without rights, subject to any choice, any touch the world offered.

She didn't want to see John or her father. Two men who loved her but couldn't shield her. She would serve them without a word. If she spoke, they would know her pain and weep in their hearts for a manhood denied.

John was right. He couldn't keep her from being trampled on as much as he wanted. He had walked her all the way to the steps, but it wasn't enough. His cover still fell short.

It wasn't fair that she expected more. Of course they couldn't protect her. They couldn't protect themselves. Lydia thought of all the Colored men sold, hung, dragged behind wagons. She thought of the welts branched on John's back. They were all subject to owners. She scoffed at the word so rightfully given. Yes, owners. They owned houses and land, slaves and cattle. They owned bodies and souls. They caught the spirit of life of the captured like one caught a firefly in a jar. Only so much time passed before the light flickered and went out for good. What was left was disposed of, dumped in woods or sometimes fields or kitchens, bound in boot or apron strings, tied down by the weight of death. Escaping was the only option. What did a slave have to lose? Not a thing.

She could still feel the master's lips on her neck, his arm squeezed around her waist, his hands. Those hands she couldn't get off her body, off her mind.

She saw John and turned away.

"I'm not getting water today?" He chuckled. She turned to him, her eyes downcast. If he saw her eyes…

"Oh, I see. I've got to get my own," he said, dipping the gourd into the bucket. "How's my Lady today?" When she didn't answer, he stopped, holding the ladle in midair. "Lydia? You all right?"

A secret between them. She couldn't allow him to carry the thought of another man touching her or worse, the guilt of not being able to do a thing about it.

Tears slipped down her face. One after the other.

He grabbed the bucket from her and set it on the ground before pulling her to him. She rested against his chest.

"What is it?" He tilted her chin up to him. "What is it?"

The most gentle eyes. Gentle hands held her in silence.

"Don't worry, Lydia. I'm right here." He cupped her head, rubbed her back. She could hear him take a deep breath and swallow. "I'm not going nowhere."

John waited until he saw Dr. Kelly walk out the front door. He dropped the rake at his feet and ran to him, catching him just before he stepped into the carriage.

"I want to get married, sir."

"Pardon me?" Dr. Kelly stared at him with wide eyes.

"Married, sir." He hated he had to ask this man. Isaiah had been different. He was honored he had come to ask for his daughter and happy for them. "I know by law it's not granted."

"It most certainly isn't," Dr. Kelly said, gripping the side of the vehicle as he climbed aboard. Red marks spotted his knuckles.

"Yes, sir, but we'd like to have our own ceremony."

"Who is it?" The doctor hesitated. "Another slave from here?"

"Yes, sir. She's right here. I won't need to go off for visits."

"Good."

"I just need permission to have her with me." He cleared his throat. "At night."

"Of course." Dr. Kelly smiled. "Why else would you get married?"

His smirk raised John's blood. Maleness did not link them. Nothing connected him to the man.

"Sure, John. That's fine."

"Thank you." *Thank You, God.* "Thank you, sir." He was already jogging, running back to the fields, lighter than he'd come.

"Who is she?" Dr. Kelly yelled.

John turned around. "Lydia." He was far in the field now but could've sworn he saw something flash across his face. "Her name's Lydia."

Of course he knew her. She was Dr. Kelly's house slave. But soon she would be his wife.

CHAPTER THIRTEEN

*G*randma, you have to stop." Lydia wiped her grandmother's tears. Lou had wept all morning in the back room of her cabin.

"I just can't believe it. You getting married. My baby's baby."

Lou lifted herself up from the low wooden stool in the corner of the room, one hand on the seat, the other against her breast. She coughed herself hoarse before walking to Lydia, her tree-trunk legs dragging beneath her.

It struck her how much her grandmother had aged. Life had waged an all-out assault against her and was winning with little resistance. Her once-prominent features had melted to dough.

Lydia wrapped her arms around the old lady.

"Grandma, I love you."

"Granny loves you, too, baby. Lydia, you better not cry!"

"Well, you're crying!"

"The bride ain't never suppose to cry on her day. Listen, here, chil', you got plenty days to do just that."

Lydia laughed.

"But today, you got to be happy, you hear me? Ain't no reason to shed a tear today. Now, go on and get ready, girl. Noon, Lydia. John'll be waiting."

"Lydia!" Her father called from the front room.

It warmed her heart to see him in his white-buttoned shirt and navy trousers, Sunday's best. He squirmed against the small wooden knob that held the collar close against his throat and smiled.

"I've got something for you, Lydia."

"You do? Daddy, you know—"

"I don't want to hear it. Now go on and close your eyes."

She closed her eyes and heard the door open and the sound of something being dragged inside.

"Open your eyes."

Lydia stared at the bench, a redwood cedar polished to perfection, and wrapped her arms around her father's neck. "Daddy, it's beautiful." She knelt before it and ran her fingers over a carved heart and letters on the backrest.

"Says John and Lydia," her father said. "Took me awhile to add that." He smiled.

"It's perfect, Daddy. Thank you."

Lou stood at the back of the room, grinning.

"I wanted something special for you," he said. "It's a special day."

"Yes. Yes, it is." Lydia kissed her father and gave her grandmother a squeeze before scampering off to the Big House.

All she could think about was tonight. Joy and fret warred, flipped, and tumbled over each other inside her belly.

In the washroom outside the manor, she scrubbed her body and hair with soap made of ashes and lard in a wooden bucket of water, drying off with a few shakes of her frayed towel. She slipped into her knee-length stockings and chemise, but when she lifted the oversized cream sack dress over her head, she steadied herself. Joy swelled as she traced a string of yellow ribbon above the pocket around her waist and tied it in a bow behind her. She had wanted to wear the gown she had made for herself but thought better of it. It was Jackson's dress now and much too formal for anything John owned. She combed through the damp tangles of her hair, wrapped it full and high, and smiled at the crown Lizzy had taught her to create.

Inside she found her friend in the sitting room, flipping the yellowed pages of a book small and thick.

"Where's your mother? Are your parents here?"

"Who knows where my father is, but my mother's in her quarters. Resting, I believe." Lizzy looked up at her. "Lydia… Look at you! You coming from church?"

"This is it, Lizzy." Lydia giggled and ran to her. Kneeling beside her, she squeezed her hand. "Today's the day."

"What day?" Lizzy tossed the book aside and scooted to the edge of the sofa.

"I'm getting married, Lizzy," she whispered. "I'm getting married."

"You're getting married?" Lizzy nearly screamed.

"Shh!" Lydia laughed, cupping her hand over her mouth, but was no quieter. "I'm all ready. I don't want to keep John waiting."

"Oh, Lydia. I want to come. I'll come with you."

"Lizzy, you can't. You know your parents wouldn't approve."

"Well, then, I'll just sit with you until it's time."

Lydia squeezed her tight. Lizzy giggled all the way down the hall to Lydia's hushes.

In the room, Lizzy sat on Lydia's bed and smiled. The dingy, thin cotton sheets crinkled around her like sun rays. Everything was beautiful today.

Lydia pulled the sheer drapes aside and sat in the rough-hewn chair at the foot of her bed.

"What about you, Lizzy? Still thinking about Jackson?" She hadn't mentioned his private conversation with her.

"He's a bit stuffy for my taste." Lizzy shrugged, then her eyes lit. "Andrew's interesting."

"He's nice, but no more sneaking around."

"Well, no, I certainly can't ask you to go with me now. Not *now*." She slurred the word and laughed.

Lydia smiled. Lizzy looked like her father. She'd never noticed how much before. She turned away.

"You all right, Lydia? Seems you should be happier. You do love him, don't you?"

"Yes. Yes, very much. Lizzy, I wish you knew him. He's wonderful."

"So what is it?"

"I just wish…"

"What, Lydia? You wish, what? I *wish* I'd known you were getting married. I would've gotten you something. If there's something you want…"

But what she wanted her friend couldn't give.

"You're a good friend, Lizzy."

"You're my best, Lydia. My best."

The beauty of The Room stunned her.

Ruth and Odessa had wrapped their heads in crimson scarves and much of the fabric on the floor was half stuffed in the cracks of the walls so that they hung down in flaps on every side. Lydia felt a tug in her heart and swallowed the lump that swelled inside her throat. She looked at the women and Old Abram inside, who wouldn't have had the opportunity to see her wed had she not decided to come to them. She stared at her father, her grandmother, and Cora smiling at her against the open door. Her family. The sacrifice, the effort of ones with little power, moved her. Tears welled up and she tried to look at, touch, take in each piece of material they had placed like feathers in a hallowed nest. Each one took breath, strength they didn't have. Lydia cried. Each one gave love, they did.

"Oh, now, what did I tell you about that?" Lou chastised through tears. "No crying, Lydia. Got me crying again and ya'll ain't even married yet!"

"Come inside." Lydia motioned but Lou shook her head.

"I can see plenty good from here."

Truth be told, there would only be room for John in the tight quarters.

Abram and Odessa sat in a half circle on the mounts of fabric that remained. Ruth, at the loom.

"Got something for you."

"Miss Ruth…"

"Ain't much, but you know it's from my heart."

Ruth lifted a woven rainbow band of cotton. When she heard her approach, she reached out and loosened the yellow ribbon from Lydia's waist and tied the colorful belt behind her.

"I had to do something." Her fingers climbed from Lydia's chin to the cheek she patted. "Had to do something."

"He's here," her father announced.

Lydia brushed past her daddy and the others and stepped outside. Her heart lifted when she saw him a few feet away.

John gripped a tattered Bible in his right hand and a red rose in his left. He ran to her.

"I made it," he said, dusting his faded black trousers and white shirt. He grabbed then kissed her hand and handed her the flower.

"A rose."

"Yes." He looked at her. "You look beautiful."

"You think so?"

He nodded, his fingers slipping over the shiny scar she hid behind wisps of hair.

"Who would've thought we'd get married in this sad little place?" She laughed.

"It's not sad today."

No. No, it wasn't. Not today.

In the moonlight near the log structures where slaves found rest, Lydia leaned against her grandmother on her new bench and watched the folds of skirts lift and spread around caramel and mocha-colored legs like the petals of flowers opening and closing above stems, thick and thin.

"I'm glad I lived to see the day," Lou said, patting her leg. "It was beautiful."

It was. Like a dream.

Lydia squeezed the walnut-shelled hand on her thigh and smiled at her husband several feet away. John clasped the tips of Cora's fingers and spun the girl until she collapsed in giggles at his feet. A yellow glimmer drew her attention away. Lizzy ambled through the crowd in her ballroom gown. She waved when she saw her and pressed her way through, sunshine tendrils tumbling left, then right as she strained to keep contact.

Lizzy clutched her hand when she reached her and kissed Lou's cheek.

"I didn't know what to wear."

"Oh, it's fine, Lizzy. It's fine." Lydia stood to her feet, happy to see her. But it was a risk.

"Did you really think I'd miss this? Your wedding?" Lizzy looked around. "But I did miss it, didn't I?"

"Just the vows." Lydia wrapped her arm around Lizzy's and led her toward the dancing. "I want you to meet John, but, Lizzy, it's not wise for you to stay."

"You don't want me here?"

"Of course I do."

"Lydia, *please*. I'm here and I'm staying."

Lydia stared at the soft image of her master and forced a smile.

"I wanted to give you something." Lizzy touched the strand of pearls against her throat and grinned.

"Lizzy. Lizzy, no." But just as Lizzy had the night she discovered her adorned in the formal dress in her room, she unlatched the necklace from her neck. Through bleary eyes, Lydia looked at the gems, the treasure, the gift in her palm and the woman at her side. "Lizzy."

"For you, my friend."

Lydia clutched the pearls in her fist and Lizzy even tighter and cried.

Lizzy wiped her eyes and smiled. "Now where is this husband of yours?"

Lydia slipped the necklace in the pocket of her dress and spotted John and Charles bantering near an old, withered oak.

"Lydia," Charles said, grabbing her hand. A smile, as wide as it was bright, spread across his narrow face before he released her. "The Lord's blessing with this one." He cocked his brow and nodded at the man at his right. "I guess this is it. I've got to find another place to lay my head tonight."

"No, it's all right." John gripped his shoulder. "We'll give you one more night."

"Will we?" Lydia asked.

"Yes. I've got things set up somewhere else."

The storehouse. She smiled.

"Introduce me," Lizzy said, stepping forward a few feet from the men. Charles's long, thin limbs shadowed like a maple over her.

"Oh, I'm sorry. John, Charles, this is—"

"This is Elizabeth Kelly," Charles inserted. "Of course we know the master's daughter."

"The master's daughter? Is that what I'm known as?" She stretched her hand to him. "I'd much rather be called Lizzy."

"I see." He was hesitant. "Lizzy, then." Tentatively, he shook her hand.

"Shall we?" Lizzy glanced at the couples swinging around them and shrugged. "It's just a dance."

"Miss Elizabeth."

Lydia's father appeared in the midst of them. The top button of his white shirt was now undone and his sleeves cuffed at the wrist.

"Daddy." She hadn't seen him in hours, hadn't even seen him walk up. She smiled up at him, but he was looking at the White men planted among them.

"Surprised to see you here," he said to her friend.

"I didn't want to miss Lydia's big day."

"Well, that was nice." He glanced around and nodded. "But it's probably best you head back over to the manor now."

"I will." Her face flushed red. "I was just going to have a dance with Charles."

Charles backed up, shook his head.

"I think you need to go home, Miss Elizabeth. We don't want no trouble."

"There's not going to be any trouble."

Lydia looked down, hated to see the shame on Lizzy's face. But her father was right. If Dr. Kelly found out where she was, it wouldn't be good for any of them. The quiver of a man she encountered the other night faded into the one with power she faced day after day.

"Miss Elizabeth." Her father lowered his voice. "I understand how you feel, but your daddy won't be happy knowing you're out here with us."

"Lydia wants me here. Don't you, Lydia?"

The joy of the day was wilting with the tension. Lydia moved closer to her friend and whispered, "Maybe it's best…"

Lizzy's eyes widened. She swung around and stumbled. Daddy's hand flashed like a whip around her wrist.

"What are you doing?"

The crowd quieted. All eyes settled on them.

She jerked her arm free.

"I was just trying to help you, Miss Elizabeth."

"Don't help me." Wet eyes stared at Daddy, then Lydia.

Without another word, Lizzy staggered past them, draped the folds of her dress over her forearm, and teetered down the road.

Lydia twirled the stem of her rose and gazed into the eyes of her husband for the first time.

They strolled hand in hand, John with his Bible tucked under his arm. The September night had turned cooler than she had dreamed it would be. Back through the murky woods they walked across a clearing. Lydia stopped at a huckleberry bush, picked a handful of fruit, and fed them one by one to her husband. The deep purple juice stained his lips like wine.

"You all right? Not too cold, are you?" John faced her and rubbed the length of her arms in quick strokes until heat rose in places yet untouched. "Better?"

"Yes." Lydia never could look just once, but tonight she let her eyes linger over every feature, every detail of the man.

Much of the way they walked in silence, Lydia so immersed in her thoughts about the beauty of the day, the journey to the storehouse seemed mere minutes.

"I thought we'd never get here," John said when they arrived. This had become their place. When he slid the door open, the familiar scent of pine greeted them.

She smiled.

Through a high window, moonlight illuminated the room. Hours earlier, he had cleared a path through the straw, made a haven just for them.

"How long it take you to do this?"

"Not long."

He lit a candle and led her behind the shelves to a puckered quilt in the farthest corner of the room.

"Not the blanket, I see."

"Not tonight." He laughed and settled beside her. "Lydia?" He brushed back the hair against her forehead and kissed her.

"Yes?"

"You ever been touched by a man?"

She dropped her head.

"I mean, it's all right. It's all right if you have."

"No." She hadn't. Not really. Dr. Kelly was no man. He was a beast. How did she tell the one she loved the little he held had been trapped, harassed, handled by hands unlike his? "No, I haven't."

"I've got you," he whispered. She could feel his lips, his breath, soft and gentle against her scar. He pulled back and looked into her eyes. "The only thing is, I don't have nothing for you. I have something I prepared, but nothing to give you. Something to put in your hands."

"What are you talking about?"

"I mean, a man's supposed to have something for his wife."

"I don't have nothing for you. Your blanket is almost done, but—"

"You're not supposed to, Lydia. *You're* my gift, but I'm supposed to have something for you."

"Who says? I say you're my gift just like I'm yours."

"Is that right?"

"That's right. John, you gave me a rose."

"That was before you were my wife. I still think you've got to have something." He looked around. "I'll be back."

Several minutes later, he returned with his hands behind his back.

"What you got, John?"

"Go on, now. Close your eyes."

He came close. Close enough for her to want him closer.

"Open your eyes." He placed the items down in her lap: a tree limb, a stone, and two crinkly gold leaves.

"What's this?"

"All right, Lydia. You've got to work with me here. This is the best I could do for now." He chuckled. "Not much out there this time of night."

"All right…"

"All right. This here"—he lifted the twig—"this is a stick, Lydia. It means I'm going to stick around." She giggled. "You see this rock? Now this rock means I'm going to rock you through life's hard times." She smiled. "And these"—he held the leaves up to the candle and twirled them by their stems—"these leaves are just what I'm doing. A man leaves his father, his mother, to be one with his wife. Tonight, I leave it all behind."

"John…"

"I know, I know. I wish I had something—"

"I love it."

He smiled.

"I love it, John."

"You *love* it?" He laughed and stroked her hair. "You are too easy."

"It was beautiful."

"One day—"

"It was beautiful."

"One day I'm going to have a real gift for you, Lydia."

"I've already got it." She thought about the pearls in her pocket. They were nothing compared to the ones shining down on her against the finest of velvet. "I've got it."

"There's something else." He opened his Bible. She loved that he was a reading man. Not many of them could open a book, decipher letters, and extract meaning from passages of literature.

> "*And on the Sabbath*
> *we went out of the city*
> *down by a river side,*
> *where prayer was wont to be made.*
>
> "*And we sat down,*
> *and spake unto the women*
> *which resorted thither.*
>
> "*And a certain woman*
> *named Lydia,*
> *a seller of purple cloth,*
> *of the city of Thyatira,*
> *which worshipped God,*
> *heard us.*
>
> "*Her heart the Lord opened.*
> *And she was baptized,*
> *and her whole household.*
>
> "*She prayed,*
> *If ye have judged me*
> *to be faithful, Lord,*
> *come into my house,*
> *and abide here.*"

"From the book of Acts." He flipped the pages closed but his hand rested on the worn leather before he set the book aside. "Lydia, you are named after a seller of purple, the royal color, of kings and queens."

She relished his words.

"You are a rich, free woman who makes the finest cloth."

"One day, I hope."

"Right now, Lydia. You are right now."

Her eyes filled. *Who is this man?*

John came closer and kissed her neck, her chin, her lips.

"That's it, Lydia. That's all I've got, but one day, one day, Lydia, I promise, I will give you everything."

She wept into light hands he placed against his heart.

"You're beautiful, Lydia. Did I tell you that?"

"Every time you look at me."

The night was misty like a dream. Every touch, every taste sweeter still, wrapped up in tangles of heat. She breathed him into every pore and fell asleep in his arms.

In the morning, Lydia sat chilled in her crumpled dress staring down at the man she had to leave. He was sprawled on the quilt in a place far away. "John. John…"

When he turned over, his eyes lit. "Lady." He propped himself up on his elbow, his head resting on his hand. He smiled. Lydia watched everything. Tried to remember every detail. She inched closer.

"I have to get back."

His eyes flashed before the smile faded. He sat up slowly and reached for her. He covered her hands in his and held them to his lips. "How do I let you go?"

A glare of light, streaming in through the same window that had blessed them with soft moonlight, blinded her. She squinted, moved back from the ray, from him.

As much as she hated to leave him, she was foolish to expect more. They would never have enough time together. Slaves never had enough of anything. The thought choked out the beauty of the night. He wasn't hers. It was just a night. One night.

When she stood to leave, she felt something against her heel. Like blood beneath her feet, she saw the rose. Trampled on.

Few words were spoken on the way back to the Big House. When he kissed her good-bye on the bottom steps of the manor, her heart broke and everything about their night, she tried to forget.

CHAPTER FOURTEEN

She heard the turmoil before she reached the door.

Lydia chased the screams around the winding dirt path to the front steps of the house. A crowd of slaves hovered together, clutching each other in the center of the withered grass. Trembling hands raced from backs, to shoulders, to faces in a haze of blue and brown burlap and denim. Heads bowed. Others tilted upward toward the high porch. Shouted prayers and quiet wails echoed in the early-morning wind from the saddest faces Lydia had ever seen.

John was in the crowd.

"What is it?" Lydia touched his back. "Can you see what it is?"

"Some White men." He stretched up on the balls of his feet and strained to see. "They have a slave." His eyes widened.

"What is it?"

He shook his head but his eyes filled with tears.

"What do you see, John?" Lydia moved closer, pressing on the backs of those in front of her. "Please...what is it?"

"Go back, Lydia. Go around back and get in the house."

"What are you talking about? Why?"

"Lydia, listen to me." He said "Lydia" strong but the rest of his words shook. "Lydia! Go inside." He grabbed her arm, but the pain in his voice drew her deeper into the crowd and she shook free. She could not see what clenched her people tighter, what caused a few to fall to their knees. She pushed aside winding skirts and pressed her way to the front.

She stumbled back.

Daddy was shirtless, his hands bound behind him. Two men in straw hats, white sleeves shoved over their forearms, swaggered around him. Their mouths in angry lines spat words Lydia strained to hear.

The tan, bearded one grabbed her father's hands and jerked him straight. He yanked on his jacket pocket and with a quick twist of his hand, flicked a shiny blade against a face that remained oddly calm.

Screams and gasps filled the crowd but Lydia's screech pierced through the uproar. Impulse shot through her veins. She sprinted up the steps, her tears flying hot into her ears.

"Daddy!"

Lydia watched her father's eyes widen, his chest rise and fall.

"That's my baby. Get my girl out of here!"

The stouter man swung his fist into her father's jaw. The force knocked his hat loose. It drifted to the ground and landed with a thud in the dirt.

Lydia grappled for her father. "Daddy!" She needed him. If they hurt him, if they hurt her daddy... They *couldn't* hurt him.

She was almost at the top when she was swept off her feet. Arms wrapped around her torso. She kicked herself free and fell two steps back. She gripped the step above her and pulled herself to her knees. An arm swung under hers on each side. Two men, like Daddy, lifted and carried her toward the weeping below.

Lydia swung. She bucked. She tried to bite, but she was still flying backward. The men stopped several steps above the crowd and held her by her arms.

A flicker of ivory drew Lydia's eyes upward. In a window to the right, a curtain was drawn. With parted lips, Mrs. Kelly stood like a ghost. Like she was somehow asleep or playing Lydia's childhood frozen bedtime game and winning without effort. Chills rushed through her as she watched the one constant. Moving forces all around, but here in this one space, stillness. The missus's eyes were on her father, but with little sign she saw him. She couldn't possibly see him struggle and not move, not do something. Suddenly, Mrs. Kelly's eyes met hers.

"Please," she begged the image in the window.

Lizzy's mother clapped her hand on her mouth as if sickness was rushing to her lips and stumbled forward, her fingers sprawled against the glass.

Please... She was her only hope.

Hope closed the curtains and walked away.

Lydia collapsed in the arms of her husband. She looked back at her daddy. Beautiful Daddy. The one who meant everything to her. How could she live without him? She reached for him, weak now, with a single arm in the air. If she could reach him, touch him somehow, she would live. "Daddy." A hot, salty tear burned her tongue as she whispered for him.

If John saw what she saw, he would release her to him. His eyes of unwavering love, her name on his lips, and glistening tears that slid, slow and steady, down his jawbone. *My daddy...*

"No! No... Please. Please!" But she couldn't touch him, as much as she willed it.

Lydia glimpsed Dr. Kelly on the porch before she was half-carried, half-dragged to her father's cabin and draped in the lap of the only blood she had left.

Never would she forget the sound of Grandma Lou's wailing. It rang high-pitched above the other mourners within the walls of their cabin, though her normal tone flowed thick as honey.

Brown faces surrounded her, their eyes saying what their lips refused to repeat. Arms embraced and hands caressed, but nothing stopped Lydia's head from shaking.

"Sit her down," one woman instructed, pulling her toward the crate, but Lydia's body refused to bend.

"Give her some water," another suggested, but she could not drink.

Lydia shook her head faster and faster, her hands pressed against her ears, trying to shake herself awake from this day of torment, this hour of anguish.

The solemn faces swayed back and forth before her like a turbulent sea. A quivering in the center of her stomach rose until it sat salty in the back of her throat.

"I need my daddy."

"You gonna be all right."

"I need my daddy."

"I know."

"Daddy..."

"Hush now."

Sobbing heaved from her chest until her eyes rolled back and all color faded to black.

Lydia awoke beside her grandmother to the smell of okra, onions, and tomatoes steaming in a cast-iron skillet.

A basket of vegetables sat on the table. A gift. A gift already for the bereaving. *Please, God, no.*

Only two remained, John and Cora, lingering near the hearth.

"Where is he? What happened to my daddy?"

"You need to eat something," Cora urged.

"Please… Please!"

"He's gone, Lydia," John said, his head between his hands.

No.

Her grandmother closed her eyes. When she opened them, tears glistened in wavy streams down the maple mountains of her cheeks. She turned to Cora. "Tell me. I wanna know. Tell me what they did to my boy."

"One of master's men…" Cora looked down, spoke slowly. "He said he needed to teach him a lesson. Teach us *all* a lesson." Cora's lip quivered. "Slashed his face. Heard they threw his body in the Potomac when they was through."

"I ain't even got his body. I ain't even got my baby's body." Lou's sniffling erupted into sobs, deep and hollow.

Cora rushed to her side and wrapped her arms around her. Together, they rocked to the rhythm of their weeping.

Lydia couldn't breathe. She sprinted out of the cabin past the other slave quarters and the tobacco fields. She stopped when she saw the pink-streaked sky and tumbled to her knees. Its beauty stung. *How can it not weep with me?* She knelt alone, fatherless, outside in a world unscathed by a broken heart.

⎯⎯⎯•◦•⎯⎯⎯

Lou fought sleep like the devil it was.

Sneaking up on her, tempting her to close her eyes, alluring her with a gift it never gave. Rest never came on nights of terror.

Tonight, her first night without her son, she wouldn't dare shut her eyes. Isaiah could come strolling in at any moment, surprising everybody, telling the tale of how he escaped, fled from evil, and made it home. The Lord had done *much* greater things, hadn't He?

She wouldn't sleep and miss her son. Or clothe her mind in those awful pictures of him Cora had shared. Why had she asked? Why did she need to know they had cut him, sliced her baby's face? She shuddered. No, that devil wasn't going to sneak up on her and force her to see her boy all bloody and beaten like an animal. *My baby...*

She wouldn't do it. She wasn't going to let sleep win. Every time a wave of exhaustion bowed her head forward, she spoke to it.

"Liar," she said when her lids grew heavy, "Yea, though I walk through the valley...," she slurred when her chin bobbed against her chest.

Her mother had given her these words to hide on the inside, said it was all she had to give. Even then, Lou knew it was enough.

In and out of liquid thoughts, she roused herself until light spilled through the cracks of their log house and onto the face of her grandbaby. The girl, balled up on her side, made Lou cry all over again.

She looked around. John and Cora had slipped away.

She needed to do something. Keep herself busy. That's how they were going to make it. One tied-up moment after the other until the good Lord called them home.

Lou strapped the faded, striped apron around her waist and marched to the crate in the kitchen, pulling out flour, lard, and sugar. In a wooden bowl, she tossed handfuls and pinches until she stirred a yellow dough that stuck to the back of her spoon.

Isaiah loved tea cakes.

"Just one more, Mama," he would plead when he was no taller than her waist. Though she knew they needed the extra for supper, she always gave in.

"Just one more, Isaiah," she whispered after the other slaves cleared the table and hurried out the cabin to their day's duty. Giggling, he would skip out on their heels, clutching the fat, round biscuit against his chest.

"Grandma?"

Lou turned to Lydia's drowsy face, still pressed and pulled by slumber like the dough in her hand.

"Why you cooking, Grandma?"

"What do you mean, why am I cooking? We got to eat, ain't we?" Lou looked at the sad eyes, dropped her hand from her hip, and confessed. "Granny's gotta keep her hands busy, baby. Got to stay busy."

But the lack of sleep was getting to her. Like an old bandit, it crept in, entered one finger at a time. Her hands trembled. She shook them steady.

She brushed against Lydia as she made her way to the hearth. Didn't make a lick of sense how they were all bunched up in the smallest of spaces with the large quarters the master had. Didn't make no sense at all.

"Grandma?"

"Yes, baby."

"Why'd they kill my daddy?"

"Oh, baby." Lou's withered hands pounded the sugary flour into perfect circles. *Yes.* They were perfect. Whatever her hand found to do...

Taste was one thing, the expected thing, that had to be present at every meal. Food with flavor was vital. Not much more pleasure a slave had, but making each dish pleasing to the eye thrilled her more. Why not take the time and make the patties as round as she could? Not too many she knew cared about those type of details. Not like she did. If she'd done it for a master for years, why not for her own? With what little her family had, her special touch made it all the better.

But now the more she worked, the more she shook. "Do something, child." When Lydia propped herself against the chair, she handed her a patty. "Knead this."

Lou tossed the dough from palm to palm. She kept her eyes on her work and off Lydia. Where eyes focused, the mind would follow.

"I needed him."

She tried to ignore it, but she saw it. A single tear sped down Lydia's cheek before others raced to join it. She smudged them with the back of her hand and sniffed. "We needed him."

"I know, baby. We did. Granny knows."

Lou glimpsed the girl from the corner of her eye and a chill shot through her. Her son sat, young, innocent, unbroken. She shuddered back into the present. Her granddaughter. She wanted to reach for her but if she stopped—if her hands stopped moving—she would feel the burning, the ripping of soul from spirit. She tossed instead and blocked the words, the thoughts, the feelings.

"It's not right."

If the girl would stop talking...

"What ain't right? Hurting your daddy? No, 'course it ain't." What happened to her perfect circles? Girl sure didn't take after her. "You ain't doing it right, Lydia. Take it like this." She pressed into the tea cakes. "Push your palm in deeper."

"I mean all of it. Treating us like we don't matter. Like we don't cry. Like we don't bleed. Like we don't have the same needs they got."

Lou nodded. She needed her to be quiet.

"But God knows."

"He sure does, baby."

"He knows."

"Hush now, Lydia. Hush." Not another word.

Lydia's hands fell still. She rocked, her eyes in a distant place. "He knows."

"I told you to hush!" Lou snatched the patty from Lydia's hands, but when she touched the thin fingers, felt the warm skin of her offspring, the shaking took over. She couldn't stop. It rode through her body like a loaded train.

Isaiah. Her boy. Her baby boy. Beautiful, beautiful boy. *Not my baby. Not my baby!* All her children taken away. Now, on this side she had none. A flood of tears surged. She slumped against the wall, slid down on her son's dark blue blanket, fingernail prints pressed hard into the cakes still in her hands. She was drowning, drowning in quivering images of a boy who stole her heart with his first breath.

"Isaiah. My baby."

She shook with her granddaughter holding her, Lydia's arms wrapped around her. She shook, squeezing the patties, harder, deeper. She couldn't fight it.

"I can't stop shaking. Please, Lord, have mercy." Lou clung to her grandbaby and wept. "Have mercy on me."

CHAPTER FIFTEEN

The next morning, Lydia dragged herself toward the house she would never call home again.

When she reached the old colonial, her heart weighed against her, heavier with each step it took to arrive. Covered in dust, her shoes slid against each plank until she was standing where her father had stood, struggled, cried out to her. She knelt and glided her fingers across dried scarlet drops on the damp wood.

No life at all.

How much more could she bear? How much longer could she remain? If she stayed she could die at their hands or worse yet live at their feet. She thought of Lou, stripped of the last child she had. *Dead is better than us alive.*

At least Daddy was free.

When she could sit, bow no longer, she rose, stronger, and marched right through the front door. She wanted them to tell her something, ask her anything, and she would give them what they wanted, whatever they needed to shut her up. She could feel the heat blazing from the pit of her belly to her chest. Let them kill her. Let them stop her heart, quench her breath. She had nothing to lose. They couldn't take what she never had.

In her room, she stretched across her bed and wrapped herself in the blanket she had weaved for John. She had only a few rows to complete but even that would prove challenging now.

Her door creaked open.

She rolled to her side. Lizzy stood under the door frame, shaking. Loose blond strands shimmied over her red eyes.

"Lydia."

She sat up and stared at her.

Finally, Lizzy inched closer. "I'm sorry, Lydia. I'm so sorry." Her words gurgled in tears.

Lydia watched her, weeping, trembling, and she knew, she knew Lizzy felt the same hurt, carried the same weight, experienced the same pain. They were not friends. They were family.

She ran to her, clung to her, and cried.

"I'm so sorry. I'm so sorry," Lizzy said. Over and over she said the words until they soothed like a balm for a wounded heart.

She stepped back and looked at Lydia. "I didn't know. I never said anything."

"I know."

"I don't know how it happened. I don't know why, Lydia, but—"

"I know."

There was nothing else to say.

When she nodded and turned to leave, Lydia wanted to scream. *Don't go! Stay!* But she said nothing and watched her slip away. Another back to her.

When she heard the door close, she stood still for a long time before her knees locked and buckled. She slid to the floor, felt the cold oak against her legs, her spine, her scalp. It penetrated, chilling her until she shivered.

As cold as it was, she remained. Didn't have the will to rise.

<hr />

Emma rocked on the edge of the wing chair, clutching the cushion that spilled out beneath her, and watched her husband ease the front door open.

She knew where he had been.

He bumped his head on the silver candelabra hanging in the center of the room and winced. He looked drained, weathered, sorely out of place in a sunlit room of lilac and crushed velvet.

"I'm sorry," he said, kneeling at her side.

For Isaiah? Or the countless women?

Even on his knees, she had to look up to him. The smell of sweat clung to his clothes, lingered around the collar of the same bloodstained cream shirt she couldn't scrub clean. He had worn it the evening before when she sent him out on the porch with his boys.

She had heard the moaning.

The sound of muffled cries from covered mouths. They echoed like screams that fought to escape but were bound by fear, shoved down deep into the pit of souls. It was this anguish that drew her to the window.

The people below moved slowly, cautiously, as if they could be stung at any moment by angry white bees swarming above.

The men lowered their hats over icy sneers as they strutted across the porch, raising their fists.

Then she saw Isaiah. Bare-chested and bound. She saw for the first time in years. She had watched the seasons change, her child grow, and her marriage fall apart, but she hadn't seen any of it. Until yesterday. It was her on the porch. She was Isaiah. Hands tied behind her back, subject to a man in control, bound to one who took her kindness for weakness.

She hadn't expected to feel anything. But when her eyes locked with Lydia's, something happened. She saw the silent horror of a girl begging, pleading. It was *her* grappling for life, begging to be saved without sound. And in that bedroom, for the first time in years, she felt her eyes blinking back tears, her heart beating, her fingers sprawled against cold glass, her hand over a mouth that had swallowed sickness for too long. She stepped back and let the curtains close on the scene she no longer wanted to play. And in that bedroom, she screamed. She screamed. She screamed until Michael rushed through the door and she yelled for him to do something. *Do something! Why don't you do something?*

But it was too late.

Emma stood up and left Michael on his knees. She was leaving him. Never returning from Richmond.

It would never be too late again.

More joy. More pain.

As soon as one caught fire, the other ignited. Joy had blazed wild and carefree in his wife, but pain flickered until it flamed in the corners of a hurt heart.

Outside their cabin, surrounded by maples and a fresh scent of evergreen, John stoked low, flickering flames before Lydia arrived. On bended knee, he leaned over the fire until it crackled and he heard the light pattering of feet on crushed leaves. He looked up into the eyes of the woman he loved. Even under the night sky, her beauty glowed against the backdrop of night.

She dropped to her knees and laid her head against his shoulder.

"You feeling all right?"

She nodded.

"It's going to be all right, Lydia. I know it's hard to see that now, but I promise." *Please, God.* He had to keep his word. "I'm getting you out of here. I'm speaking with Dr. Kelly tomorrow." He cupped the crown of her head and tilted her face toward him.

She looked at him with little emotion. He searched her eyes, her lips, then smiled for the both of them.

"Rest assured. There's nothing to worry about." Her face, his heart, said otherwise.

He blew out a breath.

"I wish I could just keep holding you. Doesn't seem right you having to go back to that house after what happened. A wife should be with her husband."

"Yes," she said quietly.

His wife. He still liked to say the word, hear the sound of it leaving his lips. He kissed her. Once. Twice.

"Maybe after tomorrow Dr. Kelly will let us—"

"*Let* us?" Lydia's back straightened.

He rubbed it in long strokes. "We're going to go just right, Lydia, and trust God to do what only He can."

Hounds barking in the distance startled him to his feet. "You hear that?" His hand locked around hers as she scuffled up, ready to run. They watched the bushes, the wind in the trees behind them, and strained to see any sign of threat until the sound faded. John breathed relief, but several minutes passed before they settled back near the fire.

"What kind of life is this?" Lydia stared into the flames.

John stretched his legs and leaned back on his palms, orange and red burning, crackling, playing softly around them.

Lydia shivered in spite of it. He drew her close.

"Don't let it go out, John."

He scrambled up and jammed a branch into the heap.

"You've got to stir it up," she said. When he leaned forward, he saw it in her eyes.

A flame building.

In their cabin that night, Lydia reached for him.

"Are you sure?"

"Yes," she said, sliding down on the quilt. He leaned in over her until he smelled lavender, breathed in peace, and surrendered to soft fingertips drumming against his back.

"Lydia…"

That night, like the others since her father's death, when he made love to her, his heart filled with guilt. It seemed wrong to find pleasure in the midst of pain, but she had begged him. Had offered herself to him each night since their wedding. Said she needed him, needed to feel him close.

She had a way with him like no other. He was amazed at how deeply he had fallen, how quickly his sharp edges broke in her softness, her love.

The cracks of day woke him. She was already dressed, ready to leave.

"Lady."

She turned to him with sad eyes.

"What's wrong? Something wrong?"

"Seeing you every night is not the same as having you."

"I know, Lydia. Soon."

"It's not enough." She knelt beside him. "This hurts. I need more."

When he reached for her, she stopped him, grabbed his hand before he could hold her. "I've got to go."

"All right. Give me a minute." He wrestled into his pants, searched for the shirt he had worn.

"I've got to go."

"Lydia, let me walk you to the steps."

She shook her head and flashed a final smile.

He ran out after her, watched her slip away, counting her every move up the planks to the Kelly manor. One hundred and twenty-seven steps later, they were a world apart.

John folded into himself and pressed the damp corners of his eyes. He took a moment to breathe it in, but peace was gone. It had followed Lydia with his love.

CHAPTER SIXTEEN

*H*ow much would it cost?"

"Excuse me?" Dr. Kelly stared at him.

All that planning, all that praying, and this was the best he had? Greeting the doctor in the early-morning hours at the edge of his colonial before he had a chance to set his feet in the place he should've been.

"I'd like to know what I'm worth. So I can buy my freedom."

"Buy your what?"

His stomach churned at the thought of purchasing something that rightfully belonged to him or turning over wealth into White hands that Brown backs labored for, the insult of which sent him running the second time. He needed money for when he made it North, he reasoned, but the thought of MaDora convicted him. It was her wish that someone walk free. Walk free, not run away.

"I'd like to buy my freedom, sir," he said again, stuffing his hands in his pockets.

"Is that right?" Dr. Kelly looked him over and paused. He cocked the heel of his boot against the side of the house and twisted against the frame. "How much you got?"

"How much I need?"

Dr. Kelly frowned. His thick, dark brows wrinkled low over his eyes.

"You've got to have a price, sir."

"Well over five hundred, John. Well over."

"Would you take a thousand for two?"

"A thousand?" He laughed. "Where, on God's creation, did a Colored get a thousand dollars?" When John didn't reply, he sobered. "You saying you got a thousand dollars, John?"

"I'm saying if I get it, would you take it?"

He was no fool.

"Sure."

John stared at the doctor, tried to read his face.

"Sure, I would. Who wouldn't accept that kind of money?"

"So we have a deal?"

"Sure. Why not?"

———•◦•———

"Free?" Lydia hunched on their makeshift bed, tugging red and yellow patches of quilt into a small hill between her thighs. She cared little about the folds of her skirt bunched up all improper around her waist. Just focused on the word they had so often beckoned that was finally showing up for good. "Is that right?"

"That's right." John smiled and nodded calmly like he was waiting until it grabbed hold.

"We're going to be free?" The thought overwhelmed her. It was all she ever wanted. For her, for him, for all the bound to be loosed. This man she loved would no longer belong to anyone. Free for Isaiah. She smiled her first real smile in weeks, one that spread from the heart.

She clapped her hands and flung her arms around his neck. "Free!" she squealed. He spun her off the bed and around like a child. Collapsing against the wall, he propped her legs up again around him.

"Free," she whispered in his ear. Her head was still spinning in another world.

In the dim candlelight, she couldn't see, only tasted salty tears. She touched her fingers to his cheek. Wet warmth trickled down her wrist.

"Lydia… This is it. What you've always wanted. I'm so happy for you."

"What *we've* always wanted, right?" She slipped from his embrace to her feet.

"Yes. This is for us."

"For us."

"Dr. Kelly said he'd take a thousand dollars for the two of us."

It couldn't be true…

"We're going together. We're going to walk out of this place together with our papers."

She imagined them in their own world and thought back to Jackson's manor. They'd never have wealth of that kind, but a place of their own, yes.

It was too good. She wanted to believe.

"Don't you see? It's happening, Lydia. It's really happening."

"But what if he changes his mind—"

"What if he doesn't?" He touched his finger to her lips and whispered, "What if he doesn't?"

What if he doesn't…?

"If he does, we'd run, wouldn't we? Together." Or apart. She could release him to go without her if she had to. Whatever she had to do.

"I don't know, Lydia."

"What do you mean, you don't know?"

"I mean, it's dangerous. You know good and well what I'm saying. They almost killed you. Lydia, they've got dogs, guns…"

She had nothing to say.

"Are you listening to me? Baby, this is serious. We've got to do this right. Lydia. Are you thinking about all of that?"

"I am but it doesn't matter."

"What do you mean?"

"It doesn't matter what they've got. I've got something too."

"What you got, Lydia?" John leaned forward. "What you got?"

"Fire." Lydia rose to her feet and paced around. "I got fire." She swiped her hand through her hair. "I don't know if you understand, but I've got this burning that I can't put out. I don't think nothing's going to put it out but being free. Not until we can live like we were meant to. Until I get free, it's going to burn. I tell you, it's burning a hole right through me and I'm serious, John, if I don't get out of here soon, it's not going to be good. Not for nobody."

"Sit down, Lydia."

She stared at him. His face was gentle but his voice was strong.

"Sit down."

Slowly, she lowered herself onto the blanket across him.

"Lydia, listen to me. Listen to me. You're a smart woman, but you don't know everything. There are folk who would kill you so quick, step over your body, and sit down to supper the very next second. They ain't thinking about you. You hear me? So you've got to think about yourself. *I'm* thinking about you." John leaned in close to her, inches from her face. "Enough talk about fire. If you got a fire in your chest, you best blow it out before they do."

Several minutes passed before she nodded, understood.

Stay put. She saw Lou's face, remembered her words. She didn't agree, but she understood.

John knelt beside her and rubbed her knotted shoulders.

Whether he grasped how she felt or not, he was hers and he loved her. She saw it in his eyes, heard it in every word.

She reached for him, wrapped her hands around his face, his neck, his back, tighter, and pressed herself into him, deeper, everything a lady didn't do, but love kept her holding on.

An hour later, she watched him slide to his side next to her on the rumpled quilt and close his eyes, his hands tucked between bent knees. She wrapped herself over him and found sleep hard to find.

CHAPTER SEVENTEEN

*I*t had been a mistake. A bad choice. An error of his ways. Simply a wrong decision.

Michael glanced back at the slave house, the dark fingers that pulled the door shut behind him, the half smile he would blot out before he treaded the path of oaks and maples home.

Each night it was a different place. Every evening he was unsure where he would lay his head. He had no inkling in whose arms he would find solace, whose legs would be wrapped around his when he awoke. It gave him a shot of energy, made the monotony of life bearable. Was it not a tedious plight, a cruel test of the will that subjected a man to move through each day doing the same thing? Waiting to aid the ill, walking the tobacco fields, riding through endless meadows of corn, seeing the same slaves, doing the same work? Strolling through the gardens? He swallowed. It was still difficult going to the bed of flowers, thinking of Beatrice sprawled there on her side. Another dead body he had stumbled upon. He had held that woman. Had felt safe, satisfied, in her arms for a while. She was the only one he had returned to, for weeks, for months, for years. One more touch. One more kiss. One more time. He had...loved her? *No.* No, but he cared. He did care for her...and their child.

In his forty years, he had never really loved anyone. Not because he didn't want to. He wanted to love, desperately. With everything, he wanted to find some kind of peace, some type of joy in the heart of another as much as the next person. Wanted to fall in the arms of the feeling and never rise again, drop deep into the heated abyss of affection like everyone else. He had gazed into the eyes of every woman he'd bedded and hoped she would be the one who would take him there. In every soft pair of arms, thin or thick, dark or light, he hoped he would find it. With each pair of lips, he hoped he would taste the one thing that was missing. He searched for it on every pouty mouth, every curved figure that came into his presence. He wanted it. Desperately. As much as anyone else. Who didn't want love? Somebody to hold. Somebody to understand. Somebody to stay by his side.

He sighed. Emma had done just that.

Michael crossed over the dirt road, deciding to take the long route back to the house and the woman he had bought with a handshake. One grip, one squeeze, and here he was, miserable in the world.

He had wanted the house, a solid piece of property with good bones on acres of land that would have taken a boy with a broken mother and no inheritance a long time to acquire otherwise.

He had so little in the beginning.

He was only nine when he found his father, a bootlegging womanizer, dead in the tall Bermuda grass beneath his bedroom window.

When he saw the back of the man, he thought to run to get his mother, someone, anyone, but he stayed staring at a head of clipped brown curls, the checkered wool shirt he had worn fishing the week before, torn and soiled now, and a pair of denim trousers with a faded circle on the back pocket where his pa's tobacco canister hid. Even still, he needed to know for sure. Anything could have happened. Anything can make it not true. Maybe a vagrant had robbed him, stolen his clothes. He hoped, held his breath and mustered up the courage to lift his foot. The heavy Brogan quaked in the air until his calf ached and he pushed the hard toe of it against the back pocket. The body rocked then steadied. Michael leaned in closer, his heart thumping against his chest like a wild hare. He stood and kicked once more, hard and deliberate, swinging the man onto his back.

He shouldn't have done it. It was a bad choice. The wrong decision because what stared back at him was an image he would never forget. The face of his father covered with black beetles, erupting out of a mouth that had praised, that had chastised, those repulsive winged insects squeezing in and out of narrow nostrils, climbing, crawling on, across the blue corneas of eyes stretched wide and looking, staring at him, through him.

Michael backed away, one step, two, and broke loose in the fields, running with his eyes shut as far as he could through the open meadow. He didn't want to see where he was going, just wanted to keep on moving. He wanted to end up somewhere, some place unbeknownst to him. Needed to find himself anywhere else. Fleeing, he discovered that what scared him, thrilled him, was this running, racing, flying through with no vision. But distinguishing danger from excitement was difficult at nine.

Old Man Henry found him hours later crouched in a rusty shed several miles from his house, his window, his father.

And so it had been one mistake after the other. He shouldn't have married Emma. Tied forever to a woman he didn't love, linked to the lie of a union, bound by the burden of returning each day to a place he didn't want to be.

He never desired her, never wanted to feel her arms around him. Nothing in him rose to touch her. Ever. The more she tried to give herself to him, the more the thought disturbed him. She was a friend of sorts, a sister, had become a mother to him. It had been an error. Just a business deal. An arrangement. And who got excited about an order, a duty, aroused over a cold, hard handshake?

He felt awful about it. Every time he saw her sitting still, staring out at the world around her, he felt his heart bleed. It was a cut on the inside, a sharp slice of truth of what he had done, of who he had become and what he had turned her into.

He still couldn't shake that evening in the rain. It played in his mind often, especially evenings when hints of gray clouded the sky. It had been years and to this day he found himself glancing around, peeking behind him, determined to never be taken off guard again. He dreamed about it. The patter of feet following, racing after him. It put a fear in him, and to be quite honest, a respect for Emma for the first time. She was not weak, but controlled, and as much as he hated to acknowledge the bitter seed of distrust he had sown in her heart, dangerous.

He had witnessed her will when she convinced him to take two injured slaves under his care, but he saw her strength the day Isaiah was killed. *Death all around him.* His overseers relayed the story of the slave's encounter with his daughter, but he knew the man. Had known him for years and was certain it had been nothing. Despite the fact, he was coerced into letting them teach his servant a lesson. He allowed it and couldn't stop it in time. He had been wrong.

That morning when he stepped on the porch, he saw Lydia being carried away and was showered in shame. He had avoided her as much he could since that night in her bedroom. He could feel the heat rise in his face, his ears warm at the memory of rejection. He was usually so sure, read all the signs of a woman's interest accurately. Hadn't she glanced over him one night on the front porch? Gazed into his eyes a little too long? And to think she'd assumed he would force himself on her. It was a disgrace. He *never* did that. Never had to.

He was surprised how easy, how eager women were to lie in his arms. It all started with a look he shot at long lashes. It only took seconds to know, to wait for the batting, the shy glance down and her lids to lift, her eyes to lock with his. That was it. A sure thing. He would love her, adore all that she possessed, until the thrill died with the break of day and left him crammed up against a log wall, staring down at pretty eyes rolled back in a head as messy as it was wild and a mouth he had kissed, drooling against his arm. He left disgusted and determined not to return. He would see her the next day, the next week, with another on his arm, and her eyes would blaze, or she would curse him if she was bold or run off. That was the most common response. Running off. He was the master, after all. No one went crazy on him. Except his wife.

He was just like his father, and though he hated it, there wasn't a thing he could do about it. It was in his blood.

One dreadful step after the other, Michael made it home. He studied the wooden frame of the old house he'd sold his soul for, then glanced up at Elizabeth's window. He had failed every woman in his life, had disappointed them all. He needed to do right by one of them. At least one.

The least he could do was grant his daughter her slave. He would simply tell John he misspoke. Lydia was to go with his daughter when she married, like Beatrice with Emma.

Would Lizzy end up broken like the other women in his life? Michael bit his lip and swallowed the thought, bracing himself against the chill of autumn with folded arms.

He watched John approach, his gait light and carefree. Something glistened in his hand, his countenance. What did this man have? Something more than money.

"Whew! Chilly this morning, isn't it, sir?" John said, tugging the frayed collar of his coat against his throat. "Seems too bright to be cold."

He nodded. Up close he could see the dented copper box. "Is that the money?"

"Yes, sir. You have the papers, Dr. Kelly?"

"Well, see, that's the thing, John. I've been thinking." Saying no proved harder with the bills so close, in a sparkly box, only a handshake away. He took a deep breath. "I don't think it's a good idea."

"Sir?" His hand dropped to his side as if the weight of the treasure suddenly multiplied.

"I'm sorry, John. Lydia needs to be with Elizabeth. I should've never told you yes. It was a mistake."

Like every decision he ever made.

He glanced into the eyes of disappointment, a look he was used to seeing, a glare that made him ashamed.

"But I do understand. Don't think I don't." He knew all too well. "You want to spend more time with your bride. Listen, that's no problem. I can ease up a little on the girl so it can feel like a real marriage for you. That Lydia is a beauty." He nodded. Looked at the man a moment too long, delivered a message he had not meant to send.

John stared at him. Michael swallowed.

"You've caused enough pain." The high-pitched voice startled him.

Michael turned around. Several feet away, Emma stood behind him. Had snuck up on him again.

She stepped forward, her eyes steady on his. "Let them go."

CHAPTER EIGHTEEN

*L*ydia knelt between Lou and a splintered crate in the corner of the still cabin. Inside the box, a wooden bowl and spoon shifted on top of a cast-iron skillet as she slid it against the back wall.

Closer now to the sleeping woman, she drew the rainbow quilt over her grandmother's shoulders and placed the thin black rope of hair into her lap. Gently, she unraveled the strand and weaved lock over lock into a tight braid. Many moons had brought them here, to this cycle of life where the latter one labored like the one who came before. It was time for Lou to rest. Lydia nestled into her, happy to do anything for this one who loved her strong.

Lou stirred before mole-dotted lids lifted.

"Grandma, you all right?"

"Fine." Lou blinked several times and smiled slowly. "My baby."

Calm, comforting Lou.

"You certain?"

"Yes, Lydia. Just tired. Help me up now."

Lydia knelt beside her and lifted Lou's shoulders from the ground. Panting, Lou struggled up. Beads of sweat slipped from her temple, curved down her cheek, and slipped into the deep folds of her neck. When her breathing steadied, Lydia leaned forward and whispered.

"John is speaking with Dr. Kelly today."

"Today?"

She nodded and grasped her fingers. "May have already done it."

"My Lord."

"Can you believe it, Grandma?"

"Yes, chil', I can."

Joy sprang Lydia to her feet. She lifted her hands and twirled herself into another world. With a spin of worn cotton, she was lifted out of the tiny log cabin into a grand hall of royalty.

"Grandma, I'm going to march out of here a free woman."

"I like that, Lydia." Lou laughed. "I like that."

"I'm going to hold my head up high." She jutted her chin forward. "Don't need to look at the ground no longer, begging, pleading, because I'm going to walk around land *I* own. Bury my bare feet in grass that is mine, Lou. *Mine.*" She wiggled her toes and put her hands on her waist. She took a step. One, two, three steps, one foot in front of the other, she strutted back and forth for the one who rooted her on. "Oh yes, I am going to eat the richest foods." She couldn't think of any. "Wear the finest gowns." These she knew well. "Satin and silk and lace, Lou, weaved, knitted, and sewn by somebody else's tired hands." Let them work for hours creating something for her back. "I'm going to go the furthest place my mind can take me." She had no idea where. Anywhere but here. And then she remembered John's words. "I am a rich, free woman, a seller of purple. You know what purple is, don't you, Grandma?" She didn't even wait for the woman to answer. "It's the color of kings and queens."

"Oh my, my, my." Lou shook her head. She was feeling it too.

Free!

It was the most beautiful thing.

Lydia fell to her knees, laid her head back in her grandmother's lap, and let the tears roll, slip into her ears. Lou caught the ones she could in her palms.

"Isaiah would be so proud knowing."

He would. That right-sided grin would light his face. Yes, it would.

"I wish you could come."

"For what? Baby, I already got what you trying to get." She hummed a slow tune before she opened her mouth and sang, "*I'm going to meet Jesus. Going to meet Jesus. Yes, I'm going to meet Jesus. Going to meet Jesus after a while.*" It was slow, but sad? Not one bit.

Lydia hadn't heard her sing the song in years. *Years.* "Oh, Lou." She buried her face into the coarse burlap against her cheek. "What will I do without you?"

"Don't you worry. You ain't never going to be without me. Not for a minute."

Lydia sat in the dark on the redwood bench her father crafted, waiting for John.

The sky was as black as the night she ran free. She tilted her head when she saw him, a shadow moving toward her, among the trees. She could see his arms, his legs lift, the outline of a man, strong and tall like her daddy. She slid to the edge of her seat and waited, watched him come to her like a dream.

"John."

"Lydia."

She rose to embrace him, but before her arms could lock around his neck, he gripped her elbow and stepped back.

"Is everything all right?" She looked at him, could barely make out the details of his face, nothing to read. "Let's go inside." By the candlelight. "Oh, and I have something for you. You hungry?"

He shook his head and followed her indoors.

"You're back late."

"Yeah, I was here earlier before you came."

"Well, how did it go?" The silence between them, the pause of that moment, waiting, waiting to hear if they had been granted life, hovered endlessly. She could feel her shoulders rise. Seemed they never did fall. "Well? Did you talk to Dr. Kelly?"

"I did."

He tormented her with each sigh, with every break in his speech. She was much too tense. She laughed. "You taunting me?"

"No. I'm sorry, Lydia."

"It's all right." She could see him now. Charcoal eyes watching her, flashing white every glance away. "What did he say?"

John propped himself against the wall, a knee bent and a foot flush against the logs behind him.

"Lydia, did something happen with you and Dr. Kelly?"

The words entered her ears, tumbled to her heart.

"What do you mean?"

"I mean, did you… Did he… I don't know, Lydia, you tell me."

She shook her head. She could see his chest rising and falling, waiting. "No," she said finally, but her hesitation told him all he needed to know.

"Lydia…" He shook his head. "Tell me it's not true. Lydia?"

"It's not. Not like you think."

"So something *did* happen?"

She turned away but could see him from the side standing for a long time with his face in his hands. When he looked back at her, his brows crinkled close and low. "Why didn't you tell me? Why didn't you tell me?"

"I don't know." She was starting to tremble. "I was scared."

"You were scared?" He rubbed his hand over his head and paced. "I can't believe this."

"Please, John."

"You lied to me?"

"Not really, no."

"Not really? What kind of answer is that?"

"I'm sorry." Would he believe her? Believe she could resist another? How she had clung to him, needed him every night?

He shook his head.

"John."

"Lydia, I've been up there in that man's face! A man who has…done what? Tell me. Tell me what happened."

"Why do you want to live that?" She didn't want to live it. She had buried it the night they wed.

"You were scared? Scared of what? Scared of *me*? What did you think, Lydia? Am I so evil? So awful? Have I ever given you reason not to trust me? Have I?"

"No. None of those things." She tried to keep her voice steady, failed with every word.

"But you were scared?"

"Yes."

"You were scared?"

"*Yes!*"

"You were scared of what?"

"I was scared to hurt you. I was scared you would feel awful you couldn't protect me. You walked me up those steps right into his hands. But what could you do? What could you do? What could a *slave* do?"

He stared at her. He didn't move, just stared until she dropped her head. She had said too much.

They were silent the rest of the night. When he crawled in front of her under the worn blanket she hated, he turned on his side, his back to her.

So sorry. So sad, she nestled close, wrapped her arm around him, grazed the back of his head, ran her palm across his neck, his ear.

"Don't you want me anymore?"

The pause pierced.

"Lydia, I don't even know who I've got."

She slid to her back and stared at the wood-shingled roof. It was true. He didn't know her. Never did. This was her life. One heartache after the other. Just her place in the world.

What could a slave do?

CHAPTER NINETEEN

*L*ydia grazed the lips of the man she loved and draped him in the woven blanket of red circles and purple diamonds she had finished. Circles and diamonds. The cycle of life. Birth. Life. Death. Rebirth. She watched him sleeping, the covering rising and lifting, freedom already giving breath.

He would have a better chance leaving without her, could save half his money for the journey and his settling up North.

She cried as she stumbled out, doubled over when she stepped under the threshold and turned to him for one last glance. How did one leave love?

Push.

It was early morning, still dark out when she stepped into her grand-mother's cabin. No one, nothing remained in the gray darkness except a faded, striped apron sprawled near the door. Panic rose inside her until she remembered the crate and her fear weakened with sadness.

In The Room, Lydia caressed creased foreheads and the sunken cheeks of the sleeping until she reached the one against the back wall. Lou among them. She kissed the old woman's temple and prayed, pouring the words like oil over her. "The Lord watch between me and thee when we are absent one from another." *Stay with your heart,* Lou had said. Lydia had tried, but failed. How did one follow a wayward heart?

Minutes later, she watched through her bedroom window as the doctor and his wife stepped into the carriage, Charles holding the reins. It was Lizzy who kept her standing, staring, watching until the sight of her friend slipped away.

Lizzy.

She let the folds of the drapes fall over the window frame as the mares trotted off.

Slowly, she walked to the three-legged table and lifted a woven chocolate dress she had made for Lizzy. And as always, it was her flesh, her skin that touched it first. She clasped the pearls Lizzy had given her around her neck and stood in front of the mirror.

There was no difference.

She peeked through the door of Cora's room and found the girl slumbering, her evergreen blanket kicked beneath her feet lush and thick like grass. *Grass that is mine, Lou. Mine.*

Push!

When Lydia pushed through the front door, hat in hand, she pushed through the pain and walked down the steps she had grappled on. There was no turning back. *The pain.* It was more than the push for life. It was the death. Like the losing of a limb.

The searing ache in her heart slowed her, but nothing stopped her from moving moment to moment, inch by inch into a new world and further from the commitment of love, the ancestry of Africa, and the twenty-year bondage of being who and doing what another dictated. Draped in the clothes of a wealthy White woman and pearls, she left it all behind.

Lydia teetered by the road in the low-heeled boots she still hadn't mastered. Before she could gather herself, a White man in a wagon stopped for her.

Though fear clenched her throat, his eyes told her he didn't see a Colored, but a woman, a beautiful woman. She traveled with him past county lines until evening, when he pulled over to the side of the road and offered more than a place to rest.

She resisted kindly and waited until his eyes closed. When his breathing gave way to a wheezing hiss, she stole away and journeyed until her legs trembled and she fell in exhaustion under a towering cedar.

She rested then walked slowly into a new day. Hours later, she heard trotting behind her.

"You all right, ma'am?" Another White in a wagon.

She froze.

"What *are* you doing out here this time of morning?" He looked behind him. "You out here by yourself?"

The terror she felt must have shown in her eyes.

"I'm not going to hurt you or nothing, ma'am. I'm just wondering if I can be of service somehow."

"No. No, you can't, but thank you," she said in her most ladylike diction.

"All right then." He tipped his hat of straw and clicked his tongue but tugged on the reins before the horses moved.

"Uh, if you don't mind my asking, where you headed?"

"Just up the road, to town." She had no idea where she was going, hadn't planned a bit of it.

"Are you going to the junction to get the coach?"

She nodded.

"Well, let me give you a lift. You might just make it before it pulls off. I hate to see a little thing like you walking alone. No telling what kind of wild animals running loose 'round here. Especially with them coons running away all the time." He peered down at her.

She swallowed hard. *Oh, please...*

"You all right, ma'am?"

"Yes. Yes, I'm fine." She was weak, feeling weaker by the moment. She needed to sit, to rest. "I suppose I will accept that ride." She let her lids flicker a few times and smiled. "If you're still offering."

"Of course." He jumped down to help her climb inside. "It'd be my pleasure."

"You're not from around these parts, are you? I've never seen you around here."

"No. No, I just got here."

"Do I know your people?"

"No. I don't think so."

"Where you from?"

Think! "Manassas. Manassas, Virginia." It was the first place that came to mind.

"Not terribly far. If you catch the coach you'll be there shortly."

She feared someone might recognize her, but right away she calmed herself. The last time she ran, she had been a slave, dressed in slave clothing. But now she was a White woman dressed as a lady, and to her surprise the only eyebrows raised when her driver helped her down from his wagon in front of the general store were of men taking interest in her beauty.

"There's the coachman feeding his horses, miss," he said, releasing her. "They'll probably be pulling out shortly. Travel safe, now. Good luck to you." He hopped back into the wagon and nodded his good-bye before riding off.

Lydia drew the bonnet close against her cheeks and dropped her eyes when the store owner's slaves assisted other passengers, two middle-aged men, inside the coach. It was the dark faces that concerned her, that she feared would see through her disguise. When they returned inside, she lifted her head but startled at what she saw in the distance.

Charles sat several feet away in the front of an empty wagon, much like the one he had driven for her and John. When he tilted his head in her direction, her heart thumped. Foolishly, she watched him dismount and walk toward her before she scrambled into the coach.

"Where you headed, ma'am?" the driver barked as he sprang into the driver's seat.

"Manassas, please, sir." She glanced over her shoulder for John's friend. Maybe he hadn't seen her.

"You know the fare already, ma'am?"

"Yes, sir." She didn't know. Wouldn't have done her any good if she had.

As the coach rolled out of town, she bit her tongue, the tip of torn flesh raw. Slowly, the taste of salt filled her mouth and she swallowed the blood of her heritage.

Lydia wept softly on the ride, her head bowed, her face covered by her bonnet. An older passenger, a woman with a thin, long neck, looked down at her, her eyes shifting, her chin lifting higher each time Lydia glanced her way. The display of discomfort danced between them for several miles before she handed Lydia an embroidered handkerchief.

Lydia glanced down at the folds of her dress bunched up into fists that had turned her knuckles white. She loosened her grip and took the cloth from the stranger. They rode in silence, Lydia rubbing the delicate flowers in the corners of the cloth, grateful to have something to do with her hands.

"Manassas, Virginia," the driver announced before the coach rolled to a stop. Passengers rose around her and the swing of skirts swept against her. A heavyset man in a tight frock coat stepped on her foot, but Lydia didn't flinch. She just sat, clinging to the cloth in her lap.

"Ma'am."

She was the last one remaining. A nervous flutter kept her still, quiet.

"Ma'am. You're here. Manassas, Virginia." His pink face scrunched. "That is where you were headed, wasn't it?"

"Yes, sir. It's just...I don't have a way to pay you. I'm sorry."

"Your fare has been covered."

"Has it?" Lydia looked around. No one knew her. She prayed no one knew her here.

"Yes."

"How? By whom?"

"The woman who sat across from you. The older one. I assumed you knew her."

"No."

"Well, you're covered."

"Thank you." Lydia rose slowly. "Thank you, sir," she said, stepping onto the arrival platform. She glanced up at the blue sky. *Thank You.*

She was here. Manassas, Virginia, once again.

Fatigue and road weariness seeped into her bones as she stumbled with quivering knees up the dusty road, yanking free the skirt stuck to her thighs. She scoped the magnificent view of a plantation grander than Kelly's land. Paying little attention to her steps, she stumbled into a burrow and twisted her ankle. A wrenching pain shot up her leg as she tumbled to the ground near the edge of the road, breaking the heel of her boot.

Lydia twisted around to the sound of hooves and gravel behind her. A covered wagon slowed and the driver, a squatty slave boy, clicked his tongue and yanked on the reins. Two chestnut mares halted and the young one jumped clumsily to the ground. Dusting himself off, he staggered to the side of the stage. Parting the tan linen tarp, his passenger appeared.

"Jackson?"

"Caroline, what are you doing out here? Are you all right?" Leaping down from his carriage, he glanced around. "Are you alone?"

Very.

"It's all right," he said to his driver, waving him off with the back of his hand. When the boy disappeared behind the wagon, Jackson whispered, "What's going on? Do you need help?"

She needed it. Didn't want it.

"I think I twisted my ankle." She held up the two-inch ivory heel.

"Let me help you." Jackson knelt and wrapped his arm under hers, lifting her to her feet. *The pain.* When her toes grazed the ground, she flinched. When she pressed the ball of her foot against the damp ground, she yelped.

"Oh yes, you need help."

"I'll be fine." She hobbled forward and shrieked.

"I insist." Jackson looped her arm around his, shifting her weight against his large frame. Lydia hopped against him into the carriage.

"Now tell me. What were you doing out here alone?"

"Leaving." How much of the truth could she share?

"Leaving? Leaving what? Leaving whom?" He stared at her.

"My father died."

"Oh. I'm sorry to hear that. My condolences. Does Elizabeth know?"

"Yes. She knows."

"Well, I'd imagine she would be glad to take you in. I'm certain you could stay with her."

"I did. I was with her, but her father, her father tried to…" She dropped her head in shame. If only she had told John.

"I understand. Enough said."

"I just left, walked away with nothing." She held up the broken leather. "But this heel." She forced a smile for all the broken she held on to.

CHAPTER TWENTY

Odessa wailed at Abram's feet.

An early winter chill whipped through the hills of the Kelly plantation and in and out of the bodies of owners and slaves alike. Days later, it settled deep in the chest of her love.

She couldn't lose him. Not now. *Lord Jesus, not ever.*

She was supposed to go first. Fall in his arms and rise in the arms of Jesus. That was the way it was supposed to be, the way it had to be because he was the strong one. The rock. Her strength. She needed him. God knew she needed him. Had never made a step without him.

"Please, Lord."

She draped herself over him, pressed her cheek against his chest, his hot, damp chest, rising and falling, higher, drawing his stomach tighter, lower until his ribs poked through the rags of thin cotton. She closed her eyes, listened to the rattling of sleep coming from blankets across from her, the wheezing of death beneath her. Ruth and Lou had stayed up until bloodshot eyes begged to close, but she had no choice. She had to fight. She kissed the scar in the middle of his palm, leaned in, pressed harder, whispered into his pores, spoke to him. Spoke through him. Her face lifted with his every breath, dropped with each exhale. Together they battled. His body, her prayers. One spirit fighting to live.

It wasn't the first time.

Decades before when she, Abram, and Ruth were on the Whitfield plantation, it was she who needed saving.

"I got you just where I want you, girl." Young master, their owner's son, stepped toward her.

Odessa squirmed in the corner of the dim work shed where she had been waiting for Abram, her love. He had promised to meet her there each day for a week, but every evening she had waited in vain.

She tugged on the folds of her dingy dress, stretched it past her ankles, sweeping it against the floor, but it still wasn't enough. Lustful eyes looked past it, saw through it. She needed a real covering.

Lord, help me.

Master Tim made his way through all the slave girls, ones she had brought into the world with her own hands, and now he wanted women, even ones old enough to be his mother. She had prayed she'd never see the day but it had arrived, streaking in as a harsh ray of light across her enemy's face. He was close enough for her to see him well. Every detail. Four beads of sweat, clinging to his upper lip, ran together when he grinned.

He stepped forward into the shadows.

Please, God.

"I've been waiting for this a long time. I've been watching you."

Another step closer.

Jesus, You there?

"Now I'm a see if you been worth the wait." His fingers trembled when he reached for her. She screamed for Abram and shrank away from his hands, from those nails. They were the shortest nails she'd ever seen, rimmed in dirt or blood, bit so deep the tips looked longer than normal. The ugliest hands she'd ever seen.

"Come here, girl."

"Please, sir, *please.* Don't do this. Please!"

"Where you going? You playing shy?" Laughter spilled from his pursed lips. "I like that." Hot words seared her face.

His fingers clutched her thigh. She screamed.

"Please, no! God, no." *Help me, Father.* She struggled to break free, to move his hand, but his hold was tighter, stronger than she could manage. She swung forward, her right hand tearing his face with her fingernails.

Two red lines stretched from his temple to his jawbone. His eyes narrowed. He threw her down against the wall. "You crazy—"

Please, Jesus, come for me.

"Leave her." Ruth's trembling voice turned their heads in her direction. She stood with a knife, holding the red handle like a pistol between both hands, her legs spread wide apart under the sway of her skirt. "Leave her alone."

Master Tim leapt toward her friend and grabbed the blade from her hands. It was the moment, the tragedy Odessa would never forget, the horror she would never forgive that would change all of them, each as much as the other. Ruth's dark brown eyes widened just before the blade sliced across them and they gaped with blood. Odessa screamed as she watched her friend collapse in the hay.

There was no sound, only the horror of a red stream trickling down a stricken face, a white shirt, a burlap skirt. The flow that would not stop, would never dry from her own eyes.

Master Tim stood staring at the injured woman at his feet. It was the last thing Odessa remembered before a scarred hand wrapped around her mouth, pulling her to her feet. Suddenly she was lifted and carried away. She slept for hours before she awoke safe on her cot, wrapped in wool.

"Sissy?"

"Child, what is it?" Her friend stirred and turned to face her, her eyes still slit from sleep.

"How did I get here?" She scrambled up and looked around. "I went to go meet Abram at the shed, but Master Tim…" *Ruth.* The image of Ruth shook her. How had she been able to sleep?

"What did that boy do, Dessa?" Sissy rose wide awake. "He touch you?"

"No. That's the thing. He was about to. He was in my face, Sissy, all over me, oh, it was awful." She bit back the pain. "I thought for sure he was going to… Oh, Sissy, I knew this was it, there was no getting away this time. I was all alone, hunched up in a corner, when Ruth came. Ruth is dead." She sobbed. "Ruth is dead, but I was saved. I was saved. Somebody, I didn't see him, but somebody with a scar on the inside of his hand, right in the center of his palm, put his hand over my mouth and took me out of that place. I don't remember nothing else, but I'm here and I'm saved."

"My God…"

"You think, you think Jesus came?"

"Who else, Dessa? Who else?"

Odessa stared at the tears in Sissy's eyes and thought of the shed blood that saved her.

But Ruth wasn't dead. Yet and still, something had died in Odessa. An innocence, a trust, a peace cut out of her. The knife had sliced through her mind, made all her reasoning separate parts of a whole. Her words came out slowly as she linked her thoughts like the pieces of a puzzle, but when she couldn't, she cried. She had cried every day since.

The next afternoon, Odessa waited for Abram at the shed and he showed up. When he extended his hand, she gasped, nearly fainted. Her heart beat double when she saw it.

"Where you get that scar?" It was the first thing she asked him.

"Ain't nothing," he said for hours until late that night when they were alone. "Last week me and Sammy decided we was gonna do something. Not just sit around and let them hurt our own. We're willing to risk our lives if we have to. We're going to save our women. That boy has to be stopped. Anyway, we used that hot poker to prove we were tough, that we could take whatever came our way. I got mine in the hand. Sammy's is in his right foot."

"It's just the two of you? Saving folk?"

"Just the girls, from that no-good—" He bit back the words. "Yeah, the two of us. We were the only two fools crazy enough to believe we could do something. The only ones crazy enough to burn ourselves." He chuckled.

A year later, Sammy stopped him, slit his throat like the man had sliced Ruth's eyes, but the price was high. Master Whitfield beat him until he was unrecognizable and hung his body out by the slave cabins and dared anyone to take him down. He stayed up there until the stench filled every log house on slave's row, until you could taste death in every bite, in every drink consumed on the land. His body stayed there until the slices of skin that were left peeled away under the boiling sun and his flesh was pecked by the wild at night.

None of it was good for Odessa's mind. None of it was good for any of them, but while the others continued walking around the swinging corpse, choosing to move through the day like it was normal to see a dead man, a friend, somebody's son twirling by a rope around his neck, Odessa couldn't. She sat and cried.

"Old Man Whitfield's an evil man and that bad seed passed right on through to his boys," Abram said. "At least one's gone. All we have to deal with now is Jackson, and he's a young one who don't seem to have a thing for dark skin. Don't want none of us in his sight mostly. Suits me just fine."

"I can't believe ya'll was so brave."

He shrugged.

"How many girls you rescue, Abram?"

His head dropped before it shook.

"Abram?"

"I don't talk about that, Dessa. I don't ever talk about that. When they killed Sammy, I let it all go. He was the brave one. He was the one who died."

And yet Abram was the one honored. The healer. So many years ago.

Odessa stared at the man lying before her. Ruth and Lou returned to her side.

"Lord, I'm so scared You gonna take my husband from me. Then what I'm gonna do, Lord? What I'm gonna do?"

"Odessa," Ruth interrupted, "you gonna pray or you gonna worry? Can't do both, child."

"Leave Dessa alone. You all right, baby. Just talk to Him the way you want to. He knows your heart."

Abram stirred.

"See there."

Ruth reached down and touched the limbs in front of her. "That you, Dessa? She's on his foot, Lou. Wouldn't you wake up if all that was on you?" Odessa threw a tattered patch at Ruth. The women chuckled.

"You all right, love?"

He coughed, struggled up, and fell back.

"Stop trying to be strong. Rest now, you hear?"

He nodded, wiggling to his side. By midnight, he lay helpless in a pool of sweat. All heads bowed in prayer. Odessa wept.

"Abram, you got to make it. For me."

Ruth and Odessa took turns wiping his forehead, keeping him dry. Tremors quaked through the broken vessel.

"Come on, get up, Abram! Get up." Odessa gripped a chunk of his flesh and squeezed, twisting his skin purple under Ruth's watchful hand.

"Stop that, Dessa, you hurting him." The blind woman slapped her fingers away. "That's a terrible way to die."

The room fell silent.

"I'm sorry. Dessa, I'm so sorry. I didn't mean it. You know I always say too much."

"I ain't gonna make it without you." She slumped over her husband's body. "You kept me here in this world," she mumbled, every word muffled against his ribs. "Without you, I would've been gone. Would've gone to Jesus a long time ago."

Lou and Ruth swayed with her, calming her with gentle hands and a thick melodic hum. A death hymn, slow and dark. She was losing him and they all knew it. Each moment, he slipped further from her and this life, this world. It would be just the women left in The Room.

The ladies dozed in a layered pile until a wind whistled through the cracks of the walls. Shifting tumbled the stack awake.

Abram lay cold and still.

"My baby's gone," Odessa cried, gripping the hands of her sisters. They sobbed over the motionless body.

When Abram's eyes flashed open, they screamed.

"Abram? Abram! You ain't dead!"

He blinked, coughed, hard and long, and sat up on his forearms. "Wouldn't you wake up with all that on you?"

Odessa put her hand on his forehead. "Fever's gone."

Lou leaned against the wall and pulled to her feet. She bounced in place, her hands pressed together, head down one moment, both hands and head raised the next. She shuffled herself breathless to her own rhythm.

"Welcome home, Lazarus." Ruth squeezed Abram's hands. "Welcome home."

Odessa let the tears come. Wet love streamed into the crevices of her face, raced through the maze fast and steady until they dripped down her chin onto her husband. She snuggled next to him and spoke to him. Only him.

"That night when I was in that shed, I know it was you that saved me." She struggled with each word. "I knew. I always knew. I saw your scarred hand, Abram, before you rescued me."

Abram struggled up and stared at her.

"When I thought you was gone, that I had lost you right now, I was sad I didn't say thank you."

"Dessa…"

"I know, Abram. I've always known. You had the power to heal. You had the power to save."

"No, love, you don't understand. I never rescued nobody."

"Sure you did. I—"

"I ain't never rescued nobody, Dessa. Felt bad for years about it, too, that Sammy died the only real savior. He killed Mr. Tim, died because he did, died a horrible death. And I didn't do nothing. Never got the chance to help one girl."

"Sammy had a scar on his hand, too, then. In his right palm?"

"You know he didn't. You saw him hanging there. Body hung for weeks. We was crazy, Dessa, but believe me, one wound was plenty enough. I stuck that poker on his right foot and he seared my right hand. Near killed *each other* when we did it." Abram coughed through a pain edged with laughter.

"But I was saved… And the hand, I remember the hand. Ain't nobody else you know scarred on the inside of they hand?"

"What are you talking about, Dessa?"

"Thank You, Jesus!" Lou hollered. She couldn't stop shaking her head. "Can you believe it, Dessa? He's alive! This here is a miracle if there ever was one."

Odessa nodded. *A miracle indeed.*

ere you are," Jackson said, swinging the bedroom door open with a flair and a movement much more grandiose than Lydia expected. She laughed.

"A little entertainment for the lady." His hand remained on the knob. "Go on." He nodded at her. "Have a look. Do you need some help?"

"No. No, thank you." She had insisted on walking, hopping up the thirty steps to the entry of the manor though she had leaned against his grip on her elbow and rested midflight. She was winded but she would be fine. She glanced around the room. Hard not to be fine in this place.

Soft blue walls rose to a soaring arched ceiling over a high bed draped in white lace in the center of the room. In the corner there was a cedar armoire with three unlit candles and an ivory straight-back chair in front of a vanity. She hobbled toward the chair.

"I—I don't know what to say. It's so beautiful." She was overwhelmed by the grandeur, the elegance, of the space. It was more than she had imagined.

"We'll get this room filled with whatever you need," he said, lighting the candles. "Let Annie know and I'll see to it that you are well taken care of." His face turned solemn. "So sorry to hear about your loss, Caroline."

"Yes, thank you."

It was a terrible loss. If he only knew how great. Everyone she loved was a memory to her now. She felt her spine curve under the weight of it. What was she doing here?

"I'm sure there are a few items Annie can gather to make you comfortable tonight. Let me know if there's anything else you need. I'll see you at supper." He started toward the door. "Caroline. I'm glad you're here." He flashed a smile and closed the door behind him.

She was grateful to have a place to stay for the night. By tomorrow, she'd think of where to go, what she needed to do next. If she could walk on her sprain. She sighed. Tonight, she would rest and be thankful she had made it.

She touched the chair's frame, running her fingertips over the curve of the backrest. The smooth wood had been buffed to perfection. She had seen Lizzy and Mrs. Kelly sit in one like it. Although this one was taller, wider, much more elegant in appearance. She sat and stared at herself in the mirror.

She was tired, weary to the bone, but beyond the structure of her features, there was something else in her appearance, a look that made her lean into her reflection and examine herself up close. There, in the wideness of her eyes, was a vulnerability, a fragileness she hadn't seen before.

She unpinned her hair, raked through the tangles with her fingers, and swooped the length of it back into a low chignon.

Her skin was whiter, her features sharper in the flickering candlelight. She glanced at the three orange flames jumping behind her. When she turned back to the mirror, she noticed a shadow behind her. Like John coming in through the trees. She startled and steadied her hand on the strand of pearls at her neck.

She moved to the bed and flipped back the covers of lace, brushing her palm across the cold satin ivory sheets. She lifted the pillow to her face and cried. No worn blanket, no purple and red one, nothing to remind her. She placed her hand where she dreamed he would lie, ran her fingers, over the pillow like it was the back of his head.

But she had made her decision. A new life now.

A tap on the door sobered her. She wiped her eyes and stood.

Annie poked her head inside.

"Miss…Miss? I don't know what to call you."

"Oh. Lydia is fine."

"May I come in, Miss Lydia?"

And then she remembered.

"No!"

"No?" Annie began to shut the door.

"No, please, Annie. Come in. Yes, come in."

Annie crept in tentatively with thick, white towels in her arms. "I'm sorry, I was saying no about the name. I prefer Miss Caroline, if you don't mind."

Annie looked at her for a few seconds before nodding. "Yes, ma'am."

"I brought a couple of things for you before dinner. Setting them here is fine?" When Lydia nodded, she placed hair pins and a brass brush on the cedar cabinet. "Master Whitfield said you're going to be needing more. Plan on staying awhile?"

"Not long. No."

"Well"—Annie glanced at her—"I'd be happy to find out what you need now or after supper, ma'am."

"After supper would be fine, Annie."

"If there's anything else I can get you, Miss Caroline, let me know."

"Thank you."

Annie stood there, her head slightly cocked, staring at her, studying her. Lydia's heart quickened. The woman nodded and stepped out.

She would be one to watch.

"Did you get settled, Caroline? How is everything?" Jackson shook out the maroon linen cloth over his lap with a flip of his wrist. "Annie get you what you need?"

"Yes, sir."

"Sir?" He looked up at her. "That's hardly in order."

She was making too many slips. It seemed easier to act the part with Lizzy at her side. It had been just two silly girls playing make-believe, but this, this was real.

"Jackson," she said, calmly, softly. "Yes, Annie was wonderful. She was a great help."

"Good."

She watched him cut into a slice of ham. The *ting* of silver sawed back and forth, sliding the meat into the hill of mashed potatoes and corn on his platter. He looked up and smiled.

"I appreciate your kindness. I don't plan on staying long."

He raised his brows. "I see." He forked the pork into his mouth then looked at her plate. "Aren't you hungry? You haven't touched your food. Like the last time we dined together. You aren't much of an eater, are you?"

"I am. Just a little tired." She scooped corn onto her spoon and ate what she could.

"How long will I have the honor of enjoying your presence?"

"I don't know. A day or two."

"Well, it will take at least that for your items to be ready. I mean, you're not planning on leaving here without clothing, certain necessities?"

"No." She hadn't thought of that. Hadn't thought of anything. "I suppose I'll need them."

"I'd imagine it would be difficult to get too far on that ankle." He raised his wineglass. "Either way, I'm a lucky man to have you even for a night." He smiled and sipped his drink, his blue eyes steady on her.

Lydia shifted in her seat and looked away. Dining alone with a gentleman not her husband. Warmth rose to her cheeks. She hoped she wasn't blushing, hoped this man wasn't witnessing the shame, the embarrassment, in her pores. John didn't deserve such disrespect.

"Are you all right, Caroline?"

She nodded. "Just been through a lot. I'm sorry I'm not much company."

"It's no problem at all." He smiled. "Enjoy your food. We've got time."

Lydia lowered her eyes and willed herself to eat, one bite at a time.

Later that night in bed, pictures of the day she had walked into drifted through her mind. She endured the blue sky of another day. She made it through, this time to the other side. And now she reclined on slippery sheets in the blackest of night. Royalty.

Jackson had turned out to be the perfect host, a wonderful gentleman in her time of need. His offer of material goods was just the thing she needed to move on once she decided where she was headed. The possibilities. As far as her mind would take her.

Her door creaked open. She drew the covers to her chest and sat up.

"Miss Caroline."

It was Annie.

"Yes?" She only saw the girl's silhouette in the door.

"Mr. Whitfield has called for you."

"I'm sorry?" She hadn't heard correctly. He had not called for her. At this hour? Lydia scrambled to the edge of her bed and blinked until she made out Annie's face in the dimness. Surely she was jesting. One of them was not serious.

"He wants you in his chambers, ma'am." When Lydia froze, she added, "Now."

"Why?" Lydia's heart raced. "Annie, please, tell him…tell him I'm asleep, all right? Would you do that? Would that be possible?"

"He's waiting," she said simply, and shut the door.

Annie.

The walk down the hall was as long as the journey it took to get from Dorchester to Manassas, from Colored to White, from bondage to freedom on a sore foot and a bruised heart.

Her hands trembled as she turned the knob to his room. She stood on the threshold in the dimly lit room in the same brown dress she had arrived in, waiting.

He was sitting on a chaise, reading by candlelight. He looked up from his book and smiled. "Caroline."

She stood silent, waiting, praying.

"Come in."

Oh, please, God.

She took a painful step forward.

"Oh, I'm sorry." He looked at her red ankle. "Please have a seat."

She looked around. There was nowhere to sit. He was in the only chair in the room. He nodded toward his bed as he sipped from a copper goblet.

She teetered on the edge of the linen, pressing her damp palms together in her lap.

"Unwind, Caroline." He placed his drink beside him and closed his book, resting it against the leg of the chaise. "I just thought you might feel like talking."

"Oh." She felt her shoulders fall, her face soften. She smiled. "Thank you, but I'm quite weary from the journey. If you don't mind, Jackson, I would love to get some rest." When she started to rise, he stood up. She stopped and stared at him.

"That will be fine. I didn't want to keep you long." He stepped closer, breathing through his mouth, the burnt caramel scent of rum. He swept wisps of her hair from her forehead.

Lydia flinched.

"What's this?"

Her fingers touched his when she covered the scar.

"You had an accident?"

"Yes. As a child."

"Ah, what a pity to have such a thing on a face like yours. I suppose no one is perfect."

"No." She was discovering that fact at the moment. She looked down. He tilted her chin up to him. "But you're a beauty nonetheless."

She slipped back from his touch. "Thank you."

"Caroline..." He reached for her again. She looked down at the hand, so like the one that grabbed her in the hall of the old colonial, and her heart raced just the same. She had been afraid then, but this time, she felt nothing close. Something else sped through. Never again would she allow a man, allow anyone, to do whatever they wanted. Folk had touched, had whipped, had killed for too long. No more. He could not lay his hands on her. She was not subject to him. She had power and she used it on the one panting in her ear.

"Jackson." She stepped back from his arms with wide eyes. "I'm not sure what you're thinking. Perhaps I gave you the wrong idea. I am under your care, but I'm sorry."

He blinked then shook his head, his eyes as stricken as hers.

"Listen, if you want me to leave—"

"No." He laid his hand across his chest. "Forgive me. I'm sorry, Caroline."

"No, I'm sorry. It was unwise for me to come into your home." She forgot about her injury and turned toward the door abruptly. She winced.

"Caroline, please." She glanced over at him, his hand against his heart. "*Please.* I want you to stay. At least until you're better."

She waited until he shifted and the tops of his ears pinked. She nodded and limped out of the room, past Annie.

Oh, yes, Lydia was a lady.

CHAPTER
TWENTY-TWO

*J*ackson could feel Michael's breath on his face.

Despite Caroline's accusations against the man, he had ridden all the way to Dorchester to see the only doctor he trusted. He hated the thought of the older man trying to touch her, but the pain left him with little choice.

He squirmed under his touch—*much too close*—swallowing the salty pool of saliva in his mouth. His eyes scanned the room. A long wooden table full of tools, instruments of some kind, and a couple of chairs. Hardly impressive for quack quarters.

"It's bad, I'm afraid." Dr. Kelly frowned. "Have you seen it?"

Jackson stared into the handheld smudged mirror. The rotten molar sank like a seed in the red flesh of melon.

"It's badly infected. How long you been in pain?"

"I don't know. Couple of days, maybe."

Yes, it had been two days exactly, since Caroline had arrived.

"Well, it's hard to believe you're just now noticing. I'm not sure how you lasted this long." Michael tugged on Jackson's bottom lip again and peeked inside. "Whew! There's no white at all. Completely black. Best thing to do is pull it out. I'll have to cut around it some." He sighed. "Sometimes, you have to cut to cure."

Jackson leaned back on the wooden stool and tried to take his mind off the throbbing. "I'm still interested in the slave trade we discussed back in June." There hadn't been an exchange among their families in years. Not since after his brother died. "It's been some time."

"That it has. The one your father sold me isn't much use to me now." Michael chuckled.

"Funny, I thought you bought more than that." He shrugged. "But I was just a kid."

"I *bought* one. I took three, but two of them went straight to my loom room. The wife had sympathy."

"I see. Women don't think much about the costs of feeding extra mouths."

"True, but you'd be surprised. That blind one kept everyone under my watch clothed for some time with her hands alone. For years. Until she taught the others."

Jackson was silent. He could care less what that woman did. Foolish enough to try to attack his brother. She had helped get Timothy killed. So what she was blind. At least she was still breathing.

"I'll tell you what, give me the right price and we can strike a deal for a few good men," the doctor said. "I've also got one or two skilled workers you might like to hire. Let me know."

"Will do. How's Elizabeth? Everything all right with her?" He ran his tongue over the tooth and winced.

He knew well enough not to say too much. He was certain her father knew nothing of the secret visits the girls made without chaperones.

"She's doing fine." Michael smiled, placing a bulging leather bag on the table beside him. "Quite well now that she's to be married. Couldn't be happier."

"Good. Good for her." Hopefully, she had lost interest in him. Good for him.

"You ready?" Michael stood above him holding a small wooden stick with a metal claw. "I've got to get in there and see how we should do this." He placed the dental key into his mouth until the metal clamped over his sore tooth. "Let me know if it gets too bad."

As soon as the words left his mouth, the doctor's thumb pressed down against searing hot gums. The pain shot Jackson's fist forward. Michael dodged the blow and stumbled back. Slowly, his widened eyes narrowed.

"Forget about it." Jackson swore under his breath. He'd deal with the pain. A little old orchard would see him through. He'd stock up on it if he had to. "I'll be fine, Dr. Kelly." He brushed past Michael, slamming the door behind him.

Seven days and three wilted candles later, Lydia remained under Jackson's roof, her ankle sore but healed.

Every night she lit thin sticks of white wax and watched them glow against the dark. Crimson tears of fire wept streams down the length of them until they were no more than a warped image of what they had been. When one flickered, she was quick to blow it out before the wind from an open window or the breeze from a swinging door extinguished the flame.

Slowly, day by day, moment by moment the new seeped in and she began to relish her life of crystal, pearls, and porcelain, dining across from a gentleman each evening who gazed into her eyes and inquired how much longer he would enjoy the pleasure of her presence, questioned if this would be the day she would leave.

"Annie." Jackson lifted his glass. Annie filled it to the rim with a clear liquid that caused him to squeeze his eyes shut and shudder. "Tooth's hurting. Can't enjoy my meal much," he explained.

Perhaps, Lydia thought. Regardless, he was a drinker, she had come to discover, and when he chose to indulge, he became much less refined than he had first appeared.

"Did you need anything else, Caroline?"

"No."

Every evening, he asked the same question and every evening she answered the same. She never needed more. She swallowed. Finally enough.

"That will be all, Annie."

Lydia looked up into almond-shaped eyes already on her. Her gaze followed the girl out. Did Annie sense something, suspect the truth, or did she simply despise her presence? Had she replaced her somehow?

"Jackson."

He pushed his plate away and looked up.

"Why do you have so few servants in a house this size? It's only Annie and James, am I right?"

"You are." He shrugged. "It's only me to serve. Looks like I'm already outnumbered." He smiled. "For now."

Lydia cleared her throat, tried to clear her mind.

"Jackson, I was wondering…" How did she ask this? "About Annie. She seems harsh toward me. Has she said anything to you?"

"About you? No. No, of course not. She's a slave, Caroline. She knows her place." He said it matter-of-factly, just a simple statement he believed, but it pumped her pulse. "Please don't concern yourself with Annie."

He swished the last of his drink around in the glass before he threw his head back and swallowed.

A few days ago, she had been Annie. She had been Annie her whole life.

"She's just loyal," he added.

"Why?" She had never felt loyal to Dr. Kelly. "Why is that?"

"Are you thinking…?" He laughed, but the sound was not the one she heard leaving him with Lizzy that night at the dinner party. This was a tone with teeth, and it jarred Lydia straight up in her seat. "You thought I was spending time with Annie?" The idea must have perturbed him because he swiped his mouth with the napkin in his lap like the filth of the thought settled on his lips somehow. "A Colored?" He threw the crumpled linen over his half-eaten plate. "Not on your life."

Lydia's fingers stumbled over a photograph, yellowed and curved around the edges. Two boys in homespun shirts and dark trousers stood near the steps of the Whitfield manor. One was a head taller than the other, their White faces solemn. The younger one's features had not changed much.

She stuffed the image back between the pages of the weathered journal, but when she heard footsteps, the book tumbled from her hand and slammed against the hardwood.

The man of the house stood on the threshold of the study.

"Jackson."

"Is everything all right?" He scanned the room, the bookshelf behind her.

"I was just looking through some of the volumes on your shelf. Dropped a book, is all." She stooped down to retrieve it. Jackson watched her stand and readjust her clothing.

"I was going into town, Caroline. I'd like you to ride with me."

Lydia bit her lip and gripped the side of the carriage as the driver turned onto the dirt road. They were riding much too fast. A pleasant ride into town for business quickly turned into a dreaded journey that forced her to crane near the side curtain for air.

"Caroline, are you all right?" He glanced up from the newsprint across his lap.

"Yes," she lied. She watched him lick the edge of his thumb and flip page after page until her stomach mimicked the motion.

They passed a small plantation, a shabby, red-roofed farmhouse, and a church, modest and white, in silence. When the carriage stopped, Jackson jumped out onto the cobblestone and waited for the driver to assist Lydia. She lifted her hand, stopping him. She felt weak. Pulling the curtain aside, she looked out at Jackson.

"I hope you don't mind if I stay inside."

"No." He pulled his hat down over his brows. "I won't be long."

She nodded and closed the curtain, grateful for the rest.

"Jackson?" The melodic call struck a chord of joy, a chord of fear in Lydia's spine. She pressed back against the wood, away from view, and waited. She could hear the approaching patter of light footsteps.

"Elizabeth, good to see you. How are you?"

"Well, thank you."

Ten days ago, Lydia would've been at Lizzy's side, ambling along the cobblestone streets, carrying boxes stacked high in brilliant colors of lime, raspberry, and cobalt filled with treasures for an only child.

"I saw your father a few days ago."

He hadn't mentioned it. Hadn't mentioned Dr. Kelly at all.

"Business?"

"Yes, and a bad tooth." He laughed. "How's your mother?"

"My mother?" she said, like she hadn't expected him to ask the most basic of questions. "Oh, she's fine. Just visiting kin. Should be back soon."

"Well, good."

"Have you heard the news? Andrew has asked for my hand in marriage. Did my father tell you?"

"No. He didn't. Well, that's wonderful, Elizabeth. I hadn't heard. I haven't seen Andrew since our dinner. Congratulations."

"Thank you. He'll be happy to know I saw you." She paused. "Well, Jackson…"

"It was a pleasure." He bid her farewell.

Lizzy married.

Lydia's heart swelled at the thought of Lizzy in a white lace gown as a wife, shriveled when she heard the soft click of her closest friend walk away.

Jackson gripped her hand and helped her teeter down from the carriage. When the driver trotted off, they strolled under a dark sky toward the lit manor in the distance, her ankle not paining her in the least.

"Seeing Elizabeth today got me thinking, Caroline." He clasped his hands behind his back and stopped. "It's time I did right by you."

Don't say it.

"I want you to be my wife." His blue eyes glistened under the stars.

"Do you?"

"Of course. I feel awful hiding you. It isn't right."

"No, it's not." None of it.

He reached for her hand and moved forward, beside her, until they stood at the top of the radiant Victorian. She glanced down the flight of steps. It had been a long way up, but here she was. She had made it. Everything she ever dreamed of.

"Will you marry me?"

It was hard to hear the words and not think of the one she left behind. See his face, his smile. But by law, he was not her husband. Their ceremony was not acknowledged, not accepted by the world. And she was here now. Had decided deliberately to come to this side of the world. She was free. There was nothing she wanted more. John knew that.

Still, a sea of guilt swam through her blood, made her feel faint, like she needed to sit down, stretch out somewhere. She gripped Jackson's hand instead.

If she left, where would she go? Who would take her in and give her *this*? Everything. She scanned the vibrant green prairie stretched before her and the man who offered her a chance to have it all. Own it all.

In that instant, she found her life with the one who offered her the world.

"Yes."

The moment Caroline said it, Lydia died.

CHAPTER
TWENTY-THREE

No one cheated Jackson.

He was too sharp, his mind too keen to be deceived. He picked up on every gesture, caught every glance, every fluster, every fidget. He prided himself on paying attention. It was the one thing he got from his old man and it served him well.

Especially at poker.

"I fold." Rex threw his cards down and pounded the table, the sound echoing in the barn, bare besides Jackson's rickety chairs and an old saddle shriveled up in the back corner. A thick layer of hay covered the floor, but it was the smell of animal flesh long gone that clung to the walls, forever reminding them just where they were.

Every few hands, Rex and Henry complained about the stench and inquired. Finally, Jackson gave in and confessed.

"You remember the ball, the two young ladies who were here? I introduced you. The one with the auburn hair. Big green eyes."

"How could we forget?" Henry chuckled.

"Well, she's with me." He nodded his head toward the manor. "Staying with me."

"Is that right?"

"Yes, that's right. Listen, I don't want anyone to know. Not until we're married. She's a decent woman. So keep your mouths shut."

"And she took a liking to *you*?" Rex nudged Henry in the ribs. "How'd you pull that off?"

"Fate, my friend." Jackson smirked. "Fate." He raked the coins together and stacked them in six neat rows. "A fool and his money." He howled.

"And ain't that just what we are." Henry pushed two bits and a dime across the table. "Letting you pay us Monday and giving you the chance to win it back by week's end. Sounds like a pair of fools to me."

"Your day is coming." The knot in Rex's thin neck bobbed as he dragged a sip of hard cider. He shook his bony finger at Jackson. "I swear, one day you gonna lose big."

"Don't count on it." Jackson heaped the cards into a pile toward Henry. "You're up."

"Oh no. I've had enough for one night."

Henry laid his hands over his swollen belly and cleared his throat. "Enough *cards*, that is." He laughed.

"What you talking about, Henry?" Rex leaned in. Jackson cared less. He was itching for another round.

"Well, boys, I found me a lady." A rusty wide grin spread across his face under the straggliest moustache.

"What's *Mae* think about that?"

Henry shrugged, spat a wad of tobacco in the glass jug at his side. "This one, she's…" He raised his brows, whistled. "This one's a keeper. Makes me remember why I'm a man."

"You better watch yourself." Jackson leaned back on his chair's hind legs and rocked in the hay. "Don't seem like Mae's the easy type. Come on, boys, let's play one more hand. I want *all* my money back."

"You're telling me something's wrong with my needing something more? Something different?"

"I don't know. Some men do. I can't imagine I will. You've seen Caroline." She was more than enough. He raked the cards together, shuffled them, and dealt with speed.

"What's that suppose to mean? Mae ain't no heifer."

"No, 'course not."

"This ain't about her." Henry snorted. "This is about *me* and what I need."

"Right." Jackson nodded. "I was just saying."

"He's saying Caroline ain't the common woman." Rex picked up his cards and groaned before curses slid out the corner of his mouth. "Caroline's a beauty. Those green eyes, I mean, he ain't lying."

"Hey, hey! Enough." Jackson threw a dime at Rex's head. "Get your own lady."

"I don't care what he says. Believe me, Rex, whenever you do hitch up with one, you're gonna always want something different." Henry leaned in close. "Ever want one of them coons?"

"Get out!" Jackson flung his cards at Henry and slapped the table.

"Come on, now. Tell the truth."

"Never."

"You ain't never thought about it?"

"Not *ever*." Jackson squeezed his eyes shut. "Makes me sick just thinking about it. I don't even want you to *talk* about it."

"There's some pretty ones out there." Rex licked his lips. "I wouldn't mind—"

"I've *never* seen one." Jackson shook the image from his head. He'd never be so desperate. Pump a bullet through his own skull first if he had to.

"Well, maybe if I wasn't with Mae. Maybe I wouldn't need more if I had a woman like Caroline."

Jackson stared at his bald friend and snickered. *Right.* Like he could be so lucky.

------·•·------

"Got some new men coming in the morning," Jackson said one evening ten days after Caroline arrived. "Few slaves, few workers, so be careful walking the grounds."

The last thing Caroline wanted was another slave.

Another Annie sneaking peeks at her in sideways glances, curtseying before her but cursing her the moment she walked away.

She tugged at the neckline of her beige chemise, stretching it loose, looser, and paced her bedroom until a plank on the wooden floor creaked long and eerie. The sound struck her and for a moment, she stopped to sit on the windowsill, gazing out at the grassy meadows two stories below.

When thoughts of John emerged, how he had walked with her, shown her the beauty of vegetation outside the colonial, she shut them out, shoved them down with new memories. The strolls, the dinners, the rides with Jackson.

Caroline walked over to her dressing table and sat. She picked up the brush and stroked the waves of her dark auburn hair, arranging a chignon at the base of her nape with steady hands. So easy now. She had done it countless times. She glanced at herself in the mirror. *Pretty.*

But something rose inside her. It was old, familiar, a flash of a feeling of who she had been. Sometimes it erupted so suddenly she didn't have the chance to press it down like the hairs over her scar, no time to cover it with loose white powder, or tie it down with the lace of her corset. Sometimes it just was. Loose, untamed, boundless Blackness, and there wasn't a thing she could do about it. When she fought it, a panic set in.

Brass bristles slipped from her hand and hit the floor. *Creak…* She startled and fought the urge to flee.

Stooped on the windowpane, Caroline watched Coloreds descend from a covered wagon. The last man in a dark cotton shirt and denim leapt from the side of the cart with one hand and joined a man in a straw hat standing, his back to her.

She froze when he turned.

A skin as dark and smooth as velvet.

Her fingers pressed against the glass, remembering, recalling the days of Midnight.

He walked with the other man toward the direction of her window, laughing, occasionally surveying his new surroundings with a glance. A dimpled face, a mouth of pearls she would never forget.

He had not run. Still a slave.

When sadness rose, she yanked it down under the folds of her satin dress. When love rose, she willed it to die under a White hand, a white lie against her heart.

She glanced down at the man below. He was staring at her. Standing there, alone, staring up at her.

He had seen her.

When fear rose, she snatched the curtain shut and walked away.

CHAPTER
TWENTY-FOUR

*A*nnie shuffled left, shuffled right, lugging the wooden bucket step by step until she reached the back porch of the Whitfield manor and set it down between her ashen legs. When the water settled two, maybe three, centimeters from the top, she smiled at the achievement. Very little was wasted trotting it down the hill. The master would be proud.

She had no idea how so many slaves could take their work so lightly. Working for the master was like working for *the* Master Himself. If He was here, she would treat Him best she could, but since He wasn't, she did what she could for the ones He placed over her. It was her job to please them.

Inside the manor, she jiggled the bucket down beside her and dipped a cracked wooden bowl into the water to wash up. Scrubbing her hands, she paused briefly to peel a blister from the center of her palm.

"Annie," Mr. Whitfield called from the dining room. When she walked in, he was already seated, his fingers interlocked, resting on the cherry-wood table, his brows furrowed.

"It's past eight."

"Sorry, sir." *Had it gotten that late, already?* "Breakfast will be ready soon."

She served her master mint tea, then scrambled about in the kitchen clanging pots and dropping silverware, desperate to serve in a timely fashion. Thirty minutes later, she brought four crinkled strips of bacon on rye and two eggs cooked over easy on a porcelain platter to the table.

"Will Miss Caroline be joining you this morning?"

"I don't see her." Annie stood back against the wall, her hands clasped together when he lifted his fork and shot a prayer to the good Lord above. *Let him be pleased.*

Mr. Whitfield continued to sip his tea and poke at his breakfast after the first few bites. He flung the deep fried pork back on his plate and sighed.

"Sir, is your food all right?"

"It's fine, Annie. But I need something stronger."

"Sir?" She knew. Didn't want to know.

"Annie, get me something to drink."

"Looks like you ain't had a bite. Would you like me to cook a little more bacon for you? Did I make it too hard? I sure don't mind."

"No, it's fine, Annie. It's my mouth."

"Tooth still hurting?"

"Only when I eat." Mr. Whitfield looked up and shook his head. He was handsome, sure enough. "I'll be fine."

She rushed into the kitchen, poured rum from a tall flask into a dainty, flowered coffee cup he had her purchase for Caroline. It proved a nice disguise. No reason to remind anyone the liquid serpent was slipping down the back of his throat this early in the morning, hours before it was deemed proper for any gentleman. She would pour the rest of the devil out little by little when she got the chance.

"Whatever I can do, you just let me know." She set the spill platter before him and handed him the cup. "It's my job to please you."

Frowning at the delicate handle he gripped with large fingers, he sighed. "Actually, your job is to serve."

"To serve you well. I give myself a little more to rise up to." Annie thought of the words of a hymn she heard one Sunday morning from the balcony of that white paint-chipped church in the woods. The first one of its kind to allow Coloreds to worship with Whites—as long as they came nowhere near one another. The tune vibrated from her lips into a hum.

"Is there something else you could do?"

"I won't be no good far off someplace else. Not trying to serve you."

"I've been served. Go. *Please.*"

The sharpness pierced a little. He had been testy ever since Caroline arrived.

The thought of that woman churned her stomach. There was something about Caroline she couldn't stand. She couldn't put her finger on it, but she felt it the moment she saw her, had served her that platter of roast.

Something wasn't right. Green eyes looking down, looking away. All that fidgeting and fretting got in her bones, made her just as restless. Every time she saw her leaning forward, her back curved in submission, batting her frog eyes big at Master Whitfield, something in Annie's bones went cold. She wanted to snatch her straight and slap those lids back in her head.

But like lightning, Mr. Whitfield took a shining to her. The feeling struck him so fast Annie hadn't seen it coming. Never in her life would she have expected a man of his class, of his caliber, to allow an unwed woman in his home, eating, sleeping under his roof for days, for weeks. It was shameful.

She watched the man drooped over his plate. He was now sipping that devil's drink, that poison at all hours. Had never done such a thing before that woman arrived.

She was the poison. One Annie had to guard them against. Slithering in here messing up things.

Mr. Whitfield took a swig from the cup.

Annie shook her head. God help them all. And to think, he had been such a nice man.

CHAPTER
TWENTY-FIVE

*L*ydia was it for him.

It was an *it* that made John glance up from the tobacco leaves, catch her eye, and in that brief moment send a message that said *I see you*. He saw her. He saw everything. Had she ever been seen? Truly looked at from the inside, known, as bare as bones?

It was that thing that at first made his heart skip when she came around with that water but now made it beat steady, strong, and sure because this was it, and there wasn't going to be no other way around.

It was the thing that kept him awake, stole his slumber earlier on, then made him lie down in the pastures of peace because he knew this one was for real.

It was that soft smile across the field for no one but him. *I see you*.

This one he knew before, had encountered her like no other. This one who could see him, sure enough, could feel him even from miles away.

When he found her beaten, bloody, in the leaves in the same woods he ran, breaking free of the same shackles, he tore the sleeve of his shirt and wrapped her head, tied it tight, bound the wound that would leave the scar that she hated. The scar that she needed. A reminder of all she had been through, how she had suffered but survived a pain great enough to snuff out her life. If she touched it and let it touch her, she would remember that a boy with black skin wanted her, loved her. She would remember who she was in him.

Of all the people in the world, many good, fewer great, finally there was one. There was one he dreamed of. He looked to find this one who knew him, who could breathe him in and keep on moving because she was him and he was her. She didn't even notice the moment he entered in, began to swim through her blood because he was always there. Always. Before the beginning, they were one. All he ever wanted was in the eyes of this one who understood, who knew him. Before he could speak, she heard. Before he could reach, she touched. Before he could cry, she wiped the tears. A breathing, a moving of spirit, that sealed for life not two separate souls but a different manifestation of one self. A oneness unlike any other.

She saw him, and he saw her. He saw her so clearly it was seeing himself. Anything, everything she needed, he would give. All of him, he would willingly offer to finally see peace in her eyes, a rest in her spirit.

He knew where she was. Charles had seen her, had followed her because he had to. Somehow, some way they would be together. Nothing would keep them apart. Like goodness and mercy he followed and he would wait all the days of his life because she was it. The crinkling of papers in his palm kept him moving toward the woman he had to go after, he had to get back.

It wasn't that he wouldn't let go, it was that he couldn't, even if he tried.

Tiny glass bottles of cinnamon and nutmeg clouded in Caroline's slippery grip. She pinched the bonnet further over her eyes with the tip of her thumb and briskly stepped from the wagon she rode in town and walked past the barn and slave quarters, pleading she wouldn't see John.

Heaven was deaf to her prayers.

She knew even with his shoulders, his back, to her, it was him sitting on the rusted fence. He sensed her. Turned to her.

"Lydia."

Slowly, slowly, she lifted her head. How could she look at him?

He was standing now, his buttoned navy shirt half-tucked, half-hanging from his denim slacks, his hands in his pockets. He carried no trace of sadness or anger, just a softness in a chiseled face. As beautiful as ever. She looked away.

"Lydia."

John. She felt herself warming in his presence. She wanted to smile. She didn't.

"You're alive," he said, stepping closer.

"Yes."

He nodded. She bit her lip and looked down. *His boots.* The same scuffed boots that had been tossed aside near their bareness.

"It's good to see you."

She stared at him. How could it be? It had been near two weeks since she'd kissed his lips. Touched those lashes.

"Don't you want to ask how could I?"

"Sure." He swallowed, shifted forward, one leg slightly bent in front of the other, his hands at his waist. "How could you, Lydia?" The words came out scratchy, gritty.

"You didn't...I didn't think you wanted me anymore."

"Did you ask me?"

"I tried—"

"Did you ask me?" There it was. The anger she expected, she deserved. She clutched the glass jars tighter.

"I just thought—"

"You didn't ask me." His voice quaked. "You're my wife. You don't just walk away."

"I'm sorry."

For a moment, they stood in silence.

"So what?" He glanced up at her. "You're a White woman now?"

"What?" She looked down at her attire. "Oh." She straightened her dress with the tips of her fingers and swallowed. She did what she had to do. Didn't know what to say. "John. I'm sorry."

"Are you? Or are you happy now? A free woman. It's what you've always wanted, Lydia. More than anything."

She lowered her head and turned back to the manor.

"Again, Lydia? *Again?* You're going to walk away again?"

His words pierced as she stepped farther away. How many tears could one shed? Hurt and shame lumped in her throat so thick, she could not swallow. Focused on her new life, she forced them down, but they shot to the pit of her stomach and soured.

When she passed the last log house and turned the corner, she doubled over, dropping the bottles of seasoning at her feet. She crouched to the ground, yanking the hem of her skirt above the shards of glass and brown sprinkles against her ankles and vomited. She squatted there coughing, gagging, until she was able to swipe the last line of spittle from her lips and stand again. But she found she wasn't standing. All day, she was still stuck stooped in her sickness.

*H*ang him."

Jackson bit down and yanked the skin from the flesh of the chicken, dangling the bone between his fingers over a cylindrical ivory candle beside his plate. He flicked the meat, swung his head to its sway, and roared at the shadows dancing on the maroon walls. Henry and Mae stared in silence. *Pompous dolts!*

"Jackson," Caroline whispered. "Annie, dessert, please." She lifted her fingers at the girl at the back of the dining room, then slyly tugged on his sleeve.

Jackson pulled away, annoyed. He had every right to jest, to say what he wanted, to give his friend some advice without interruption from anyone. This was *his* house. She wasn't even his wife yet. He shoved breast meat into his mouth, winced, and grabbed his jaw. His tongue slid over the mount burning in his gums and locked down angry words that verged on erupting. Numbing potion. It kept him smiling, laughing more and more, but its power to soothe had worn off in a wild way. He needed a stronger concoction. And for this dinner to be over.

"I don't know what to do."

"I'm telling you what to do, Henry. You've got to get him before he gets you. It was people like you who that wild Nat—what was his name?"

"Nat Turner."

"Yeah, it was people like you he slaughtered."

"I don't even remember that, Jack. We were kids."

"We were kids, but we weren't fools. You remember the fear folk had. I remember my pa getting ready. Loading up all his guns, getting all his boys together in case that coon showed up here." The panic he had seen in his father's face angered him still. "I'm telling you, Henry, if you don't get your slaves under control, they'll turn on you. Slaughter him before he slaughters you. If your boy is sniffing around, congregating with those other Coloreds, you best believe he's trying to run away. You know that. Take care of it. Unless you're thinking about becoming some kind of Quaker or something."

"Me? A Quaker?" Henry laughed loudly. "You know I could blow one away as quick as I could a possum. Only thing is, his mama treated me like her own until her death. She was a good woman."

"So that gives her son the right to sneak behind your back and plan his escape? She did for you what she was supposed to do and now she's gone." He shrugged. "If you don't show him who's in charge, you're not going to be able to control any of them. Watch and see. You've got to put the fear of God in them." Jackson leaned back in his chair and crossed his arms. "I'll tell you what. I'll help you. I'd love to help you get your place in order. I could be there Saturday." He glanced at Mae, then back at Henry. The two had been together so long, looking at one was looking at the other. "If that works."

Mae leaned over, her red curls springing over her heavily painted eyes, and peeked at Caroline. "Is that all right, dear? A wife's not apt to give up her husband so soon."

Caroline's eyes widened before her cheeks pinked.

"It'll be fine, won't it, dear?" Jackson placed his hand over hers and patted. "I won't be gone more than a couple of days. Back by Monday night."

He hadn't told her the lie. When he invited them to dinner, Henry made it clear that Mae would not break bread with sinners. Jackson had sneered. She was doing more than breaking bread with one every night. Fine. *Fine.* Tell her they were married. They would be soon enough.

"I don't know," Henry said. "I just think there's a better way."

A better way. He'd sure like to see this better way.

"I'll be over Saturday." He was alone in a world of weak men.

Both of the women were quiet, knew well enough not to speak, but he could see Caroline out of the corner of his eye, looking at him, judging him. He turned to her and bore into the icy green daggers of her eyes. "Didn't you call that girl? Annie? Annie, get over here."

Jackson tugged at the neck of his collar. It was so hot. *Is it hot in here?* He glimpsed the open windows, the people from across him and the one at his side. None of them were perspiring, dripping, melting like he was. He was burning up. Never comfortable lately. Under his own roof.

Annie rushed to his side with a golden brown lace pie. The smell of warm cinnamon rose and floated over him, lured him in, distracting him from all discomfort. Enticing him.

"Dessert, sir?"

"No." *Blasted tooth.* "I'll pass."

He watched Caroline crumble the flaky crust and spoon creamy slices of apple into her mouth. She licked her lips. Her eyes closed a moment too long.

It wasn't right. How could something so sweet cause so much pain?

———•◦•———

Caroline was still seated at the table, in the same chair she had sat in during dinner, afraid to move.

"Caroline."

She watched Jackson approach, screeching the leg of a chair back behind him. Her heart pounded at the stranger falling into the seat across from her.

"You did well tonight," he said.

"Thank you." She bowed her head, afraid he would see in her eyes what she had witnessed in the last hour. A beast of a man. His beautiful appearance marred by his rage for her people.

If he knew them, Cora and Lou, John... If he knew them... If he knew Lydia...

Annie entered the room from the kitchen. Jackson nodded at the girl.

"Get me a drink."

Caroline sighed. She hated to smell the liquor, the rum, the whiskey on his breath, in his pores. He was not the man she had sat across the table from the first time with Lizzy. Mean and cold when he drank. Not himself at all. She glanced up at him. Or perhaps he was more himself. His eyes met hers. She hadn't a clue what was true.

"Must you?"

"Must I what?" His tone was calm, but the question was a threat. Without doubt, she knew, could hear it in the simmer of the words. He was changing, turning from the inside out. She pressed her back against the chair until her spine was flush against the wood. *Careful, Caroline, careful.*

"Drink. Must you drink, Jackson? I was thinking maybe you've had enough for tonight."

He paused, then laughed bitterly. "You amuse me, Caroline." He stared at her until she looked away. Annie returned with a glass that he lifted in Caroline's honor. "This is to my beautiful wife-to-be." He tipped his head back and gulped the drink in one swallow, flinched, and handed the glass back to Annie.

"I was wondering about something." Caroline waited until the woman cutting her eyes at her left the room. She needed to be wise, lay her words softly at his feet.

"What is that?"

"I was listening to you at dinner."

"All right." He frowned.

"You seem to have a real dislike for Coloreds, I noticed."

"*All right.*"

"And I was wondering…why?"

"You want to know *why*?"

"Well, yes."

"Am I wrong in my dislike? Let me ask you a question." He leaned forward on his elbows and clasped his hands together under his chin. "Do you like all animals? Do you? Probably not. If I'm not particularly fond of one type, does that make me a bad person?"

Caroline clenched her hands, hidden in her lap. The pulse in her temple throbbed.

"Listen, Caroline. It's my last night here for a few days. Let's just make the best of it."

But there was something more. There was always something more behind such harshness. "I was just wondering if something happened. Did something happen, with a Colored, I mean?"

He shook his head.

"Are you certain?"

"*Yes!*"

Fear clamored in Caroline's throat.

"Don't say anything else about it." He grabbed his jaw and cursed under his breath. "Forget about it." He stood from the table. "Go. Go, Caroline. Get some rest." He swayed into a chair, steadied himself with a firm grip against the headrest, and left the room.

━━━━━◆◆◆━━━━━

For the third time, Jackson rolled over on his left side. He stuffed the thin pillow into a ball that he pounded, squeezed, flattened under his neck, squirming until it sealed the curve between his head and shoulder perfectly. The discomfort was more than a sleep position. With every pound, every squeeze, he tried to flatten the feeling, squash away the thoughts that plagued him.

And now he couldn't get rid of them. Images ran through his head, as dark and wild as the people he despised.

When intoxication and torment ran their course, sleep came and the memory of his brother filled his dreams.

They were just kids.

"Hey, wanna see something?"

Jack grabbed Tim's arm and pulled him down the dirt road near the blueberry patch. Pebbles and debris bit into the flesh of their bare feet as they ran in the sweltering heat of summer.

"Look there, 'cross the river."

Tim brushed aside the tall blades of grass.

"See her?"

A slave girl knelt bathing in the water. Her plaits, erect as soldiers, saluted the sun as its rays beamed a shower of gold against sable skin.

Jack giggled at the sight, but Tim gawked in silence. "Funny, ain't it?

We better get back before Mama comes looking for us." Tim didn't move. "You hear me?"

Jackson woke up in a sweat, his hands shaking, his mouth throbbing. He closed his eyes and tried to stop the story in his mind.

Every chance he got, Timothy returned to the same spot and watched the girls, the women with black skin, even when Jack wanted to chase squirrels or trap fireflies. Nothing compelled him more.

The moment whiskers sprouted on his chin and his laughter deepened, he took them, mothers and daughters alike, one after the other. He forced himself on them until one of their men sliced his throat a red river in the middle of the night.

Those dirty women had lured his brother to an early grave. Their darkness brought death. He was grateful his father lynched the slave who killed him. His only regret was he hadn't done it, hadn't strung up the coon himself. It was his only regret. And showing Timothy that wench in the water in the first place.

CHAPTER
TWENTY-SEVEN

*A*s soon as the early-morning rays of Saturday spilled into the corners of her room and she heard the pull of gravel under carriage wheels, Caroline stretched across the white lace of her bed and sought rest, but as it had done for days, sleep teased and weariness taunted.

She could dine every night with a man who hated her only if she imagined it wasn't so, but pretending was exhausting. Capturing every thought, reining in every impulse, pulling in every emotion, pressing down all honesty at all times—it was more than exhausting. It was suffocating, killing her. Every truth she bit down against, she swallowed until her belly swelled. She feared after a while, Jackson would take notice if she didn't burst before.

Caroline felt the weight of her lids close, only to open again moments later at the sound of a tap. She glanced at the door, waiting for Annie to knock again. When she didn't, she rolled over on her back and closed her eyes. She was as worn out as the first day she arrived, as weary as she had been as a slave.

Another tap. At the window. She dragged herself to the edge of the bed and sat with hunched shoulders and a hung head until she mustered the strength to rise.

She crept across the wooden floor and peeked through the drapes. *John.* His face lit hers before she fought the impulse.

Even from two stories above, she could see what she had always seen in his eyes.

He didn't say anything, didn't wave. He just stood there waiting, waiting until something in his stare, something about the way he looked at her, stirred her and made her walk away from the window to him.

Caroline headed down the back steps of the manor for the fields. When she saw him, she smiled.

She lifted the hem of her skirt over her ankles and made her way toward him.

He simply waited.

In the dark corner of the stable, Caroline watched John light a candle.

Two days. Two days he had been on the same land with her. When he turned to her, she could feel a sprout, one tiny sprout of life break through.

He sat leaning forward, his elbows on denim-covered knees crossed in front of him. A thin cord around his neck peeked from inside the collar of his dark shirt, navy, black, she couldn't tell in the dimness, but she could see his sleeves were cuffed. She nodded. Always cuffed.

He watched her head move, her hands fidget. Finally, she spoke.

"I left because I thought you didn't want me anymore."

"Is that right?" He didn't believe the lie.

"I didn't tell you about Dr. Kelly because I was yours. He tried to take the only thing you had. He had so much, so many women, and what did you have?"

"I had everything."

His words cut, they always cut, made her heart bleed. "I'm sorry."

"Nothing had changed, Lydia. I was angry, but nothing changed."

"I wish…" But the words broke off in her mind. She didn't even know what she wished anymore. The thing she had wished for, she had wanted all her life, she now had. Didn't she?

He looked at her for a long time until finally she could feel the corners of her mouth lift. "I'm glad you're safe."

"You too." He nodded.

She was glad he was alive, but speaking with him, meeting with him at this place, on this land, was unwise.

"You have to be careful, John. Careful here."

"I come and go as I please."

"No, you don't understand. Jackson hates Coloreds."

"Does he?" She watched his eyes glance over her.

"He doesn't know, of course." If Jackson found out, if he discovered the truth… She could feel an unrest, a panic creeping in, bubbling in her veins. "You won't tell him, will you?"

"Who do you think I am, Lydia?" He shook his head. "I don't know who you think I am."

"I was just making certain. I'm scared."

"Be scared, that's fine, but don't be scared of me."

She looked at the face of the man she loved, she had loved. Quickly, she swallowed the feeling. She couldn't feel it and stay where she was. She batted away the tears.

"How is everyone? I heard Lizzy's getting married. How's Lou?"

He shook his head.

"John?" Her heart thumped. "Something happen?"

"No, but she's not doing well. A bad sickness fell in The Room a couple of weeks ago. She's been asking for you. I don't know. Looks bad, Lydia."

"I've got to see her."

"Lydia…"

"I have to."

"Do you know how dangerous that is?" He leaned forward. "Do you know how dangerous *this* is?"

She knew. He had no idea how much. What she had seen, the change in Jackson's demeanor, the loathing in his eyes. She knew, but she had no choice.

"I'm going."

"Now?"

"Tomorrow. Tomorrow night. Please, will you come?"

CHAPTER
TWENTY-EIGHT

Cold settled in Lou's chest like a web, thin at first, practically unnoticed, but slowly it netted and weaved itself around her lungs until she felt trapped.

It was freezing lying on the ground, no matter how close she was to the others, no matter how many covers she wrapped herself in. Although several young slaves had filled as many cracks in the walls as they could with mud to keep out the air, there was no getting warm in the winter. She could see that now. She shivered. What would night bring?

The knock startled her. No one knocked here, especially this time of morning. They just walked right on in whenever they felt moved to do so.

She eased her quilt down low enough to peek at the sleeping faces of her friends and saw Cora walk in with a wooden bowl and a cup.

"Miss Lou, you getting better, right?" The girl squatted next to her, flashing a bright smile. "Yes is all the answer I'll hear, I hope you know."

"You gotta give me some time to get better. I'm old now. This body don't do like it used to."

"Try and eat something, Miss Lou." Cora sat with a bowl of okra in her lap and smiled. "Maybe some tea would make you feel better." She lowered the hot toddy to her mouth. "Can you sit up?" Lou pressed her lips together and shook her head.

"You seen my baby yet?"

Cora's smile faded.

"Ain't she ever coming back?"

Please, Lord, send my baby.

"Drink."

"Where's my Lydia?"

"She'll be here."

"When she coming?" Lou coughed. The web tightened, refusing to break. A fire fought on the inside of cold limbs. Panting, she shifted to her side.

"You're going to be all right." Cora patted her hand. "You're going to make it."

"Yes. God's going to do it." *On this side or the other.*

"And if He don't, this here hot toddy will." Cora laughed.

"If God don't do it…," Lou whispered. She shook her head. No more words. No more moving.

"You need some doctoring. I'm going to see what I can do to get Master over here to see about you. Get you some tonic. Don't seem like nothing I'm doing is working much."

"I'll be fine."

She didn't need no doctor, no man poking and prodding. Just some rest and Jesus. If God didn't do it, it wasn't going to be done.

When Cora waved good-bye, Lou didn't pray for her, didn't say a word.

"You sure you all right, Miss Lou?"

"I'm fine." *Just don't want to get up!*

But she was far from fine. Couldn't get up if she wanted to.

CHAPTER
TWENTY-NINE

*S*unday night. *Finally.*

Caroline slipped out of the still house through the back door and dashed down the steps. A rush flared in her chest so hot, she hardly noticed she needed more on her shoulders than the cotton shirt to ward off the night breeze.

Her heart pitter-pattered when she brushed past the roses. From the hill she couldn't tell how low and tight the vines hung. Thorns grazed her cheeks, her arms. She ducked under its mild assault until she reached the fence. A withering oak.

When Caroline wiggled through the bushes, the throbbing leapt to her throat. She was suddenly back to the night she had escaped. And here she was escaping again. Once again fighting the tug between life and death. This time, her life, Lou's death. With a hard swallow, she shoved down fear and exhaled. She was here now, standing before the small log house where she had arranged to meet John.

With him at her side, she ran across the green meadow, past the hill, through the garden, and didn't stop until they were at the wagon at the back of the stable, winded and weary.

John hitched the horses and they traveled back to their old plantation.

Lydia watched the way. Folk would find it odd for a lady to travel without a companion, but none would stop her because of the color of her skin. They avoided the ones who might question by journeying late at night.

She was traveling through time. Back through history. Back to being a Colored girl named Lydia. Back to a world of passion that had drawn a well of love from the pit of her. And pain. She would never shake the horror of her father's murder. But she was back for a reason. And in all it could cost her, Lou was worth the risk.

"Grandma."

"There's my girl. There she is." Lou chuckled, coughed. "I've been worried."

"I'm fine, Grandma."

"Then why you just now seeing me?" Her voice was hoarse, strained.

"I'm here now." She patted Lou's hand and kissed it.

"We all missed you, Lydia." Odessa hugged her before bumping Ruth off the loom.

"This place wasn't the same." Abram grinned. "You make this place special, girl."

"Oh no, it was that before I came, but I did miss all of you. So much." Lydia gazed at each face. Her eyes settled on John. She turned away. "You hurting, Grandma?"

Lou struggled to sit up on her forearms, failed, and collapsed back on the mat. The sound of her heavy wheezing filled the room.

Lydia's hands traveled from Lou's forehead to her cheeks, then traced the swollen fingers she brought to her heart. She prayed until sleep fell on everyone, until her own head nodded, but she fought it and nestled into her grandmother.

"I'm here, Grandma, I'm here."

Lou stirred.

"Don't move. You don't have to say nothing. You're going to be all right, Grandma. I prayed. I've been praying and God's gonna do it. Just rest."

There was a draft. Lydia drew the quilt at her grandmother's feet up over her waist. When she knew Lou had fallen asleep, she twisted around on her back and stared at the cracks between the logs in the roof. She turned to John. He looked like a young boy sleeping, curled up into himself, his mouth a perfect circle. They were so far apart. No matter how close they wished to be, life had set their place. Like logs trying to block out the cold, the cracks remained and the chill always broke through.

Lydia squeezed closer to Lou and shut her eyes tight. *Please, seal the cracks.*

Lou couldn't breathe. She tried to flail her arms, kick her legs. She grasped for Lydia. The girl was no more than a few inches away. *Lydia!* Her reach fell short. She panted, wanted to scream, but had no air for sound. Lifting her head—it felt so heavy—she scanned the room. Everybody sleeping deep like she wasn't dying.

She settled back, settled down, and slipped in and out of consciousness. *So be it.* She hated the thought of breathing her last breath in this place, but at least she wouldn't die alone.

Visions of the past clouded Lou's mind like a bad storm, looming, threatening to destroy all signs of peace. Isaiah's murder, Lydia's tears.

Smells bombarded her, from the fresh scent of newborn skin to the musk of blood and sweat in open wounds. Steaming okra stew to the hum of neediness. *Oh yes, indeed.* There was a smell to poverty, sure as there was a sight to it. The crowding, huddling of a burdened people could produce a stench of hopelessness, and if it wasn't fought off, it killed instantly, clung to skin, and embedded itself deep into pores. She'd never forget the smell of despair or the odor of her own flesh.

Life had been hard. More suffering than joy filled her days, but the good shone like stars in a blanket of darkness. She clung to those moments she would soon live forever. See her mama and papa again. Her children. Her baby among them. *Isaiah.* Her baby boy with her again.

Lydia stirred at the break of day as John stepped outside the cabin. She watched him pull the door closed behind him. Funny how it felt like nothing had changed. Like he was meant to be here with her. Like she had never walked away.

She was the only one awake when she returned to her grandmother's side. She sat, legs crossed, watching, waiting for the Lord to move. She placed Lou's head in her lap. Flickering eyes.

"Grandma?"

She blinked.

"I love you."

Double blink.

"I know you don't feel it, but you're going to make it."

Lydia caressed her face, brushed back sparse eyebrows with her fingers.

"I couldn't lose you. Not now. I need you, Lou."

Lou's lips parted. No sound.

"I already know, Grandma, everything you want to say. I know you love me. Just rest and get your strength. Rest, Grandma, all right?"

Tears slipped down the sides of her face. Misty hazel eyes here then gone.

"Don't cry, Lou. Don't cry."

The weeping further labored her breathing. Lou twisted Lydia's skirt in her fists.

"Lay back and rest." Lydia tried to pry the clamped hands from her skirt but her grip was strong. *A good sign.*

Lou's lids slowly began to close like night falling, her moles like stars.

"Stay with me, Grandma."

"Lydia."

"Grandma, don't talk. Rest. You'll heal faster."

"Lydia…" Lou's eyes focused on her. She frowned, continued. "I want you to…"

"What?"

"Lord, have mercy."

"What, Grandma?"

Lou's weeping overwhelmed her, turned her face red, blue, purple.

"Stop it. Stop crying! You're making yourself sicker."

"May God show you."

"Show me what?"

"The truth. My dear God…"

"Grandma."

Lou coughed hard. Couldn't stop coughing. And coughing. Lydia rubbed her head and prayed with all her strength. *Please, God!* She prayed until her words were gurgled, saturated in tears, until only she and He understood. The coughing stopped.

"Stay put."

"Stop talking. You've got plenty of time to tell me whatever you want to say." Lydia rested her hand on her forehead. Lou pushed it away.

"You stay put and let me go. Let me go."

Lydia shook her head. "Stop."

"Let me go, now."

Lydia stared at the life in her lap. Her grandmother, who had made her tea cakes and braided her hair and never complained about the stiff branches that sprouted from her hands. Lou had shown her what it was to be a woman, had explained the ways of a man when no others would dare speak of it. Had even giggled with her at some of the parts. There was only one Lou. Only one who had believed in her beauty and taught her to love her difference. It was Lou who had told her she'd always be all right because someone would always be there to lift her up. Lou was the one who saw beyond the surface to the bone and marrow of all people and loved them anyhow. She was the one who loved her.

She was leaving, already giving up the fight. This woman was lifeless, only a shell of what she had been, though she still breathed and moved and whispered.

But Lydia refused to believe it. She lifted her grandmother, cradled her head against her chest, and begged, pleaded for her healing.

"Lord, please, I can't do this again. Lou, I will die if you leave me. I won't make it." She sobbed into her. "Please, I need you."

Lydia heard the door creak open and the footsteps that followed, but she continued to rock Lou until she was surrounded by love. John rubbed her back and whispered peace.

"Please, God."

"Lydia."

"Please."

"Lydia…Lydia!"

Lydia looked up at the stricken faces on all sides. Abram reached over to Lou, uttered a prayer, and closed her eyes.

She wanted to scream, to run. Again. *It happened again.*

"She's gone, Lydia."

"But, but I prayed…"

"Yes, baby." Ruth nodded. "You just prayed the wrong prayer."

Lydia slid Lou off her lap, rose slowly, and drifted out of the room. *Another loss.* The world was spinning, whistling a solemn song. Staggering, she reached for a withered oak—*I need my daddy*—and collapsed into the dead leaves of dawn.

CHAPTER THIRTY

$\mathscr{J}$ohn carried his wife to their old cabin, at first cradled in his arms like a child, then over his shoulder, his arm wrapped around her knees. The trek through evergreen and oak seemed days long with the extra weight. He laid her on their bench, studying her thin frame. She was no heavier than his heart.

A pang of guilt shot through him as he stretched red circles and purple diamonds over her, thankful the gift he had purposefully left behind was still here after several days.

"Lydia, I want you to sleep. Get some rest. You hungry?"

She shook her head.

"Lydia…I know you're tired. Try to sleep." He kissed her softly on her head and sat beside her. "You're going to make it through this. You know that? You believe me?" He stroked a wispy curl around her ear. Tears glistened. Hers. His.

"I'm going to see if I can get you something to eat."

Thirty minutes later, he returned. John stepped into the cabin, scanned the room.

She was gone.

"I'm going to meet Jesus. Going to meet Jesus. Yes, I'm going to meet Jesus. Going to meet Jesus after a while."

Lou's song whispered in Lydia's head like the wind. *Going to meet Jesus…*

Her hair had fallen loose from the pins that held it in place, and in the afternoon breeze, it swarmed around her. She tucked it behind her ears and walked closer to the water. Her thin cotton dress, lifting and bending as it rode the waves of the wind, hung loose on her sunken shoulders. She shook off her shoes. What normally would've caused her to shiver had no effect.

Going to meet Jesus. The One they all left her for. Her father, right here. His body right in this place.

Lydia gathered the hem around her knees and stepped closer, closer to the riverbank. Mud slid between her toes. She would wash it away. The water tossed around her calves, her knees, her thighs.

Going to meet Jesus. Wash it all away.

She swayed—water splashed above her waist—and yielded to the matter that engulfed her.

Lydia...

Lydia...

"Lydia!"

She turned when she heard him, but she staggered under the pull.

"Lydia!" John screamed, swimming, splashing to her, his eyes wide. "What—What are you doing? Lydia..." He grabbed her and waded with her back to the muddy bank, stepping on and ripping the corner of the blanket he tried desperately to wrap her in. Out of breath, he collapsed beside her, and then he cried.

Lydia drew up, wrapped her arms around her legs, laid her head on her knees, and rocked. Every ache in her heart flowed through her, moved her. Until she heard him.

John's weeping stilled her. She looked at him shaking, his large hands covering his face above quaking shoulders. She watched for several minutes, then crawled near, the strip of blanket in her hands. She placed it in his. When he spoke, she listened.

"I'm here, Lydia, I'm here."

If only for the moment, he was here. Right here with her.

What had she done?

John held her in the broad sunlight; on the brisk winter day they were free. If only for the moment.

Outside the manor, Lydia coughed her lungs clear and waited until her breathing steadied and her mind refocused. She had a role to play.

She had sobbed at the thought of Lou, how she wouldn't be able to attend the funeral, the burial of the one she loved, then she caught herself, dusted off the soot of sadness with the back of her hand, and reined her tears in tight under a clear head and a thin smile. Never would she end her days as the others who came before her. Never would she allow herself to die at the loom. She would do what needed to be done. She would walk the fields with a confident stride, stand in the path with her head high, and sit in the seat pulled out for her, for Lou, for Isaiah, for all who were stripped of the right.

With the damp blanket still wrapped around her, she climbed the back steps of the manor and entered from the rear. Still going through back doors, even as a White.

In the hallway, she heard a door creak but saw no one. Like she had heard the footsteps of Dr. Kelly that night, she waited, but this time no one came.

When she was safely in her room, she wiped the dried blood from the scratch on her face likely from the fall outside Lou's cabin. She wondered how she would explain it, wondered how she would have the courage to face Jackson again at all.

She shoved the blanket under her bed and sat in front of the mirror, a mess. Her hair was in disarray, her eyes bloodshot; the scratch, though, looked better than it felt. Could easily be covered with powder.

It would be several hours before night, before Jackson's return, she thought, but she was alarmed when her door swung open two hours later. She was just finishing her hair.

"Where were you?"

Lydia's brush paused in midair. She could see Jackson's long legs behind her in the mirror. She wiggled upright in her seat. "Pardon me?"

"Where were you this morning? I heard you were gone."

That Annie!

She continued brushing her hair. Her hand moved slowly over the waves, but everything internal raced. He winced. She could see his hand shoot up toward his face. "How's the tooth?"

"Don't ask. Caroline, answer me."

She laid the brush down on the cedar stand, her fingers still loosely wrapped around the handle, and twisted toward him.

"Rode in one of my wagons, did you?"

"I needed to talk to Lizzy."

"Is that right? You're on friendly terms with her again?"

"Of course. Always. We'll always be friends. Just because her father—"

"What did you speak to her about?"

"I talked to her—"

"About what?"

"Womanly things, Jackson. Don't tell me you want to know the particulars."

"Well, did you?"

"Did I?"

"Talk to her?"

"Of course I did."

"It's so easy for me to confirm this, Caroline. You know that, don't you?"

Lydia could feel fear trying to escape through widening eyes or a dropped jaw, but she reined it in, harnessed it deep, until he whacked the back of the chair. She held tight, but a measure of terror rushed through her blood and a single vein in her hand jolted. She gripped the brush tighter.

"Talk to me, Caroline!"

She stood up and turned to him, running her fingers over the buttons of his white shirt and a throbbing heart. "There *is* something I've been keeping from you."

"What is it?" He gripped her shoulders and pressed her back. "What is it? Tell me."

"It was to be a surprise." *Think, Lydia, think!* "I was planning our wedding."

He stared at her. Through her.

"Is that right?"

"Yes. When you said you were going to Henry's I knew it was the perfect time to get the plans underway."

Lydia brushed past him and sat on the bed. Leaning back, she dangled her legs off the edge, playfully. Auburn locks cascaded around her.

"Why now? You haven't mentioned a thing about it since that night on the porch. I was starting to question if you even wanted to get married. Most women would've jumped at the chance."

"I'm not most women." She waited for the arrogance to slip from his cocked brow. "Regardless, isn't it what you want?"

He searched her.

"Should I proceed?" She watched him watching her, hoped she had said enough, done enough, to convince him.

He nodded. One small bead of pressure released down the back of her neck.

"Is that a 'yes?' You would like me to continue planning our wedding?"

"I suppose."

"Well, fine." She clapped, clasped her hands together, and grinned.

"When are you trying to do this?"

"I'm not sure yet. Soon. In a month."

"In a week."

"In a week? Jackson—"

"In a week, Caroline." His head was bent toward hers, his eyes narrow. There was no convincing him otherwise.

"In a week." She nodded. "After Christmas, then. Just something very small. Intimate." She thought of the Kellys. "No Michael Kelly. Only family. Yours, of course."

"Of course. That's fine. So, did Elizabeth have any words of wisdom? You did speak with her, didn't you?"

"I did." She leaned forward on the bed and grinned. "Never mind all the details, Jackson." She smiled until the rigid edges of his face softened, melted. She could see he wanted to believe her.

Kneeling in front of her, Jackson leaned in close—she breathed his breath—but before his mouth touched hers, his head fell back. He squeezed his eyes shut and bit his bottom lip blazing red. Mumbling curses hissed low through a cupped hand.

Lydia stood up, moved away much too quickly for a woman in love. "What are you going to do about that thing?" she asked to distract him.

"I don't know." He gripped his jaw, rubbed fiercely before pulling himself up. "It's killing me." When he grabbed the doorknob, he stopped. "You're sure there's nothing else I need to know?"

"No."

"You're not hiding anything, are you, Caroline?"

"No. Why?"

"I've got a feeling you're not telling me everything."

"What do you mean?"

"I mean there are some things you're keeping to yourself. Secret."

"No."

"Not one? Not one secret?"

"I don't know what you're talking—"

"Your story, Caroline. Your family story. Everything's not adding up."

"I lose my father and you doubt me? I don't believe you, Jackson."

"Funny." He stared at her. "I don't believe *you*." He jerked the door open, but his hand lingered on the knob and his fingers tapped. Tapping. She was suddenly on the porch with Dr. Kelly.

"Caroline, I just hope you're not lying to me. About anything. I hate to think I'm marrying a liar." He paused. "Or something worse." The door slammed behind him.

Lydia stood frozen until she heard his footsteps fade. When her heart settled, she moved back to the chair and looked in the mirror. She could see, in the right-hand corner behind her, a strip of red and purple.

She turned around and saw the blanket under her bed. She needed to hide it well. But before she rose, she glanced at her reflection and startled. A withered soul stared back at her.

The reaping had begun.

CHAPTER
THIRTY-ONE

*E*verybody deserved to see what was coming.

Lydia peeked through the window of the Whitfield Loom Room. Three women snuggled together quilting in a corner, and a man sat on a wobbly wooden stool winding strips of fabric around a peg. She walked around, fascinated by the beauty of her roots and the window in which to see them.

"Nice," she whispered more to herself than to them.

She spotted Annie near a corner in front of a floor loom. "How are you?"

Annie tugged her head rag over the top flap of her ear and looked up at Lydia with surprise. Lydia smiled at the memory. How she hated those scarves.

"I'm doing fine, ma'am."

"You mind?" Lydia sat beside her and started wrapping pieces of yellow yarn around wooden pegs. "What are you making?"

"Umm...a rug." She could see Annie in the corner of her eye, staring at her. "Just something for my room. To keep my feet warm. Is that all right?"

"I think that's great. It's going to be beautiful."

Lydia hadn't realized how much she had missed the string, the yarn, the fabric between her fingers.

"You do good work, Miss Caroline," Annie said, but the look on her face unsettled Lydia, causing her to scramble quickly to her feet.

"You carry on now. Let me know if there's anything else you need in here. I can ask Mr. Whitfield for you like you did for me when I first arrived."

The girl kept her hands and eyes on the loom. Finally she looked up and nodded. "I got everything I need."

Empathy rippled through Lydia's flesh.

Not everything.

It was dark, late, or as early as morning could get.

Abram sat up in the middle of the night, coughing, staring at the back wall where Lou had lain only two days before.

He cupped his hand on the wrinkled forehead of his wife. She wasn't warm, though he knew each day, each hour, they both crept closer to their last breath. His thumb quivered over eyes shut tight, like she was trying to block something out even in her sleep. She stirred under his touch and turned to her side, nestled her head against his thigh. He stroked the wiry gray hairs of her head and smiled. He had fallen so easily for her.

A young, innocent girl with hope, a pureness. That's what he had loved about her. The beauty of wonder in her eyes and an easy smile still present after the other girls her age had hardened under life's toil. Not his Dessa. She kept right on grinning and laughing. He chuckled. A laugh so light, so sweet. *Silver bells.* It was the best part of her. He hadn't heard it in years, many years, not since she witnessed the torture in the shed. It was a faint memory now. Like the many things that had passed on. What did they really have left?

Why?

Abram shook his head, tried to shake the word free from his mind, but its beckoning sank him into a sea of unrest.

He hated the word. Hated it more than the beatings, more than the deaths. It was useless, a cruel, dirty word that made him question his life. He shut his eyes. It was more than that. It made him question his God.

Abram coughed and slid down beside his wife under the wool blanket he pulled up beneath his chin. He needed to stay warm, rid himself for good of the cold that near killed him. He was glad he had made it for Odessa's sake. When he had awakened and seen the look in her eyes, the flow of grief that never ended, he was glad he hadn't left her alone. She was so shattered. Nothing left to break. One more tragedy, and she would die. Death was all that was left for both of them.

It still bothered him, bothered him all these years when he had the power to lay hands on and heal children, that he could never heal grown folk. Not even from a sore throat, an ache, or a pain. Not even from a tear. Nothing. He had tried countless times with Odessa, had thought she was innocent enough, that if anyone of age could be healed, it was her. But no. Not even Dessa.

Abram turned on his side behind her, slid his arms over her waist, over the body that hadn't changed much in size, just in weariness. It had been the inside that changed, that had seeped like poison through the pores of her face.

It made him sad to look at her. She was too fragile for this life. Her mind, her heart, had cracked under the cruelty. Witnessing Ruth's assault had sent her over the edge. She thought she was the cause of it even after everyone insisted it was not so. But when reassurance ceased and people moved on, then what?

He didn't understand why.

What was the point of having a gift and losing it? Of losing everyone, everything, you ever loved? *For what?* For what purpose did they live in death? One was supposed to walk through the valley of the shadow, not dwell in it.

Why?

Abram thought of the faces of the children, the burst of tears that shot into praise from parents on their knees. It had been a sight to see. To be used by God so greatly. But now…

He closed his eyes, didn't want to see where he was, where he had ended up. He had nothing left.

If only he could have one moment. One more moment. If he could gather his strength just once more to be used, a vessel in the hands of the Potter. Just one more, Lord, he heard himself saying as he faded off to sleep. Just one more.

"Abram?"

"Odessa." He opened his eyes at the sound of her voice. "Baby, what is it?"

She was crying again. Nothing left, Abram wept at her side.

Something was undone.

Lydia sat in front of her vanity and studied the cloth across her lap, examined every stitch near the loose thread. She had to find it. Somewhere, something was no longer attached. Her eyes strained and her fingers searched.

It was a silly thing. Just one thin, white handkerchief handed to her by a stranger on a coach. What difference did it make? Jackson had given her a dozen others. She wrapped her hand around the fabric and traced the delicate embroidery of flowers in each corner. Someone had taken time, precious time, to create such a beauty. The detail. She smiled. Important enough for her to search a little longer for the missing knot. One tug and it would all unravel.

She sighed. She had been sitting too long. Thirty minutes? An hour? She needed more light. She looked up toward the window and caught a glimpse of her face in the mirror in front of her.

Moon crescents under her eyes made her life appear much weightier than the time on earth she'd endured. She touched her lips. Pretty lips full of lies. No more, she promised the lady across from her, but the face was cynical. She didn't believe a word of it. And why should she? Lying was what she did best.

Lydia tossed the handkerchief on the stand and wrapped her hands in her hair. Twisting it around in a knot, she secured it with a pin and powdered her face. Powdered her face white.

Shame seeped pink into her cheeks. If John could see her now. She thought of him, what he was doing, what he ate, where he slept less than a mile away.

Things were becoming more difficult, had become much more complicated than she had ever dreamed.

Lydia picked up the cloth and held it to her cheek. There was only one choice. She had to see him again soon. At the right time.

When she stood, she bumped into the vanity and the airy rectangular cotton fell from her hand, floating to the floor. She snatched it quickly by a thread, just before it landed, and just as quickly witnessed the result.

Undone.

CHAPTER
THIRTY-TWO

*S*he begged for blood.

Oh, please! But when Lydia ran clear out from the dining room table to the washroom gagging from the smells, too many smells of the morning meal, she knew it would be a long while before she saw the flow of fluid she'd cursed month after month.

She missed last month's cycle, but she thought worry kept it away. It had happened once after the incident with Dr. Kelly. Before she had ever been with a man.

Lydia glanced up at Annie. She was walking back and forth in the sitting room, dark, despite the open drapes. She hadn't heard a word she said, just sat on the edge of the sofa with her arms wrapped low across her waist.

"We need to be certain we have enough poinsettias. Those would look nice. Unless you want a softer look, but there's not much growing this time of year so we can't be too choosy. Let's see, we could... Miss Caroline, are you listening?"

Lydia stared out the window, hoping to catch a glimpse of the father of her baby somewhere on the grounds.

"I was just thinking, Annie."

"Ma'am? You all right? You ain't yourself. You're different to me."

Lydia's eyes filled with tears.

"I'm tired, Annie. Ever been tired?"

"'Course I have. Every night I just fall out, almost too tired to close my own eyes."

"I mean a tired on the inside." She leaned forward and stared at Annie.

She was saying too much, but the words continued to tumble out of her mouth. "Like you're dragging on the inside."

"I can't say I have." Annie stared at her. "I don't think I've ever felt like that."

"It's awful, Annie."

"Why you so sad?"

"I've lost everything." And now she had a baby on the way with a man she had deserted. The truth she swallowed, had thought she hid, had rooted in her and would sure enough make itself known before long. She could feel the tears welling in her throat. "I don't know if I can make it."

"You can make it."

For a moment, Lydia sobered. She looked up into the face of a woman she thought hated her and saw something else entirely. A knowing, a kin. She looked into the face of the slave she had been. "How do you know?"

"'Cause you're doing it, Miss Caroline. Breath after breath, you're doing it."

Lydia stared at Annie. She wanted to say something, thank her, but nothing rose on the inside but sorrow.

She couldn't move and she couldn't stop thinking about the pain she endured, the pain she had caused. Despite the house and the freedom to come and go at will, she was lost, still bound after all this time. Not one breath closer to life.

Thought upon thought, her past wove her weary until night fell. She laid her head against her knees, closed her eyes, and begged for sleep, a sweet escape from the torment of the past few months.

She made it to her room somehow and stretched out across her bed. Her lids fell heavy.

Echoing voices and vivid colors painted pictures of all things beautiful in the mist. She smiled at her good fortune as she strolled barefoot past green meadows set against an orange-red sky, violets and daffodils dancing at her feet.

Then she stepped on something. She could feel it was round and solid but small enough to continue moving forward. But with each stride it dug deeper until she recoiled. She turned to discover a trail of blood that stained every place she had been, soaked the grass limp so that even the flowers died.

Heartbroken, she sat to examine her raw foot, to discover what had caused so much harm. She saw it instantly. In the center of her ripped flesh, there it was, glistening white in all its glory: a pearl.

"You're beautiful, Lydia. Did I tell you that?"
Every time you look at me.

Lydia still heard the words from her wedding night, still felt John's fingers dancing along her face, sweeping her hair back. Could still feel herself locking her fingers with his and submitting to his touch.

Her head was spinning. Too many dreams. She sat up in bed, pressed her fingers against her eyelids, and stopped the tears before they ever had a chance to flow. She was good at that. Cutting things off before they took hold. Even still, she had to be careful. One wrong move and she could end up buried under the whole stack of lies.

CHAPTER
THIRTY-THREE

John flipped the wool collar of his navy coat up over his ears as he jogged to the stables. As much as Lydia loved this time of year, to him, bare trees and shriveled plants always made the world appear dark, ominous. There was a reason Christmas fell in the middle of winter. Just before everyone plunged into a pit of depression, it arrived just in time to warm everything with lights and love. He glanced up at the sullen skies. From the looks of it, an early November snow was possible. He rubbed his hands together and shoved them in his pockets. *No gloves.* No doubt taking care of the mares was much more pleasant on warmer days, though he wasn't sure he could bear the heat, sweating as he was already.

"John…"

He turned slowly. "Lydia." She stood shivering in a black hooded cloak with eyes as innocent as a child's. "What are you doing here?"

"We need to talk," she whispered.

"You shouldn't have come." But he was happy she had. Her glassy eyes moved him. *Those eyes…*

"I had to."

He looked around, wiping the beads of perspiration from his brow with the strip of fabric in his pocket.

She smiled faintly at the keepsake from the blanket she had weaved.

"All right," he whispered. "All right. Follow me."

In the shadows of the stable, he let the tension in his face, his neck, and his shoulders fall to his hands. He gripped his fingers. Then hers.

"You all right?"

"I–I'm fine."

"No, you're not." Her hands trembled in his.

"I didn't know where else to go."

"I know."

"Sometimes the weight of it all, the pressure…"

"I know."

She burst into tears, and his heart broke.

"I didn't think. I didn't think through any of it, and I'm sorry. I knew it would be hard, but I'm not sure how much more I can bear." She paused long enough for him to see her sitting on his worn blanket, long enough to remember the way they were. "Do you think about us?"

"Always," he said before she could even finish the question. *Always.* He smiled. "Look, Lydia, I'm here, all right?"

"All right." She dabbed her eyes with a rumpled handkerchief.

"You just have to be careful."

"He's gone. Won't be back until morning. Can I have you for the day?" She smiled faintly.

She had him for life.

Lydia felt a warm tingling, a flicker of heaven she hadn't felt in a long time. Afternoon rays seeped through the cracks of the stable and lit the corner of the place like gems. They sat together in the riches of light.

John.

She missed him desperately. Earth's beauty in one body. She could feel him watching her, studying to see if she was all right. She was fine. Today she was the best she had been.

"You've been eating all right out here? Have you had enough food? I could have Annie bring what you want."

"Don't worry about me. I'm worried about you in there. Is he…" John blew out a breath. "Is he touching you?"

"No. No, he isn't. He hasn't." Not her body. Not her heart. No one touched her like he did. "John, I need to tell you, I need to tell you why I left you." It hurt to look into his eyes and say it but she kept staring, held his gaze until her eyes streamed. "I left that day because I wanted to be free, married or not. Even though I loved you, I always…"

"Loved it more."

The words pierced. So difficult to admit, even harder to say. "Loved it more."

"And now?" He waited.

"But now." She sat up on her haunches and moved closer to him. She needed to be closer. "But now I know." When the words came, she bowed her head. "Now I know." She looked at him, swiped her hair back from her forehead, but when her fingers grazed the scar, she stopped. "You're the only one who can see this thing and I'm not ashamed." She laughed. "You're the only one."

"I love you." He said the words simply but they rose, lifted, engulfed her. "I do."

"Even after—"

"I do."

She laid her head in his lap and wept. Soft strokes on her head healed her heart. He was all she needed. "What have I done?"

"You can make it right."

"I don't know how. Where would we go? Run together? Would we run away together?" But now in her condition it would prove much more challenging. "He wants to marry me. I told him I was planning the ceremony, but I won't." He had to know. "I won't do it."

"What do you want, Lydia? You have to choose."

She sat up on her knees.

"What do you want?" He was looking at her, waiting.

"I want you."

"Do you?"

"Yes."

He stared at her.

"I want you, John. It's you." She looked into his eyes. "It's you I want. I need *you*."

His face, his eyes, were serious like they were the first day they sat with their people.

"Do you know what you're saying? You've got to lose everything to be with me. You certain about that? This place is beautiful, Lydia."

"Yes. Yes. I'll give it all up."

She lay against his chest.

"Do you love me, Lydia?"

"Yes, I love you."

"Do you?"

"Yes, I love you, John. I do."

He held her away from him and looked into her eyes. "Do you love me?"

Her heart was grieved because he asked her a third time.

"Yes. Yes, John. I love you."

He caressed her face.

"Are we going to leave? Run away?"

"Trust me."

"You never did tell me about the second time you ran. What happened?"

He pulled her closer. "Something drew me back."

Through the forest Lydia walked hand-in-hand with the one she loved. Amid maple and redwood, a milky-white shimmer danced on the river before them. She slipped her fingers free from John's and moved toward the bank, its splendor drawing her closer until she stood staring at the pearl of moonlight and the black velvet stream, her reflection against her husband's. She shone bright in his beauty.

When she leaned forward, John snatched her back, his grip strong around her.

"Don't worry. I'm better now."

"I should've gone another way."

"I'm glad you didn't." She turned to him and gazed at the image of herself in his eyes. "I'm much better."

John nodded, grazing her brow with his lips. He fastened the top button of her cloak and lifted the hood over her head like a veil. A loose auburn strand fluttered against her cheek. Gently, he caressed it behind her ear. "Let's walk."

They strolled along the river, their fingers interlocked, swinging between them. This time with him was what she had been missing, what she had needed for weeks. It was what she had needed her entire life. She looked up at the man by her side, thought of his child in her womb, and smiled.

"I have something to tell you."

"What is it?" John squeezed her hand and froze. "Did you hear something?" He swung around, his stance wide and crouched. Before she could turn to see, he pushed her forward. "Go, Lydia, go!"

"Wait just one minute there, *Lydia*," a man said.

She froze, her back to the stranger, but she tilted her head slightly to see out of the corner of her eye.

A man in a large straw hat swaggered toward them. *Henry.* She closed her eyes and prayed. *Please, God. Please!*

"What you two doing out here?" He swished a wad of chewing tobacco from cheek to cheek, then spat. Brown saliva dripped down the side of his moustache. He wiped it with the back of his hand and flung it to the ground.

"Nothing," John answered. "Nothing, sir."

Another man with a tall, thin frame in a plaid jacket stepped out from the shadows. *How many were there?*

"You ain't trying to skip on out of here, now, are you?"

"No, sir. We were just talking a stroll."

"A *stroll*? Look at this, Rex. We got ourselves a clever Colored." Henry chuckled, ribbing his buddy. "Who taught you your letters, boy?"

Rex and Henry. Jackson's boys.

"Sir?"

"Who you belong to? Let's see here? We close to Whitfield's land. You Whitfield's boy?"

John didn't answer.

Henry stepped forward.

"You hear me, boy?"

"I hear you."

"You answer then. Jack Whitfield your master?"

"You're asking who I work for?"

The men howled and slapped each other on the back. Henry straightened, narrowing his eyes. "You don't work for nobody. You a slave. You serve, boy. You got that?"

"Who's this you with?"

Lydia tugged the hood farther over her head.

"What the—" Rex walked up closer to her, but John stepped between them. "You ain't with no White woman, are you?" He flipped open a switch-blade. "I don't want to have to kill nobody tonight."

"Neither do I." In one quick motion, John kicked the knife out of the man's hand. It landed in the leaves upright. Lydia could see Rex running and tumbling forward out of the corner of her eye.

"Run!" John grabbed Lydia's hand and pulled her through the thicket. Terror pumped power through her lungs.

John's muscular legs lifted with ease through the tangles of the woods. Lydia was at his heels, pushing, pressing forward, slapping tree limbs out of her path.

They sprinted through the forest, Lydia several steps behind him. Her lungs burned, and a piercing pain seared her side. She squeezed her hand around her waist, but it slowed her. Had they run a mile? Lydia looked back. They were far from the river. No one in sight.

"John…," she breathed.

He stopped and allowed her to catch her breath.

"We got to make it back to the house. We've got to get you back safely. It's not far."

Another mile, maybe, but in the dark, how long would it take?

"We've got a little ways to go. Maybe halfway there."

A little was all she had left. She leaned forward, her hands on her knees. She wanted to sit but was afraid she wouldn't be able to rise.

John stretched his legs.

Escaping together might not be the best thing, she thought. She was slowing him down considerably.

Huffing, he bent over, his hands on his waist. He looked up and swiped a trickle of sweat from her forehead with his thumb. His eyes surveyed their surroundings. "We better go. You all right?"

"I'm good," she lied.

They ran until she collapsed. She managed only short, quick breaths. "This is as fast as I can go. I can't catch my breath." She was suddenly worried about the child in her womb.

"I'm sorry, baby, but we got to keep moving."

"I can't. I can't move."

"Well, I'm not leaving you." John's hand braced her arm and pulled her to her feet like a rag doll. "Even if I have to drag you."

Lydia winced. The twisting of her flesh and the pressure of his pulling ended in a pop they both heard, a flash of lightning only she felt. She screamed as she fell to the ground, her arm motionless.

"Lydia!"

John knelt beside her and touched her shoulder. She cried out.

"Shh. I know, I know. I got to put it back in place, Lydia. You hear me?" He lifted her chin. She couldn't stop shaking. The pain seared. "It's going to be bad, but you've got to keep quiet. As quiet as you can, understand?"

John placed one hand across her collarbone and the other across the back of her lifeless limb. Swiftly, he shoved the joint into the socket. She screamed. He covered her mouth and curled into her.

"I'm so sorry, Lydia, I'm so sorry. I didn't mean—" John's head whipped around. "Listen."

She rubbed the throb and held her breath. She could hear it. Faint, but certain. Barking.

"We've gotta run!" John swept Lydia into his arms and ran, tripping over tree branches, stumbling over rocks.

She shut her eyes, clamped her arms around his neck tighter, and prayed, amazed at what fear could ignite. Most times it just sat yellow in the pit of her like a trembling child, but now it sizzled red hot through her veins. They were in the middle of a childhood nightmare: pitch-black darkness—where had the moon gone?—rustlings, wild animals, whistling wind, and evil men who wanted blood. A nightmare she had lived once before. She could hardly breathe.

The hounds were getting closer, but before she could determine their direction, John's foot slid and knocked them off balance.

Dear God, help us!

The dogs were closer.

"Get on, Lydia." John knelt over. She climbed on his back but he rose before she could steady herself. She rolled over and landed on her hurt shoulder. She bit back a scream. She'd never felt such pain.

"Lydia, get on, hurry. They're coming!"

She pulled up and threw her leg across his back and flung her arms around his throat. She clung to him, her head bobbing forward as he sprinted toward the back of the house. Lydia kept her gaze behind them. She saw small circles of light coming through the shadows of the trees when she tumbled off his back to the ground.

"John, they're coming!"

"Run inside, Lydia, go!"

"John!"

"Go!" He ran off into the woods as she raced up the steps.

Against the inside of her bedroom door, her heart thumped hard against her chest, her shoulder throbbed, her hands shook, but she was breathing. She was alive.

CHAPTER THIRTY-FOUR

*R*ex huffed through Jackson's front door on Henry's heels, drenched despite the cold weather. The warm blood at his fingertips lit him hotter.

"What is it?" Jackson frowned, dismissing the butler. The tie straps of his silk housecoat hung loose at his side, dragged against the floor as he swung the door behind them. Hanging and dragging. Exactly what he wanted to do with that boy.

"We're looking for a Colored and we need your help."

"'Course." Jackson nodded. He'd be glad to. "What happened? What'd he do?"

"Cut me." Rex spat out the words through a clenched jaw, lifting his shirt. "Now it's time for me to do some cutting of my own."

Jackson swore under his breath and ignored the men on his heels.

"So what are we going to do?" Henry asked.

"Kill him." Rex shook his fist. "String him up, hang his body out for the world to see."

Jackson couldn't focus. He was desperate for a drink. Rum, whiskey, anything to kill the root. He should've had plenty left. Already he had scavenged the cellar but found nothing but empty kegs. He searched behind bottles of oil, among pots and pans, rummaging through the glass cabinet in the corner, flipping over wooden crates trying to find a taste, just one taste to calm him.

The constant toothache had stolen his appetite for everything he once craved. For months he enjoyed nothing, but now it was much more serious. It was robbing him of his hearing. He could barely make out words over the vibrating throb. Leaning against the counter next to Henry, he gave his ear three hard slaps and opened and closed his mouth, trying to break up the fog.

"That tooth still got you, eh?" Henry crossed his arms, brown chew stains smeared along his right cuff. "You better do something about that thing before it kills you."

"Too late."

"We're talking serious now, Jackson." Rex was anxious. And angry.

"So am I. I need one of you to shoot this sucker clear out my mouth. Get me out of this pain."

"Now, that I can do." Henry chuckled, pushing his index finger with raised thumb against Jackson's jaw. He pulled the trigger hard against his cheek.

"What, are you crazy!"

"It's a tooth! Come on, Jack. How bad can it be?"

That was exactly what he had thought the first day, the first few days, but now, weeks later, he was in more pain than he had experienced when he was grazed by a bullet hunting as a teen. His arm had hurt for some time back then, but this, this small toothache had moved up his face, gave him headaches every day, and had traveled down and become a pain in the neck, a pain in the—

"You ain't the only one hurting, you know? Boy, I'd just go over there and slaughter him if I knew which one he was, if they didn't all look alike. I'm thinking he's your boy. Your place's the closest to where we found him."

"We'll get him. Don't you worry about that."

"I want both of them."

"Them? There was more than one?"

"A girl," Henry offered. "Small thing. I couldn't see nothing but her white hand, but I think he called her Linda."

"Lydia," Rex corrected. "He called her Lydia."

"He was with a White woman?"

"It looked that way. All I know is I want this settled by evening. You in, right, Jackson?"

"Yeah," was all he could muster. He pushed away from the cabinet and kicked the screen door open to a gray sky. His unbuttoned jacket flapped in the wind around him. Clouds hovered and a cool breeze whipped through, flowing into his gaping mouth, sweeping into his cavity. He whimpered, grateful his boys were inside.

He'd hoped Michael Kelly was wrong about the tooth. Hoped it would've gotten better not worse. One thing for sure, he wasn't going to let the doctor know how right he'd been, especially after Caroline asked him to distance himself from the man. Besides, the deal was done. He had his men. No need to contact him further.

But he had to do something.

He extended his right index finger over the infection he could now smell. He howled, swore against the heavens. *The pressure. The pain.* He blinked back hot tears. He'd never needed a drink more in his life.

He felt foolish. Something so small, so delicate, made him want to weep like a baby. But of course. It was planted in him, rooted deep within.

Jackson dug inside the pocket of his work trousers and flipped open his switchblade. The splintered red handle trembled in his hand. He closed his eyes, inhaled, then sliced wildly through the rotting flesh, piercing and carving until he swallowed a sea of blood. He yanked on the tooth. Tears poured down his cheeks. It didn't budge. His heart thundered. He had to go deeper. Deeper still. His knees shook at the thought.

How could he? He choked on the salty liquid gurgling in the back of his throat. Coughing, he knelt and tore into what was left of his back gums until the dead tooth lay hopeless and shattered in the palm of his hand.

Jackson stared at it and then, howling relief, hurled his agony across the patchy dirt road with incredible speed, dust rising at its landing. Now, the pain would deaden.

He spat, wiped his chin against the arm of his jacket, and walked away.

———◆———

He was gone.

The moment she knew she needed him, loved him, wanted him more than anything, he was gone.

Lydia strolled through the path they had walked the night before. She tried to set her feet in the same place his had been, tried to touch the leaves from the branches that grazed his skin. She tried to relive everything.

She hadn't slept last night, terrified that he was captured or dead or hung, thrown in a river somewhere. Rex and Henry and Jackson, her father's murderers all over again.

So now she walked. If she got close to where he had been, she hoped she could draw near to where he was going.

She stepped out of the stable into a light mist and wrapped herself up in her shawl. It was too light for this time of year, but she didn't dare wear the hooded cloak again. She needed to rid herself of it, take no chances.

Jackson's land was truly magnificent. Hill upon rolling hill, the sound of horses trotting in the distance. The first time she saw it, she had been amazed, but now, she was struck with a different emotion. An emptiness.

She lingered. Though the rain had stopped, her hair was damp and strands slipped loose from the chignon, wrapping around her neck in the thrashing wind. She would certainly catch her death if she didn't hurry inside.

And yet she lingered near the slave cabins, drawn to a place she had once known, compelled to stay a few moments longer.

When she saw the Loom Room, she peered into the window. *A window in a room for a slave.* Still it intrigued her. Two brown women worked around a long wooden table. One man sat with his back against the wall, bowing over something in his lap. A bowl of—

"Caroline?"

She froze. *Please, no…* "Jackson."

She forced a smile, waved at Rex and Henry a few feet away, dismounting from their horses. Her heart raced.

"What are you doing here? Can't imagine you'd be making wedding plans out here."

"No, actually."

He looked behind her.

"Were you at the slave quarters?"

She shook her head. She had no idea how long he had been behind her, watching her.

"Caroline…" Jackson glanced back at his friends. "*What* are you doing out here?" he whispered. "Don't lie to me, please. I mean it, don't lie."

"I have something private to discuss with you."

"About what?"

She had to tell him she had decided to leave. This had been a mistake. She was sorry she had hurt him. Sorry she had hurt them all.

"About the wedding."

Jackson stared at her.

"I wanted to talk to you about the wedding, Jackson."

"All right?" He paused. "What is it?" He scanned her face, searching for answers, searching for a lie to indict her.

"Can we talk about it inside?" She held her eyes steady. Minutes mimicked hours as Jackson slowly gazed at her, and she tried to hide from predators a few feet away.

When he looked back in her eyes, his were bright. She breathed relief but still wrapped the shawl tighter around her shoulders.

"Sure." He grabbed her hand and kissed it. "Caroline, where are your gloves? You're so cold." He rubbed his hands over hers, blew warm air into them. "I've got to get you out of this wind." He brushed a wet lock from her forehead, coiling another behind her ear. As John had done. "Are you all right?"

She nodded. She had no idea how she would tell him, but she knew she needed to soon. She shuddered from the cold, from the truth. If he knew her lie…

"You seem sad." Jackson searched her face. She looked away. "Can't figure out what would be sad about a wedding. Caroline?"

She nodded, afraid her voice would betray her.

"You all right?"

"I'll be fine."

"You all go on." His face darkened when he looked at the men. "Do what needs to be done." They nodded as they returned to their horses and galloped away.

"What needs to be done?"

"A lynching."

No…

"You ready?"

"I need a moment." Just a moment to steady herself. She leaned against the log cabin behind her, her fingers sprawled across the glass.

She blinked.

Suddenly a shadow whirled by, moving so fast, Lydia had to catch her breath. It only took seconds to know it was the hunted one.

Run, John, run!

Lydia's world stopped, spun, and then suddenly went black.

CHAPTER
THIRTY-FIVE

$\mathcal{L}$ydia wrapped herself in a cocoon of covers in the warmth of her quarters. Despite them, she shivered. Her head was still wet from the rain, but the chill she felt rose from the inside. Cold in her bones. She snuggled tighter into herself and squeezed her eyes shut. When the door creaked open, she peered out from under the quilts.

"You all right?" Jackson stared at her. "You really scared me out there. You sure we don't need someone to take a look at you?"

"No." She sprang up. "I told you what he did. Jackson. Dr. Kelly—"

"Not Dr. Kelly, Caroline. Someone else, anyone besides him could have a look."

"No, no. I'm fine." She smiled. "Really, Jackson. I promise." She peeled back the layers.

"You wanted to talk to me about the wedding?"

"Is it all right if we do it later? I'm not up to it."

"Of course, of course. It's not important. Is it?"

"No."

"Tired?"

"I am." She closed her eyes and squirmed back under the covers. The image of John running, of their hour of terror, of her father on the porch, all of them returned when she closed her eyes.

"I'll let you rest."

When the door closed, she cried. *Gather yourself, Lydia.* She took a deep breath, willed strength, and rolled off the bed.

She opened the rosewood armoire. Behind a row of boxes stacked five high, two deep, in the base of the hand-carved furniture, lay her treasure.

She touched the red circles, handled the purple diamonds, and rubbed the place where the piece had been torn. She thought of it with her love now.

"Miss Caroline?"

"Annie." She startled and jumped to her feet, shoving the blanket inside the cabinet. "Umm…come in." She yanked the narrow door shut and turned to the girl. "Did you need something?"

"No. I was checking on you. I thought you was supposed to be lying down."

"I am. I *was*. How can I sleep with the wedding on my mind?"

Still pretending, still lying, but she had to say something, do something, until she knew where to go, how to find John, how to follow peace. "There's still so much to do. Listen, I know I had a rough start the other day, but thank you for your help." She returned to her bed and patted the spot beside her. "Sit, sit."

"I can't sit, ma'am. Not on your bed. Not with you."

"Why not?"

"I–I'm… Miss Caroline?" Annie cocked her head to the side and studied her. "You all right?"

<hr />

John dashed through barren fields of corn near the main road toward Dorchester. He flew into the deepest part of the forest and ran for hours. He knew the path, had traveled it too many times, and even under the starless sky, finding it impossible to see what was in front of him, he moved north with confidence.

For hours, he ran and knew he was now close to the Kelly plantation. His muscles tensed when he heard horses and the sound of a carriage approaching. Had they heard him? He ducked farther into the woods.

His arms swung with power, propelling his body over stone and stubble with ease until he was several miles from the sound.

Safe, he made a place in the dirt against a tree. He hadn't realized how cold and how tired he was until now, his tendons throbbing under the stress. Within minutes he felt his head nod, nodding. A little rest would do him good.

What was that? Rustling. Dead leaves blowing. Were they blowing or was something, someone—

He didn't even have time to complete the thought before he heard feet too close for him to stand, for him to think. A sheet was dropped over his head and he was dragged—punching and kicking—away.

Captured like an animal.

Scratching at the inside of the tarp, John wondered how much air he had left in the back of the wagon, how much longer he'd be able to survive.

He'd spent more time trying to stay alive than he did living any day. It was the main task of the Colored.

He flailed against the cloth that kept him from the outside world.

Tonight he was an animal. A beast in their eyes. A fearful, angry brute that needed to be tamed. Anger and sadness rode with him, one leading, then the other.

"*Speak up,* boy. *You hear me,* boy? *You better move,* boy." The man in the plaid jacket had spoken the words as sharp as the blade he'd flicked. One thing he knew for certain, had confirmed in some twenty-plus years, he was by no means a boy. None of the captives were. Not ever. They were born grown, staring death, hopelessness, and fear in the face the first day their eyes began to focus.

"Watch your back." "Pay attention." "Can't trust nobody." These were the sayings breathed into the slave spirit, hovering over every experience. But there was something more.

Deep down, buried under the heaviness, far beneath the wounds, there was this thing. For many years, John couldn't explain it. It was mysterious. A presence. A sense. He felt it special when the old folks prayed. Somewhere between the bowed head, the whispering and swelling of the lyrical call to the One, the pleading requests and the bleeding hearts laid out in the altar of the henhouse, the beating on the breast and the river of tears, somewhere in the midst, between the gratefulness of making it through another day and the "amen," he felt it, knew something was there, even as a child.

Peace.

Sweet, sweet peace. Peace was the only hope, the only friend of the slave. It was what carried them through the day. It flowed in the downbeat of the songs they hummed, made joy swing in the upbeat.

John thought of the mothers. Though only one suckled him, many had saved him. Only one had pushed him into this present life, but many had birthed him into a place still and sweet that kept him from losing his mind. Because of the love of so many, he had made it. He had not been broken. He was not shattered because someone spoke a word, someone uttered a prayer, someone somewhere believed in him and carried him when he couldn't carry himself. At some place along the journey he got planted and rooted in peace.

Caged and trapped in body, he squeezed his eyes shut, capped off the hurt, shut out the noises, and he prayed, hard, deep, and real, pulling every weight up and out of his tears, until his vision hazed and his fingers wiped fat lids. He cried for every lie, and he wept for the truth. In many ways, they were right. He was nothing. He didn't have the strength, the ability, to fight on his own. But he didn't have to. Because something deep on the inside strengthened.

His heart filled with warmth and that peace that used to graze him, that would float away moments after the tune was hummed, remained, strong and steady, the presence of God in him. *Jesus*. He called the name, until, layer after layer, he was clothed safe enough to fall asleep on the bumpy road to wherever.

CHAPTER
THIRTY-SIX

*J*ackson stood in his undershirt and trousers at the front door, whispering airy clouds of breath.

"Can't be too far on foot."

Lydia tried desperately to hear all the words exchanged, but the night air was making the house unbearably cold. How Jackson could stand it with nothing on his arms, she had no idea, because it drove her quickly out of its way, made her hurry to her room, just to get her blood moving.

The tapping of her heels against the wood floor whipped his head around.

"Caroline, what are you doing?" His voice was stern. "You need to stay off your feet after that fall."

She started to explain, but he turned back to the voices on the other side.

When he leaned against the frame, the door opened wider and she saw Rex and Henry. Rex's eyes widened.

She marched to her quarters and held her breath. A few minutes later when the bedroom door flung open, a red-faced Jackson scanned the room.

"Rex and Henry need to speak to you."

"About what?" She cleared her throat, trying to keep her voice from shaking. It wasn't the only thing disclosing her fear. She propped her trembling hand against the bed for support.

"Caroline…"

"Can't we do this tomorrow? It's late, Jackson. It's been a long day for all of us."

"And our night will end as soon as you speak to my men."

"I can't do that."

"Why not?"

"What do they want with me?"

"Caroline, they're just trying to find answers. None of us is happy about what happened."

"I'll talk to them tomorrow." She turned away.

"You think this is some kind of game?" He grabbed her, locked his hand around her arm, but his breathing was slow, controlled. "One of my boys got hurt. We need answers. Now."

"Please, Jackson." She didn't want to push him. "I promise. I will talk to them tomorrow. It was some day for me."

She witnessed the moment he relinquished. He nodded. Even still, he was not one to dismiss. She knew that. All too well.

———•◆•———

Every step to the foyer lit Jackson angrier and angrier. He wanted that boy as much as they did. Henry stood against the front door, his arms folded above his bulging belly. Rex paced, his shoulders in two sharp points under his shabby coat. He turned to Jackson.

"Where is she?" His eyes were wild, like a cougar ready to strike.

"She's not coming."

"What do you mean, she's not coming?" Rex's brows drew into a single line.

"I mean, she's tired."

"*Tired?*" Rex's tone grated Jackson's nerves. He hoped he got it under control real soon. For Rex's sake.

"Yes."

"Why is she so tired?"

"Don't you concern yourself about what's going on under my roof. What did you want to speak to her about, anyway?"

"How well you know this Caroline, Jackson?" Henry inquired.

He was getting hot.

"Well enough to know you'd better leave it alone."

"So she's too tired to talk to us."

"I hate to tell you this, my friend, but she looks like the girl we saw last night with that boy." Henry looked down.

"What?" The words seared through him. "Are you out of your mind?" Jackson suppressed every swear, held down every curse under his tongue. *Impossible.*

"I'm not saying she is. Just from the side. We only got to see a little of her from the side."

"I don't care how you saw her, it wasn't Caroline. Are we clear on that?" He had no idea where she was. He hadn't even been around. But he knew who to ask, knew exactly how to find out.

"Let's see what she says." Rex spat. "We'll know right away if she's lying."

And they would. She was a terrible liar. He wanted to know the truth, too, but he didn't want to face the shame in front of his boys. No, this he needed to find out alone.

"I said she's tired."

"Tired, huh?" Rex rose up against him. Whiskey blasted in his face. "You sure she's not tired from running around with that boy?"

"You better watch your mouth, I swear." He was a trigger away...one trigger away...

"I want to speak to her, Jack! She's not even your wife! What difference does it make?"

"All right, that's enough." Henry muscled between the men. "We're all tired. Jackson, hold it down here tonight for us. Maybe we can talk to her in the morning. We'll be back first thing."

"I want to talk to her now!"

"Come on, Rex. We need to respect the man's house." Even Henry was losing patience. He patted Rex's back. "It's getting late. Let's get out of here. Don't worry. We'll talk to her."

The three of them stepped out onto the porch.

"Tomorrow," Jackson said, stuffing his hands in his pockets. She'd better have been where she was supposed to be or they might not ever get the chance to talk to her—if he got a hold of her first. It was cold. Awful cold. He wished he had grabbed his coat.

"Tomorrow," Henry nodded.

Rex murmured under his breath.

"What'd you say?" Jackson leaned forward, fuming. They had him out in the cold, dealing with this mess.

"I said, better be. It better be tomorrow."

"Or?"

"Or I don't know who might get cut next."

"That's funny." Jackson howled. "That's real funny. You think I'm worried about being cut? Tell you the truth, I'm not worried about none of it." *Come on, take the bait. Give me a reason to whip you!* "It's not my problem."

"It's not your problem?" Rex chuckled, his breath hovering like smoke in the air. He moved in front of Henry and stepped in close to Jackson's face, inches from the tip of his nose.

"Oh, it's your problem, Jackson. I think it's your problem, especially. You better hope your girl's not tired from something else she was doing with that coon."

Before Jackson could raise his fist, Rex slammed into him and punched him in the throat. Jackson bit his tongue and felt his mouth fill with blood. He lunged into his friend with all his might. The force sent Rex staggering back, knocking Henry off balance. A loud thud pulled them apart.

Jackson and Rex jogged to the bottom of the stairs and found their friend bucking wildly in the dirt, his neck snapped and twisted.

The sun gleamed down on Whitfield's narrow face, warping his smile, as he dragged Lydia away. John ran toward his bride, but laughing men in plaid coats grabbed him and held him down.

He woke up swinging.

The tight space jarred him alert. Still in a cage. He saw sunlight breaking through the corners of the tarp and heard life on the outside. And breathing.

Someone tugged, then grabbed the edge of the tarp and yanked the cover back.

John held his breath.

"Charles?"

"Shhh!" His friend pushed his head down and draped the tarp back in place. "Someone's coming."

Through a corner, John could make out they were in a field. He could no longer see Charles. Just a coach and a plump woman with springy red curls under a large flowered hat approached. She had been crying, her quivering lips stained as brightly as her hair. Her driver walked over to Charles, but before he opened his mouth, the woman behind him spoke.

"You seen a Henry Drake in these parts? He's a smart-looking fellow, a little stout. Always chewing. Ain't never without his tobacco."

"No, ma'am."

The woman patted her eyes with a crumpled handkerchief balled in her palm. Bits of white cotton lint clung to her lashes.

"I'm sorry, ma'am." Charles nodded at her and then spoke to her driver. "I'll be on the lookout."

"Will you, now?" She sniffled. "I appreciate it."

The lady bowed her head, and her hat tipped forward. Wiggling it straight, she followed her driver to the carriage and rode off.

After several rocky minutes of riding, Charles pulled the tarp off and hustled John into the storehouse.

"We need a safer place. I think it would be easy for someone asking questions to find you here. You all right?"

"I—yeah, I'm fine. I just didn't expect to see you." John huddled in a corner and blew into his hands. He reached for the strip of blanket he carried with him. He dug in and out of his front and back pockets, pulling them inside out into tiny ghosts at his side. It was gone.

Charles looked over at him. "Looking for something?"

"Must have fallen out somewhere." He shook his head. "I've got to tell you, last night when you grabbed me, I thought it was over."

"I spotted you a few times through the thicket. You're fast, but you ain't much match for a wagon. I knew I needed to grab you before someone else did. You thought it was over?" Charles laughed, his grin stretching the width of his face. "I'm sure you did."

But it was far from that. John smiled. Far from over.

———•◦•———

Jackson and Rex knelt under the porch over the dead body.

"What did you do?" Rex quivered.

"You mean, what did *we* do."

"Nooo, no, I don't mean that at all." The knot in Rex's thin throat bobbed up and down. "No, *you* did this. You alone."

"You're crazy!"

"If you would've just gotten us the girl... I can't believe this! We would've been gone. And Henry wouldn't be..." He slumped over, heaving until vomit covered his worn boots and spittle dangled from his bottom lip. "What are we gonna do? What are we gonna do, Jack? Our friend's dead! Our friend—"

"Would you lower your voice!" Jackson whispered harshly. *This was not happening.*

"You're not even sad, are you?"

"What are you talking about?"

"You're not even sad!"

"Shut up! Shut your mouth. I feel as bad as you do." He just needed to think. There was a dead man on his property, and as much as he wanted to run, somebody had to figure out something. "We've got to get him out of here."

"You don't care, do you?" Rex stared at him and wiped his mouth with the back of his hand. "You don't care about nobody but yourself."

"You're being ridiculous."

"No, I'm serious. We were just your hired help. That's all we were to you."

"You've lost your mind."

"We were never your friends."

"If you don't shut your mouth—" Jackson jerked him by the collar. He needed to get ahold of himself. He loosened his grip. "I'm sorry."

Rex was whimpering, sucking his bottom lip in and out like a mindless child. *Pitiful!* He had enough to deal with.

"Look, you go on. I'll take care of this."

"What does that mean? What are you gonna do with him? Should I go to Mae?"

"No! No…I need to think. Maybe." After all, it was an accident. But would she believe him? Would she care? Either way, her husband was dead. "Let me handle this, Rex. Go on now. Go home. I'll handle this."

Back inside, he questioned whether or not to go to the sheriff, but then thought better of it. Too much probing. With all the liquor he had been purchasing, it would be foolish to draw attention. He would deal with it himself.

Hide the body.

He knew where to look. Annie had given Caroline all sorts of blankets when she arrived.

"Caroline?" She was asleep. He searched in the armoire for a covering and raced back down the steps, the wind stinging his face. It was the first time he felt the cold since the accident. Odd how that was.

Rex was still there, pacing, whimpering. "What are you going to do with him? Where did you get *that*?"

"What?"

"The blanket?"

What difference did it make? "It's Caroline's."

He looked at it now in his hands. Why had he grabbed the brightest blanket ever made? *This was ridiculous!* "Just help me, will you?"

"What are you going to do? You're going to wrap him in that?" Rex fell against his chest. Jackson gave his back a quick pat.

"Listen. You just go on home." He would get nothing done with him around. "Take care of yourself."

Rex just stared at his half-covered friend.

"Go on now. Take care of yourself. How's your stomach?"

"It's hurting more. It's really hurting," he sobbed, pulling up his shirt. The wound oozed yellow.

"Go on home. You're going to be fine."

"What about Henry?"

"I'll take care of him."

Slowly, Rex staggered away, turning back again and again to the man sprawled on the ground.

"Don't worry, Rex. You'll be all right. And I'm going to talk to Caroline."

"You are?"

"Yeah, sure."

"When?"

"Soon. Don't worry."

"Promise?"

What did he have to do, cross his heart? "Yeah, I promise."

Jackson stood at the riverbank.

Guilt washed over him as he tossed his friend into the shallow water and watched him rise to the surface, bobbing under circles and diamonds. *The blanket!* He needed it in case someone linked it back to him. He waded through the murky water. It was freezing. He stroked midway and yanked the cover off the body. Henry was faceup, his eyes stretched wide like he was looking, staring at him. Jackson scrambled back, falling into the water. *What had he done?*

He scurried from the bank back home, whipping through tree limbs and leaves, swatting through branches and the image of Henry in his mind. He threw the soaked blanket on a heap of hay outside his barn and set it on fire, blazing the night sky up in smoke.

When he shut the front door, he didn't know how he had made it home. In the foyer, he started to peel off his wet clothing when he heard a soft patter, a woman, Annie or Caroline, coming down the hallway.

"Jackson?"

How would he explain…?

His shoes and one sock were as far as he got when Caroline's silhouette appeared several feet from him. If he couldn't see her, she couldn't see him, he hoped.

"What are you doing up? Go back to bed."

"I can't sleep. Your boys got me all worked up."

"Don't worry about them."

She stepped closer. "Were you outside?"

"No."

"I heard the door."

"It was me. I was looking out. I thought I heard something."

She moved closer.

"Go back to bed."

"Jackson?"

He moved deeper into the shadows, hoping she wouldn't notice what a mess he was. He jumped when she touched his hand.

"You're freezing!"

"I—"

"Jackson! What happened to you?"

"What do you mean?"

"Your face. Your face is all scratched up."

He smudged his cheek. He must've scraped himself against the branches.

"Are you bleeding?" She gazed over him. "Are you wet?"

"I—"

"Jackson…" She searched his eyes. "Jackson, what happened to you?"

What happened to him was that boy. Somebody always ended up dead because of them. Coloreds were a looming shadow of death. He swore, if it weren't for them, everything would be fine, just as it had been. The thought of Henry, Timothy, buckled his knees. "Oh, Caroline…" He fell into the arms of one half his size and allowed her to hold him up.

So, you haven't seen him either?" Mae craned her neck and peered past Jackson to the left, to the right, into the foyer, dabbing her eyes with a handkerchief. "It's awful cold out here this morning. Mind if I come in? Maybe I could rest awhile before getting back on the road."

"Weather's suppose to turn ugly, Mae." Jackson frowned up at the sky, grateful for the hints of gray in the distance. "Probably best for you to head on back. Last thing you need is to get caught up in it. But if I see him, I'll be sure to send him right over. After a swift kick in the rump for scaring you like that." He forced a smile. "But I'm sure he'll be home tonight. Might be there now."

"Is Caroline here? It'd be rude of me not to speak." She pushed him aside and plowed through. "Caroline?"

Jackson gritted his teeth, slammed the door behind him, and followed Mae into the parlor.

The women pecked cheeks and sat back on the sofa.

"Look at you! As beautiful as ever," Mae said, crossing her legs. Her shoe dangled off her foot, inches above the floor. "How ever do you keep such color in the winter?"

Jackson rolled his eyes but noted Caroline's sudden unease. He stood above the two with his arms crossed until Caroline raised a crinkled brow.

"Is there something you need?" she asked.

She was becoming too familiar, much too bold in her regard, teetering on a disrespect he wasn't about to tolerate. Not in his house, under his roof. He'd handle it as soon as the nosey one staring at them went her way.

"Oh, you don't have to go, Jackson. I'm not planning on taking over.

Not entirely." Mae giggled. "I'm not staying long. I was just asking about Henry." She leaned in close to Caroline and whispered, "He didn't come home last night. I've been wondering about him. Gone all the time." She sniffled and wiggled farther back onto the cushion.

"Well, he was here last night," Caroline said.

"He was here?" Mae twisted around to him, her mouth a tight red line. "Jackson!" She whipped back around toward Caroline. "He said he didn't see Henry last night. That's what he told me." She crossed her arms and waited.

"What did you want me to say?" He blew out a breath, deep and long. His heart thumped, but he reassured himself. He had nothing to worry about. "I didn't want to hurt you, Mae."

"Hurt me?"

"He was here. I did see Henry last night and he told me he wasn't going home." The words came fast and with ease. "He had another stop. Might stay all night, depending on how things went. He winked and left. That's it. That's all I know. I don't know who, I don't know where." Jackson studied her face as she searched his.

Mae wailed into the balled-up cloth in her fist but contained herself moments later with a grip of Caroline's hand.

"I'm sorry I didn't tell you the truth," he added. "I just didn't want to see you upset."

She fanned him quiet and wiped her eyes. Jiggling the lines of her dress straight, she stood with lifted chin. "I'm fine." She walked swiftly to the door and turned toward them. "I'll be just fine."

"If there's anything I can do…" Caroline followed her to the foyer, Jackson a few feet behind.

"Thank you." Mae squeezed Caroline's hand and glared at Jackson.

"I'm sorry," he said. "I just wish there was more I could do."

"There is. When you see your friend, tell him it's best not to come near me." She narrowed her eyes. "Or he might end up dead."

Lydia snuggled under a blanket on Jackson's back porch. It was certainly an improper gesture, a lady sitting on the ground in the open. It would've been much more appropriate to sit in the wooden swing several inches away, but swinging didn't feel right, not now. Much too joyful, too carefree somehow, for a sad Christmas Eve. Besides, she was alone and after the terror of the last few nights, she could care less about custom. A few days ago, custom had her and John running for their lives. She shuddered. *This place!* She looked out over the fields of land Jackson owned. Miles and miles of land, the haunting trees in her periphery. She wouldn't allow her eyes to stray there, not yet, lest she never venture near them again.

She laid her hand across her stomach, grateful no blood stained her garments despite the rigor, the running, and the tears. Their child remained safe. She prayed the same for the father. He carried a bit of her in the blanket she weaved as she carried a piece of him. Even apart, they were knit together.

She looked out over the fields. She would have to leave this place before too long with or without him.

Shivering, she twisted to her side and leaned back against the foot of the rocker as she had so many times before with Lou. She pulled layers of blanket up over her arms, her chest.

The night was dark, as black as it was beautiful, but without John, she was uneasy, much too nervous since the men… She hated to think about it.

She lay back and gazed above until she fell asleep against the cold wood and dreamed of her husband. She couldn't see him, only heard his voice, but with such clarity that she felt his breath on her face. Though she had sat shivering, she awoke damp, her dress clinging to her chest.

His presence had been no more than a game of the heart played on her in the middle of the night.

"Anything else I can get you, Miss Caroline?"

"No, thank you, Annie."

"Mr. Whitfield, sir?"

Lydia glanced at him. Jackson shook his head and gulped a spoonful of succotash. Frowning, he pushed it away, wrinkling the maroon tablecloth under the friction. "This is a bunch of—"

"I'm sorry, sir, if you ain't pleased. I tried to do right by you, today especially. Tried my hardest to make you happy."

"Well, you didn't."

"Sorry, sir."

"Just go."

"Miss Caroline?"

"That would be fine, Annie. Go on. We're fine."

"I'll just be around this corner if you need me."

The clinking of silverware against plates echoed. After a swig of wine, Jackson cleared his throat and rubbed his right cheek.

"How's the tooth?"

"Better." He glided his tongue over his back gums.

"Long gone, but I haven't gotten used to the empty space." He looked up at her. "You feeling all right? Your hair…"

Lydia's hand grazed over her head. Strands had fallen loose from the high chignon. Warmth rose in her chest, under her cheeks. "I suppose I didn't pull myself together so well today. Just tired."

His eyes flashed before dropping down to her stomach. She tugged the crimson napkin in her lap higher against her waist.

"Forgive me," she added.

"Anything you want to tell me, Caroline?"

"Such as?" She dabbed her mouth with the cloth.

He buttered his second slice of rye and shrugged. He was watching her. She could see him watching, waiting to see if she would squirm under the scrutiny.

"Such as?" she asked again, willing herself confident.

"Such as this wedding of ours."

Her heart thumped. He saw it. Fear must have flickered briefly across her face because his demeanor changed. He disguised it with a smile.

"What do you want to know?"

"I want to know why you don't talk about it much. For a woman, you don't seem to be that happy. I thought you would've been thrilled."

"Well, Jackson, I'm still not feeling well and the wedding is only a few days away. I'm hoping I'll be better by then."

"You never did tell me what you wanted to say that day. Out in the rain."

She still hadn't told him anything. She was waiting, hoping to get word somehow that John was alive. She had no idea what to do. If she left this place without him, how would he find her again? So she did nothing. She stayed put.

"It wasn't important. Besides, I didn't think you were the kind of man who'd want to sit around and talk about weddings all day."

"So who do you talk about it with?" He leaned forward.

"I didn't think you'd be interested—"

"Try me!" Jackson slammed his glass against the table. The wine swooshed high, over the side of the flute, staining the arch of his hand red.

Lydia's trembling hands brought her glass to her lips in small jerky motions.

"You've been different lately," he challenged.

"So have you." A filthy rottenness corroded the little good he had left. She couldn't tolerate him for much longer.

"What are you talking about?"

"Since that night Henry and Rex were here. When you came in wet and bloody and Henry ended up missing."

"I told you, I don't know anything about that. I don't know where he is." He pierced a carrot with his fork and kept his eyes on his plate.

Lydia watched him. He had his own secret. At least it kept him from meddling with hers. "Merry Christmas, Jackson."

"Merry Christmas." He didn't look up.

Lydia chewed on a rubbery carrot. Out of the corner of her eye, she watched Jackson reach for his fourth piece of bread, his umpteenth glass of wine.

"Annie! Get out here. Bring us the whole loaf of whatever you've got. It's the only thing that's decent."

Annie returned with a warm platter of pumpernickel, rye, and gingerbread.

"Where've you been hiding this?" Jackson grabbed slices with both hands.

"I'll just leave it here for you, sir. The whole platter of it."

"Good."

"What would you like more of, Miss Caroline?"

"Nothing. Thank you."

"You sure? Looks like you ain't ate much. Was everything all right?"

"Yes."

"You certain, ma'am?" Annie's eyes scanned their plates.

"I'm certain."

"Looks like neither one of you enjoyed your Christmas dinner much."

"It was *fine*, Annie."

"You're upsetting Caroline," Jackson slurred.

"The dinner was just fine, Annie. I'm not upset. Go on now and rest. It's Christmas. Who are you spending the day with?"

"I ain't spending it with nobody."

"Oh." Lydia looked at Jackson.

"Don't even think about it. Go on now, Annie, and find some family, find some friends. There's plenty of slaves finding something to do with themselves today. Go with James and his family."

"Do you want to sit—"

"No! I'd never sit and eat with a Colored. You can't eat at my table, Annie. You can take some of the food you made and go somewhere. I don't mind. You can take the rest of it as long as you don't ever think about parking yourself at one of my tables."

Annie's eyes watered just enough to put out the fire that raged in them.

"I'm sorry, Annie." Lydia could barely contain herself. When the footsteps faded, she twisted around to Jackson. "Why are you so awful? Nobody deserves—"

"And you're a liar."

"What?"

"How many times did you tell that girl you liked the food? Did you? Why did you lie?"

She swallowed. "Because I didn't want to hurt her feelings."

"Is that what you do? Lie to save feelings?"

"Annie's a hard worker. Very loyal to you—"

"As she should be. I take care of her. What would she do without me?"

He didn't ever need to drink. Lydia stood up and flung her napkin on the table.

"I'm not done. Sit down."

She didn't move.

"We're *not* done. Sit down, Caroline."

She glared at him.

He shot up and grabbed her by the wrist. She tried to squirm free but every pull locked his fingers tighter, clamped his hand harder around hers. His flaming eyes bore into her. "You better be glad I don't beat my women. Don't ever disrespect me again." He flung her loose. "Annie!"

"Yes, sir." Annie walked into the room with her hands behind her back and her eyes low, not as if fear bowed her head but a mumble, a prayer, or simply a will not to witness the scene playing out before her. "Everything all right?"

Jackson grabbed a corner of the tablecloth and with a flash of his hand, yanked everything—bread, wine, bowls, plates, glasses, silverware—to the floor.

"Clean this mess up."

CHAPTER
THIRTY-EIGHT

*S*omething wasn't right.

Lydia paced the sitting room. She smoothed the cushions of the pale blue sofa with her palm, propping her toes webbed in pale stockings against the clawed foot of wood. Running her fingers over the curved back of the velvet armchair, she knew nothing had changed. But something was clearly wrong.

"Let's do it again, Annie." Lydia shook the starched linen open. "It's not right."

And it wasn't the Irish folds in the napkins.

"Ma'am, I've done it I don't know how many times."

"Just once more."

Lydia marched around the room, her rambling interrupted only by an occasional deep breath or a momentary collapse on the couch.

"Did we state the time?"

"Yes, ma'am, we did."

"Who's not coming? Do we know?"

"Yes. If we go over the list again it will be our third time." Annie paused. "Maybe you should rest awhile."

But in forty-eight hours, she would be Mrs. Whitfield if she didn't leave, if she didn't do something. "I don't have time to rest."

"I think it would help."

"What else do we need?"

"We have everything."

"You think so?" A tremor, one small tremor, crept into her fingers. She squeezed her hands together and tapped them against her lips. Steady, steady, she slowed her breathing.

"Miss Caroline, I'll do whatever it takes to help you. It's gonna be real nice."

"I'm just not feeling good about it. Maybe...maybe we should postpone."

"You think Master Whitfield is gonna allow that? After all *this*?"

Annie was right. So much had been done. Too much to turn back at this point. Perhaps this was the way it was meant to be. A granting of a wish, a punishment of a will. This was the world she had dreamed of, had craved all her life, and she had it now whether she wanted it or not. It was simply her plight to live in the world she chose. For everything she wanted, there was the thing she didn't.

Lydia glanced down. Her hands were shaking. The tremor had slipped out from under her control. Truth kept showing up. Real kept peeking, piercing through, appearing unannounced, until she knew it would come out of hiding for good and she couldn't play the game anymore.

"Well, perhaps there's nothing else to do but clean," she said finally. "Start with the windows."

"Ma'am, I did the windows three hours ago. Maybe I can—"

"You did the windows?"

"Yes, ma'am."

"I'm sorry, Annie."

Annie stopped and looked at her. "Please, Miss Caroline, get some rest."

"I will. After everything is done."

Annie and James hustled through the house streaming vines sprinkled with red berries across doorways and mantels. They scrubbed on ladders and on knees. They dusted every antique, every brass, silver, and wooden fixture, and fluffed every pillow. They shined glasses and silverware until they reflected their tired faces. They polished the floor until it was dangerously slippery and wiped every surface, swept every crumb. They worked until every corner of the manor brimmed with excellence.

On counters, they stacked dishes, glasses, goblets, silverware, a wine-colored linen tablecloth, embroidered napkins, and lion head napkin rings, and ivory and maroon candles with gold stands, every item they would need.

Seven hours later, when James retired to his quarters, Annie slumped to the floor in the dining room. Lydia poured herself into a chair and joined her.

"I don't think I ever worked so hard," Annie said.

"The place looks wonderful." Lydia glanced around the room. "I can already see it. To think in two days this place will be filled with folks, all dressed up. Glowing and laughing and flashing their big ol' smiles. They'll toast, throw their heads back, and let out the most delightful squeals." Lydia held her hand to her chest and slipped into a proper Southern accent. "Why, I do declare, it's mighty right. It's mighty right."

Annie giggled. "What's 'mighty right'?"

"I don't know, Annie. They don't either." It was all a facade she cared little for now.

Annie's eyes darted from Lydia lounging in the chair, to the dining room entrance. "You don't want Mr. Whitfield coming in here, catching you talking to me like this."

Lydia didn't move, didn't even answer.

"Miss Caroline, you hear me?"

"What is he going to do?" What else could be done? Truly, what else? She had been peeled, pricked, devoured slice by slice. There was nothing left to take but the core, and no matter how deep anybody cut, what was left was in her for good. "What is he going to do?"

"Well, it ain't the same for me."

"It's the same, Annie." She wanted to tell her the truth. Tell her who she was behind the powder and the pretense. She wanted to trust her. Instead she said simply, "For me and you, it's the same."

"Me? They would punish, they'd kill. They wouldn't try to kill you."

But hadn't they? Lydia ran her hand over her scar, the scars they all carried. Even Lizzy had scars. "And if they kill you, Annie?"

"Then I'm dead."

Lydia laughed. "Good and dead and gone to be with your people."

Annie scraped the sole of her shoe against the oak wood floor.

"Where's your people, Annie?"

"I ain't got no people."

"You don't know not *one* person a part of you?"

"No. I never knew none of them. I had another master before I was sold here. It's my third winter with Whitfield. He was a decent man before…" She tugged on the tongue of her shoe, drooping it over the side like someone gagging.

"I'm sorry, Annie." One choice, like a spring in a garden. Some lives doused under it, others sprinkled with it, but all were touched by it.

"It's all right, Miss Caroline. Things are just the way they were meant to be."

Lydia looked away. It was much too painful if everything that happened in life occurred exactly as planned. *Everything?* How did she look in the face of a slave and accept that? She turned to Annie and smiled. "I admire your will. You get up every morning knowing nothing is going to change, and you work hard with not one complaint. You know, I don't think I've heard you complain, not one time, Annie."

Not even Christmas Day. Lydia had stooped to help her clean the mess, the ridiculous result of a grown man's tantrum, and not once did Annie say anything bitter under her breath. "And he's so awful."

"No worse than the rest of us."

"I beg to differ." Lydia rolled her eyes and bit back words on the edge of her tongue.

"Do you?" Annie laughed, fell back against the wall, and laughed, hard and loud, her almond eyes mere slits above her cheekbones. "Depends on how you're looking. You looking from the inside out or the outside in? Either way, if you look hard enough, you'll see yourself after a while." She sobered and sat up real serious and wiped the tears of laughter from her eyes. "I don't do nothing for him, if that's what you're wondering."

"I was. I was wondering exactly that. How do you do it? How could you stay a slave and be happy? Are you happy?"

"We're all slaves to something. Whitfield don't own me. Never did."

Lydia sat quiet for some time breathing the words in. Annie's head was tilted back, her brown scarf pressed against the rose-colored walls. "I didn't think you liked me, Annie."

"I didn't." She didn't even open her eyes. "I didn't."

Lydia smiled.

CHAPTER
THIRTY-NINE

*S*he should not have come. Never should have come to this place.

Lydia walked out of the dining room to hers. But once she was clothed for bed, she couldn't sleep. John showed up in her dreams.

She had become a woman who relished the day. Her nights, the darkness she had loved, was now filled with terror, torture, and nightmares of the past.

She was in no condition to host a celebration, to go through such a fuss for a wedding she didn't want, for a man she could hardly stand. She had suffered through all of it to cover her lies, but they kept slipping out no matter how much she stretched the truth.

She fell back on her bed and kicked the quilts around her, glad to be alone. Jackson had gone out early, where, she had no idea, couldn't care less. Just happy to have a moment to herself without a facade.

She rubbed the tips of her fingers in the deep crescents under her eyes, touched her sunken cheeks and thought of Mrs. Kelly. She was as exhausted as the woman had always looked. Lydia wondered if she appeared the same. Perhaps it was the plight of being a mistress, simply a cross one had to bear whether slave or free.

She wondered what her own face looked like at the moment but she didn't move. *Why make matters worse?* It couldn't be good. She hadn't concerned herself with the detailed rituals of beauty in weeks. Not even for her favorite holiday had she arranged her hair and clothing with care.

She crawled under the covers, vowing to stay there until she felt better. A few hours of rest would get her thinking straight.

Lydia slept for two days.

Annie rushed to her side, pressing cool cloths to her brows. Jackson kept his distance.

"You're gonna be all right, Miss Caroline." The girl faded in and out of focus.

"We need you to drink something." The young woman lifted her up, placed a steaming drink at her lips. She burned her tongue and winced. Pushing the cup away, she splashed hot tea on Annie's hands and on her own thigh.

Annie used the blanket to wipe and cool her fingers and the red, tender mark on her leg.

"I'm sorry, Annie."

"It's all right, ma'am. We just need you to eat and drink something. Anything. The wedding's this evening." She patted her back. "You've got to have your strength to make it. I'll get you cleaned up and bring you some crackers. We'll see if that'll get you going. You need food. You've had plenty sleep."

But not real sleep. That was what she needed, sound and deep, but the dreams invaded her peace, left her fighting the feeling every time it came.

Annie rubbed her with a wet towel, cleaned her like a baby, sat her up, and wrapped a robe around her shoulders.

"But you're gonna be all right. Crackers, ma'am. Let's try them."

Lydia stuffed the dry wafer into her mouth. It was the first thing she had eaten in days. She consumed it feverishly, holding her hand out for more. She pressed the crackers into her mouth so quickly the edges crumbled under the pressure.

"It's good?" Annie smiled. "You'll drink now."

By evening, Lydia had eaten five champagne crackers, eight grapes, and half a bowl of cold tomato soup. It was enough to raise her out of bed and allow her to flutter around the house anxiously.

She slid her fingers along the tables, the chairs, the lamps, and surveyed the silverware. She stopped to count the white candles Annie had purchased special for the occasion. One hundred flames. She thought of the ones that had flickered for John and smiled.

In her bedroom, Lydia stood before her armoire and tugged on the strand of pearls as Annie clamped the clasp shut.

"Here it is, Miss Caroline." Annie pulled the white gown she had made from Lydia's armoire and fluffed it across the bed. Endless folds of satin draped under full sleeves and a corset bodice.

"It's beautiful, Annie." Just what she had wanted, had dreamt of for John.

The girl smiled as she walked out of the room, closing the door behind her.

Lydia determined that even tonight, she would not fret in front of the mirror for hours. She swooped her hair into a high knot and pinned it in place, but as she slipped on her pearl earrings, she caught a glimpse of herself in the mirror and froze.

She couldn't remember a time she looked more beautiful. She looked again, this time examining, studying every feature. Besides a few thin lines under her eyes, she was perfect. Her hands were steady. She rubbed them together and said a prayer. She had no idea what was to unfold, how she was to untangle herself from the mess she had created, but confidently, she stood. Tugging on the waist of her dress, she pulled the pleats full and wide around her, lifted her head high, and strolled out to meet early arrivals.

"Where's Jackson?" Lydia whispered to Annie, scanning the dining room.

"Not here yet. Left early this morning. Ain't been back since."

Probably drunk somewhere.

"That's fine."

Perhaps he wouldn't show up at all.

Lydia watched the field slaves Annie had recruited to help with the event. They mumbled and fumbled with everything. She could care less. She was just waiting to see what she was compelled to do. Until then, she would stay put.

"I'm here about Jackson."

"Come in, Rex," Mae said, swinging her front door wide open. The smell of pork wafted through. "You all right? You hungry? You look terrible."

He hadn't bathed in days, mostly out of fear of wetting the silky red snake that bit every time the wind blew. And his mind had been on other things. Like a lynching. It would be the best revenge.

Mae's eyes were painted sky-blue from lash to brow.

"You going somewhere?"

"No."

"No?" *You just sit around all caked up for no good reason?* Her puckered pink lips made him heave. A salty wave watered his mouth. He swallowed. "Well, I was on my way to the Whitfields' and decided to pay you a visit." Rex flopped back on the low sofa and crossed his arms. "You're not going to the wedding?"

"Wedding? Who's getting married?"

"Jackson's marrying that Caroline gal."

"What? I thought they were already married." When she narrowed her eyes, it looked like the sky was falling. "That Jackson's a big liar."

"Oh, he's more than that." Rex leaned forward into the pulsing at his waist. "And I'm here to tell you."

———•◦•———

Lydia watched Annie and the other servants swarming around the room, greeting guests and offering stem glasses of white wine while James stood near the foyer armoire, hanging coats. The house had filled quickly with a crowd larger than Lydia expected. Jackson had apparently invited more than his family, but he himself still had not arrived. Every few minutes, she glanced at the door, waiting.

"Ma'am, a couple is looking for Master Whitfield," Annie informed her. "A Mr. and Mrs. Brewer."

"Who?"

Lydia turned. Behind her, Andrew helped Lizzy shrug out of an ankle-length, dark gray wool cloak. She should have run, she should have hidden, but she stood staring at her friend.

When Lizzy saw her, she startled, then walked to her, the space between them closed in seconds.

"Lydia? Is that you?" She touched her face with the tips of her fingers. "I didn't know where you were! I didn't know where you had gone. You're alive." Lizzy wrapped her arms around her, then stepped back. "And you're the bride?" She laughed and cupped her hand over her mouth. "You look beautiful. I would've never thought in all my life I'd see you again."

Lydia gripped her hand and smiled. It was so good to see her.

"What happened to John?" Lizzy whispered.

"I don't know." It hurt to say.

"You and Jackson…"

"Are you angry?"

"No. I'm quite happy. Happy with the husband I have and happy to see you." She beamed, then leaned in close. "So he doesn't know…"

"No."

"Then he never will." Lizzy nodded and with her arm linked through her husband's, moved through the crowd.

———•◦•———

Rex dragged, holding his stomach, across the field to the Coloreds' quarters, hoping the boy was dumb enough to return. He fingered the snake. It was waking up. Sharp, piercing pain stabbed him again and again as he staggered on. He stopped when he felt the tongue and looked at his wet fingers under the moonlight. It oozed, yellow, green, he couldn't tell, but the throbbing made him want to shoot somebody in the head. Why hadn't he brought his gun? Could've taken care of everybody at once.

He thought of Caroline and spat. Now, he just wanted that slave. Wanted to stab that boy right through the heart and let the blood rush like a river. Death was the only price for what he'd done. It didn't matter he had stumbled on his own knife, because he never would have had to pull it if that boy would've known his place. Out there with a White woman. And now Henry…

He pressed the water back that tried to seep through the corners of his eyes.

Or maybe he'd just break his neck like his pal's.

———•◦•———

Jackson scanned the dining room when he entered the house. Caroline had done a marvelous job instructing the servants while he was out nursing his final bachelor hours with healing drink. Made all things right.

"Excuse me, Mr. Whitfield," James interrupted. "We have an uninvited guest."

"Handle it, will you?"

"Uh, yes, sir." The butler's face tensed. "But she's pretty upset. A Mrs. Mae Drake. She said she would like to speak with you. Should I tell her—?"

"Tell her…" Jackson looked around, trying to think. That was all he needed. Mae with her questions. "Tell her I'll speak with her later."

"She says it's important."

"I'll talk to her when I talk to her!"

Mae pranced into the room, her hands on her hips. "You will speak to me right this moment!"

Jackson glanced at the few guests in the dining room, watching.

"That's fine." He nodded and smiled at the observers. He needed a drink. Badly. "Mae, I'm so glad you could make it this evening."

"To your *wedding*, Jackson? Henry told me you had already married the girl."

"I did. It's just a formality. This evening."

"Are you lying again?" She stepped closer and closer until her breasts pressed against his stomach. He stepped back. She inched closer until he was against the wall and forced to look down into her glaring eyes. "You hurt Henry, Jackson?"

"Mae, of course not." He grabbed her arm, whispering over the hushed voices around them, "Let's go into the other room so we can talk."

"I'm not going nowhere!" She yanked her arm away and stumbled backward. "Did you kill my husband?"

All fluttering stopped. Everyone stared. Jackson could feel the blood rushing to his face.

He unbuttoned his black jacket and walked into the foyer, nodding and smiling at guests as he marched by.

"Where do you think you're going?" Mae chased after him.

He whispered in James's ear and waited at the entrance.

Seconds later the butler and a field slave had Mae by the elbows. She kicked and flailed and screamed as they carried her out the door. "Put me down! I mean it, put me down! Jackson, yours is coming!" They whisked her down the steps and around the corner.

Jackson turned to the spectators and grinned. "Not to worry, she won't be back." He turned to slam the door when he saw a frail-looking man on his property in the distance. He squinted. *Rex?* This was ridiculous.

"Excuse me a moment, won't you?"

Jackson skipped down the steps and jogged over to him.

"Rex, what are you doing here?"

"You told me you were going to talk to Caroline. You lied to me. You wasn't never gonna ask her, were you?"

"Actually, I was, but somebody sent a crazy heifer to my house."

"I was just mad."

"I don't care what you were. You knew you were supposed to keep your mouth shut. So no, now you won't get to speak to her. You're going to get nothing but an old-fashioned beating if you don't get off my property right now."

"I can't. I think I'm dying." Rex slithered to the ground.

"Your choice. Get up or I'll—"

"Break my neck?" He squirmed into a ball on the grass.

"If you're not up and out of here by the time I get back upstairs, I'm going to send some of my boys to take care of you."

"Isn't that funny? Me and Henry used to be your boys."

"Get off my land."

"Yeah, we was your boys, but now, now, you're for the other side just like your wife!"

"That's where you're wrong. I've never been for nobody. Just against most." He spat at him. Rex flinched out of the way. "And tonight, it's me against you."

"You sure about that? I've got something for you."

"I'm leaving. I've got a wedding waiting on me."

"I don't think you do."

Jackson stormed into the house, slamming the door behind him. He had to keep it together until he got to Caroline. He needed to get to that woman.

"Jack!" Andrew walked up to him, gripped his shoulder. "Great seeing you, friend."

"You too," Jackson murmured, still moving through the crowd.

"Whoa, slow down. I haven't seen you in months, and this is the kind of greeting I get?"

"I'm sorry. I've just got a lot on my mind."

"Nerves getting to you? I understand. Listen, I just wanted to congratulate you."

Jackson extended his hand and smiled. "Thank you."

"You and Lydia—"

"What did you say?" He blinked.

"I'm sorry, I meant Caroline."

"Who's Lydia?"

"Caroline." Andrew chuckled. "Elizabeth calls her Lydia sometimes."

Jackson couldn't move. A dagger. That was all he felt. A dagger straight through his heart.

"What did you say?" His words came out shaky. He cleared his throat.

"Jackson?"

He stormed into the living room and downed two glasses of wine as he scanned the crowd of dark-haired women, searching for one.

He marched back into the dining room. A tall blonde in red stood near, laughing loudly and wagging her finger at the man beside her. When she stepped aside, the hairs on Jackson's neck raised. There she was. Caroline. In perfect view.

He dangled a woven cotton patch of red circles and purple diamonds in his hand and stepped closer. "What is this, *Lydia*?"

"What?" In the back corner of the dining room, Caroline stood, trembling.

"You heard me. Rex found this in one of my worker's cabins."

Her wide eyes, her tremor, told him everything, weakened him at his core.

"I'm sorry." She stepped away from him.

"Were you with that Colored? Did Rex and Henry see you?"

Jackson leaned into her. "Answer me, Caroline!"

She stumbled backward over the hem of her dress into the wall.

With a sweep of his arm, he slid the tablecloth and the candles to the floor, the sound of glass permeating the room.

But that was all Jackson heard. Glass falling. In all the movement of men and women slipping by him, scattering through the room, grabbing coats and stoles, servants rushing, smoke rising and flames igniting, all Jackson heard was glass. Shattering. His heart breaking. He watched Caroline clutching her necklace, crumpling to the floor.

A pearl clinked against the wood, then another. One by one they fell, like a flood.

Lydia scrambled out of the dining room, slipping on pearls.

"Caroline!" Jackson yelled from the smoky dining room floor, stumbling and staggering toward the one disappearing down the hall.

Smoke billowed into the hallway and quickly filled his lungs, but it was the fire that frightened him. It had flared so quickly, he could see flames raging from the dining table to the foyer. He would have to figure another way out. "Caroline!" After he got to that woman.

She was a liar. But he knew that. He always *knew* deep down she was dishonest. In time, he could feel it, feel her lies rotting inside him. Knew it the day he found her on the side of the road, but lust kept him coming.

Jackson dragged himself down the hall toward Caroline's quarters. Halfway there, he propped himself up against a wall, panting. He was panicking. He could feel his chest closing up on him. Coughing, he doubled over with his arms wrapped across his stomach. He was weak, weaker than he'd ever remembered. He tumbled to his knees. On his stomach, he crawled, slithered his way to her room. Out of breath, he glanced up at the doorknob several feet away.

He should've never let her in his house. None of them. Annie. James. They were bad news. He coughed. The smoke was burning his eyes, altering his vision. Timothy had died because of them. Jackson couldn't breathe. He was getting light-headed. Timothy died because... He inched his way forward, stretching for the knob, but his fingers slipped.

He died because of me.

Jackson's breath was fading.

Why did that Colored have part of Caroline's blanket? Was she...? He wouldn't allow his mind to go there. He knew he hadn't made the same mistake as Timothy. He went for the whitest skin, the greenest eyes. She wasn't... She couldn't be. He was suffocating, gasping for breath. *No!* But she cared too much for them, knew their ways too well. *Had he fallen for a...* He tried to rise but everything went black.

There was smoke. Lots of it. Lydia could smell it coming in from under the door, quickly clouding the room gray.

She had to get out fast.

A rock crashed against the glass. Lydia startled. She ran to the window and pried it open. Annie paced among dozens of panicked slaves and wedding guests.

"Miss Caroline! You all right?" She waited for her nod. "Listen, you gotta get out now!"

"I smell the smoke."

"No, ma'am, it's bad. The whole thing could burn down any minute. We see the flames coming through the windows and the front door from here. You gotta get out fast. It's moving quickly."

"Is everyone else out?" *Lizzy. Andrew.*

"Yes."

"Miss Caroline, you hear me?" Annie yelled. "You gotta get out now. Jump. It's not so far down."

Lydia wept as she stood in front of the open window. Frightened for her baby, for her life, she stood waiting.

"Miss Caroline!"

But this was it. The moment she had waited for had come. She was not Caroline. The truth had surfaced. She was Lydia. She was the same woman who had survived before. And in that second, when the breeze brushed against her face and she slid out onto the sill, she knew she would make it again.

Lydia jumped.

How she so easily left it all behind, leapt from a house that she had dreamed of all her life, left the world she had so desperately wanted, she didn't know until she was falling, flying through the air, freeing herself from the weight of it. Sometimes you had to lose life to find it.

Tangled in yards of satin, Lydia felt Annie's hands helping her to her feet.

"I ain't seen Master Whitfield." Annie looked from the window to Lydia, her eyes wide and worried.

"Annie." Lydia shook her head.

"What? Ma'am, is he still in there? Is he still in the house?"

"Annie, I'm so sorry," she sobbed.

"It's all right. It's my duty, not yours."

Annie sprinted toward the blazing house. Lydia chased after her.

"Annie! Annieee!"

At the base of the steps, Lydia caught her by the hem of her skirt. Annie tripped, falling forward.

Lydia blew out relief, her fingers still gripped around the coarse wool. "I got you."

The moment she said it, Annie broke free. She bolted up the stairs and burst through the glowing door. A laid-down life fading in the flames.

CHAPTER FORTY

A blue-eyed Black.

Ruth knew as well as all her community, it wasn't uncommon for a Colored to have light eyes like Lydia. But to match it with dark skin, now that was something different. That was something different entirely.

At the loom, Ruth's hands rested, not on the wooden posts, the beams, nor the side panels, nor the spun silk she would soon weave into fine cloth, but on her face.

She had seen the reflection of her chocolate skin many times in the ripple of the river, inside the dim silver of spoons she polished when she was a girl, and once in her mistress's looking glass. Many times she had admired her complexion, smooth as the pudding she craved at Christmas.

Even now it still felt velvety, her fingertips slipping only into shallow smile lines, which she was happy to have. All she had endured and she still had joy.

"What does this look like?" she asked Odessa and Abram. She knew they were awake, though at times they feigned otherwise late at night. Folks were so silly. Very little was hidden from blinded eyes. She saw more now than she ever did with sight.

"What's that, Ruth?" Abram asked. Ruth could hear him rising, shifting into a more comfortable position.

"My eyes. What do they look like? I know they're blue, but what do they look like in my face?" She laughed at the question. She knew good and well what she looked like from the screams, the panting, the gasps, the shattering of glass, the stumbling, the fumbling of feet, the mere disturbance of children and parents alike. Still, she couldn't imagine.

"They're just blue, Ruth. That's all. If you like blue, you're fine."

She laughed. He chuckled.

Her friend rose from the place where she sat quilting and walked to her. She placed her withered hands over hers.

"What do you say, Dessa?"

She didn't answer for a while, just stood rubbing her hands over Ruth's. Finally, she cleared her throat. "I'm sorry."

"Oh, Dessa." Ruth pushed her hands away. "Don't start that, hear? I know you're sorry, but there ain't no reason for it. I don't know how many times I've got to tell you. Stop all that." She could hear the whimpering that streaked her nerves. "I'm fine. I just wanted to know what you see."

Odessa returned her fingers to her face and smiled. *Yes.* Ruth could feel her smiling down. "Pretty, Ruthie. Pretty."

Still? She had been beautiful, had been told by many just that. And that beauty had kept Master Tim's hands on her at all hours. She lost count of the nights, the afternoons, the mornings he came to her. But she had had enough. Had stolen the knife of her enemy from the back pocket of the trousers crumpled next to his drowsy body one night. When his eyes shut, she hid it under the washbasin until the day at the shed, led there by Odessa's cries. A cry, looked like life would have it, she was cursed to hear every day for the rest of her life.

She wanted to see her eyes for herself, but she was fine settling for the view of her friends. She wasn't one to fret about injustice, the things that kept many of her people bound in anger. What she couldn't change she left alone and sought peace in other pleasures. The loom was her love. When she touched it, handled it, the tension she carried was released, but tonight she sought a different pleasure.

"When's the last time you been outside?" Ruth clasped her hands. "Lydia's wedding?" But they had not ventured outdoors even then. "Both of you. I'm talking to both of you. Come on, get up!"

She stood up, shifting the bench back with the force of her thighs. "Come on now. We're going out."

"But you can't see."

"But I can feel. When's the last time you felt some air on your face, Dessa? Seen the world outside of this here place?"

"Long time. Ain't had the strength to, not after…" A whimper. "How long it been, Abram?"

"Can't go back that far."

"Well, this is it. Tonight we're going out."

"How we getting out there?" Abram asked. "Can't walk worth nothing. Legs so weak…"

"One step at a time. Come on, Dessa, help me up."

Odessa placed her hand on Ruth's shoulder, but she slipped forward and fell into the loom. Ruth could feel the frame of it shake, she could feel her lover toppling, the heavy weight of it falling forward. She tried to catch it, hold the side panels up, but she couldn't balance the load. She heard Odessa scream, the loom tumbling on top of her, knocking her to the floor.

Abram was at her side fast, quick for a sick, old man.

"Ruth! Ruth, are you all right?"

"Abram!" *Asking her foolish questions!* "I'm trapped. I can't move from under it."

"I'm going to get you out. Hold tight."

To her surprise, she wasn't panicking, just uncomfortable. At least she could move her arms. If he could just get his wife to be quiet, she would be all right. Odessa couldn't even speak for the wailing coming out of her mouth.

"I need to get help."

"No you don't. You ain't leaving me here like this. You just said you could barely walk. I might be dead by the time you get back here."

"Dessa's with you."

She didn't say a word. Didn't have to.

"All right, I won't leave you, but I don't know what to do."

"You don't know what to do? Get this thing off me!"

"I don't think I can."

"Try, Abram. Try."

Ruth could feel Abram pushing, prodding, straining, until he let out a big breath over his panting. "I don't know, Ruth. Without help…I need help."

He was quiet. Anxiety was building now, masking her ability to detect, discern. "What are you doing? Abram?"

"Asking for help. Look, Ruth, I need to do this a different way." He scooted behind her, knelt near her head.

Sliding his arms under hers, he pulled her to him. The loom wobbled forward. Ruth could hear it coming down before it hit, crashing against her skull.

She could hear the gasps, the cries, the uttered reverence of the Lord's name.

"Is she dead?" Odessa asked.

From the pain deep inside her head, she wished she were. It seared like lightning behind her eyes. But when she opened them, she blinked. A fuzzy figure behind the wood moved toward her.

"Abram...Odessa?"

"You're all right. Thank God."

Ruth blinked again and again, every shadow becoming light, every fog clearing. She swung at the wood over her, scrambled under its weight, energized, renewed, strengthened by what was happening to her from the inside out. The couple pulled her legs from under, and she wiggled free.

"Abram. Odessa." She said each name slowly, slowly, taking in the vision of the faces that were becoming more and more clear. She pulled herself up and sat at her friends' side. It was strange seeing them. Though they had been together for more than twenty years, she had last seen them as young folk. Abram's thick hair was now gone, but his gift, his strength, was back.

"I can see."

"What? What did you say?"

"I can see." Ruth nodded at the gray-haired woman. "I can see you." She reached out and touched the face of her friend. She saw, as she had often felt, the toil of the years. She saw the pain for the first time and wept.

"You can see?" Odessa's hand gripped hers. Her eyes widened just like the eyes Ruth remembered. "You can see, Ruthie?"

But she couldn't answer. She nodded. For the first time in twenty years, it was her nodding and crying, staring into the dry, steady eyes of a woman who smiled. Odessa smiled until she laughed, light and sweet.

"She can see, Abram. She can see!"

Abram sat with his head in his hands, his shoulders sunken. He looked up with red-stained eyes.

"It couldn't be."

"I can see you, Abram." Ruth grabbed his wrist. "I can see the hands that healed me." She touched the scar on the inside of his palm.

"One more," he whispered. "He gave me one more."

Ruth didn't know what he meant, but it didn't matter. She was seeing for herself. She shook her head. It was too much. The blessing. This wave of grace.

"I was blind...," Ruth said, but the rest of the words caught in her throat.

EPILOGUE

*E*very pull of death pushed her closer to life.

With tears, Lydia pulled her way forward through the black night. Scuffed, battered, and soiled in her white gown, she moved through the maze of oak and hickory, through the path of pines, over stubble, patches of worn blue grass, fallen twigs, moss. The beauty of the things that bred around her, these natural wonders she had first come to recognize as a child, she could now see. She knew them like she knew her own flesh. Through the wiry thicket she ran, her breath catching in her chest until it rose to her lips in a soft pant.

With every step forward, Lydia was freed. She knew it, even now. In the midst of her flight, she knew she was finally unleashed from all she left behind. Every cruel word, every hateful glare reserved for a slave, Dr. Kelly's hands, her father's blood, Lou's death, the loss of John, from all of it, she was loosed.

Lydia swatted past oak limbs and evergreen branches, no longer bound.

Only minutes had passed since she soared through the window toward freedom. Her heart thumped at the thought of that first move, the decision to fly, that choice that brought her here alone scrambling through the forest once again. Already she was at rest against an oak, bark crumbling over her shoulder as she glanced up at the Virginia sky. A full moon and a blanket of stars lit the night. Everything in the heavens guiding, leading her. Every sparkle, every glimmer on her side.

She knew she was moving slowly, moving easily through the dark. Her breath, she could hear her breath, flowing from her. She was stirred, compelled, drawn to something that pulsed boldly through her veins, pumped her very heart.

Tonight Lydia was ready to live. Life would surely come. Not a life of nothingness, but one rich and full that blossomed beautiful in her hands. It would surely come. Life soared through souls, filling the earth with love and a force so strong it changed the world. John had taught her of this love, had walked it out, breathed it into her, and now she carried his seed.

And so it was, every price had a prize. For everything she didn't want, there attached to it like the rose of a thorn was the thing she did. But the loss was worth the life, no matter what the risk.

Lydia smoothed the folds of her dress against her chilled skin and looked around. The sound of night creatures and the crunching of leaves reminded her that inside she carried the words, the music, of a people she loved.

She slowed her pace and began to meander, loose arms and knees swinging softly. There was no pressing, no pulling, just the gentle sound of her own breath. Oh yes, she could breathe. She was *breathing*.

The night's wind and the salt of her tears soothed, healed, as it streamed down her cheeks.

As the night passed, she grew stronger. Arms that had months before swung with vigor rose to swat tree limbs with grace. She was fearless. She was found.

And then she saw it.

One small round, dim light. High and far away. She moved toward it, focused and resilient. She floated toward it. When she was close enough to see the circle did not grow in size, she was touched by the hands of a man.

"John?"

"Yes."

"John, where did you come from? I didn't hear you."

"I was watching, waiting for you."

She ran to him. Clung to him. Finally, loved him with everything.

He kissed her scar.

"You came for me."

"I did."

"Where were you? Where have you been?"

"Preparing a place."

He tugged at the cord around his neck, yanking a small leather pouch free from the inside of his shirt and coat.

"What is that?"

"Papers. My papers."

Lydia hadn't even noticed he was holding something in his other hand. In the bright night, she could see a dented copper rectangle with hinges.

Slowly, he opened the box and unwrapped the creased folds of a document. "And yours."

She looked at him, waiting.

He handed it to her. Slowly, she read the words.

"You're free, Lydia."

"John…"

"You're free. You've been free since the day you walked away. Lady, you're free."

She froze.

"Live. Live. Live," he whispered. Like a dream.

She felt something rising, lifting in her. Her spirit flew high above the night sky. Flying free for Isaiah, for Lou, for Lizzy. *Free.*

She lay against his chest with his arms wrapped around her. She had flourished, a single black rose among lilies.

She looked into his eyes. It was him, her love.

It was Midnight.

At midnight, I will rise to give thanks to You.

AUTHOR'S NOTE

*T*he tale of a fair-skinned woman "passing" into White culture is not unfamiliar to the African-American community, but the first time I heard it had occurred in my own family, I was a teenager. And like many legends in a family's history, the words were breathed in hushed tones over the passing of plates. But a couple of years ago, I decided to inquire further. I discovered that it was my great-grandmother who had walked away from her family. Relatives claimed they had seen her living years later as a white woman up North, far from her home state of Mississippi. There wasn't much more I could learn, but this story became the basis of my book. Though this topic has been covered in other writings through the years, I wanted to tell the story from a different perspective. I wanted this to be a love story that explored the question: Is what is gained worth what is lost? From this premise, the theme of *The Loom* surfaced, revealing a story about discontentment, a desire to find freedom at any cost for a character who, much like any of us, fails to realize that she already possesses the very thing she is striving for.

As I wrote, I kept thinking about a biblical passage from the book of Ezekiel. Chapter 16 depicts an unfaithful lover, representing the children of Israel's waywardness. I was also drawn to the book of Hosea, in which the prophet's wife Gomer walks away from her marriage. Although my character Lydia does not stray sexually, she doesn't become one with her husband John in mind and spirit until their final time together before they are reunited in the epilogue.

I imagined John as the faithful and forgiving Hosea, and like the biblical character, wanted him to represent a type of Christ.

So inevitably, I wanted the antagonist of the story to represent evil. I wanted a character that was beautiful to the eye, much like the Lucifer of the Bible, who would cloak himself in kindness to lure and deceive. Jackson offers Lydia the chance to gain the whole world but lose her soul.

Another character inspired from the Bible was Abram. He was a spiritual father of many, like the biblical Abraham, but I formed him with Samson from the book of Judges in mind. He, too, was a man of strength who loses his power (and his hair!) and begs the Lord for one more victory, which the Lord grants for Abram with Ruth's healing. The scar in his hand was more for Odessa, who thought of him as her savior, a snare I find many married women fall into regarding their godly husbands.

But many times the people or the problems in the story were inspired from my own life. One of the characters in The Loom Room I sketched from an image of my aunt, who suffered an eye injury as a child that resulted in a blue, blind eye. Thus, the character Ruth.

Lydia's scar is mine. I have had reconstructive knee surgeries and have gone through several periods of concealing my scars since I was an adolescent. At times, I have been ashamed of the injuries instead of seeing the blessing of mobility the operations allowed me. I now reveal what I often hid.

I wanted many of the characters to have the same initials: John, Jackson, James; Lydia, Lou, Lizzy. This is rarely the case in novels. Generally, writers are encouraged to avoid doing this very thing for the sake of assisting you, the reader, in early character recognition. However, I wanted to show that there was little difference between these souls. All of their lives were intertwined. As much as John was free, Jackson was bound. Many of the characters, both Black and White, were gripped by something, whether it was slavery, hatred, marriage, discrimination, or money. As Annie states, we are all slaves to something.

Of course, to write this book, I needed to not only glean facts from the Bible and my own life, but to spend an ample amount of time studying history.

From a set of history books I won years ago as a pageant winner, I stumbled upon several references to a loom room and became fascinated with the idea of this place, this space where expectant women and elderly slaves spent their time weaving when they were no longer productive in the fields. It was this latter group in particular that stimulated my imagination. Who were these folk, and what would they feel knowing that their arrival to The Room indicated their days on earth were few? What was shared in this place for the dying? I was simply intrigued. In the book, I used the loom room as a place of no escape to add to Lydia's desire to flee the world of slavery.

John's copper box filled with his inheritance was another sweet nugget I found in my research. Slaves in Emporia, Virginia, buried and later retrieved such treasure chests. But the most fascinating fact I discovered was that of a slave named Francis "Free Frank" McWorter, who became a leased worker, earning more than fifteen thousand dollars over the course of his life. With his savings, he bought the freedom of sixteen members of his family in the early 1800s. Amazing.

Lastly, I colored *The Loom* with symbolism. Light and dark images prevail throughout the pages, in the sky, in the skin, in the pearls, and in the velvet. One find you may or may not have noticed was the fact that Jackson's bad tooth was a metaphor for Lydia. "Completely black," Dr. Kelly informs him. The poor man is plagued the moment she arrives, much like Pharaoh in Genesis 12, when Sarai, Abram's wife, is under his roof. In addition, there are many references to flames. A fire builds, literally and figuratively, in Lydia's desire to flee so, inevitably, the story ends up in smoke.

The wedding and Emma chapters were two of my favorites to write and to read aloud (which I do for every scene). I would love to hear which scenes you found the most memorable. Please feel free to share this and any other comments at shellagillus.com. It is my hope that you enjoyed *The Loom* as much as I enjoyed writing it. I am grateful you took the time to travel this journey with me. God bless!